Bodacious

and

Miss Ally

By:

Mary McCartney Dulany

Cover image: *Thoughts of a Swing* © by Charles Plant, photographer

See more of his images at: www.redbubble.com/people/charliep

Cover design by Joe Dulany, graphic designer

ISBN 0-9839186-3-5

ISBN13 978-0-9839186-3-9

Library of Congress Control Number: 2012936357

Printed in the United States of America

RevMedia Publishing
PO Box 5172
Kingwood, TX 77325

A publishing division of Revelation Ministries

www.revmediatv.com
www.revministries.com
www.revmedianetwork.com
www.revmediapublishing.com

Dedicated to the memory of

Ernest William McCartney

"Ernie Bill"

My mentor

My Example

My Dad

Table of Contents

Chapter One   13

Chapter Two   31

Chapter Three 39

Chapter Four 51

Chapter Five 63

Chapter Six 79

Chapter Seven 91

Chapter Eight 105

Chapter Nine 113

Chapter Ten 125

Chapter Eleven 135

Chapter Twelve 147

Chapter Thirteen 157

Chapter Fourteen 175

Chapter Fifteen 191

Chapter Sixteen 199

Chapter Seventeen 205

Chapter Eighteen 221

Chapter Nineteen 231

Chapter Twenty 239

Chapter Twenty-One 247

Chapter Twenty-Two 259

Dear Readers:

Then they that feared the Lord spake often one to another; and the Lord hearkened and heard it, and a book of remembrance was written before him for them that feared the Lord, and that thought upon his name. Malachi 3:16

Bodacious and Miss Ally is set in the year 1950, in a fictitious town in southeast Texas. For decades, great revivals swept across this nation, especially in a large area of the south. This area came to be known as the Bible Belt. There were "churches on every corner," and most of them held at least two revivals each year, some of them in tents. These meetings lasted for two weeks, but were often extended at the request of those attending. People frequented the revivals of other churches, as well as their own. This constant reminder of God's Word and of his will helped keep his children strong. They literally "spake often one to another," and "thought upon his name." Young people, and even children, could be found discussing scriptures and praying together. People tried to carefully follow the rules set down by God in the book he had written for his children.

Not everyone who attended the revivals responded positively to them, but multiplied thousands did. I was among this number, as I accepted Christ as Lord of my life in a 1946 summer revival. Our lives were forever changed, and our eternities were joyfully settled in one instant, when we chose to accept God's unspeakable gift— eternal life. I offer you, here, a glimpse into those long ago days, as we see God at work in the lives of Bodacious and Miss Ally.

Mary McCartney Dulany

Jesus answered and said unto him,

Verily, verily, I say unto thee,

Except a man be born again,

He cannot see the

Kingdom of God.

John 3:3

Chapter One

Bodacious spied the deserted house and breathed a silent *thank you* toward the sky. She was at the point of collapse, but with weary eyes fastened on the house she began walking rapidly. In her haste she tripped in a small hole and fell. She lay still for a moment trying to regain her composure; then, bittersweet tears came unbidden as realization washed over her. She was finally home.

Some instinct, which would not be denied, had driven her to return to Texas. After her money had run out, she had reluctantly turned away from the bus station and started out on foot. She had been walking for more miles than she could remember. On and on she had traveled, hardly noticing anything around her. Nothing else had mattered. She simply had to get back to Johnston.

Arriving at last she had skirted the city, afraid that she might see someone she knew. On the far side of town she had noticed this narrow lane, and had turned into it, hoping against hope for some sort of shelter for the night.

The ramshackle house now seemed like an answer to prayer. Picking herself up from the ground she began running toward it with new energy. Overhead, dark clouds left no doubt that there would be a "soaker" before many minutes passed.

A homey picket fence surrounding the house made her feel almost welcome. Many of the pickets were on the ground, but the old gate, closed and latched, looked sturdy. She opened the gate a bit timidly and walked through it. Without conscious thought, she latched it behind her. Grass and weeds stood two feet tall around her, but she didn't pay them any mind. The front door was ajar, and that was all the invitation she needed.

Thunder followed a brilliant streak of lightening, and she quickly scooted onto the rotting wooden porch, just as the late May rain became a deluge. Not pausing to knock, she went in and dropped her travel-worn bag onto the dusty floor.

She stood in a medium-sized living room, noting with surprise that the room contained a couple of pieces of furniture. An old sofa, which looked to be in fair condition, brought a relieved smile to her lips. A small table beside it had only an empty oil lamp on it. To her right were a vacant dining room and a doorway which led to the kitchen. In front of her was a hall, which obviously led to bedrooms. As she started down the hall she noticed a tiny, pocket-sized calendar that had been tacked onto the wall beside the dining room doorway. She paused to look at it for a moment. *Nineteen-fifty,* she thought, shaking her head. She looked for the month of May on the small square, and found Monday, the twenty-ninth. She shook her head again. *I can't believe I'm back in Johnston, she thought. Oh, my, it doesn't' seem possible that I have been gone for twelve years. How I loved this town! I remember how proud I always was that it had been named for my husband's great-grandfather. Now I just feel like an interloper...*

She started down the short hallway, weary shoulders bent in despair. "Oh, if only there is someplace to sleep," she wished aloud. Passing by a cracked, full-length mirror that was hanging on the bathroom door, she was shocked by her own appearance. Her sweater was old and worn. She had lost weight, and her dirty dress was hanging loose. Strands of gray streaked her unkempt brown hair. Sighing, she shook her head. She hadn't realized how much older than her fifty years she looked. Life had not been good to Bodacious for a very long time.

Peeking through the first doorway, she discovered a bedroom. Best of all—she found a bed there. The mattress was bare, but that didn't matter. She sat down on the side, then lay back and breathed

14

a great sigh. "A real bed," she said thankfully. "I'll surely sleep well tonight."

Almost before she could finish that thought, she was fast asleep.

❧❧❧❧❧

The small girl unlatched the gate and hopped up onto it to swing into the yard. She didn't smile, but the simple act of swinging on the gate gave her pleasure. Jumping down, she ran through the grass, which was still wet from the early afternoon rain, and into the house. She shut the door behind her. Sitting on the old sofa, she removed a much used canvas bag from her shoulder. She pulled a couple of apples from it and laid them on the couch. A soft "mewing" preceded the removal of a small white kitten which had also been riding in the frayed bag. She lifted it out and kissed its tiny head.

"It's gonna be okay, Mews," she said. "We're home now, and look, I shut the door. No more dogs are gonna come after you in here."

The girl held the kitten up high and smiled at it, then hugged it close to herself. The look on the child's face would have broken the heart of anyone, had someone been watching. She was small, and incredibly thin. Her dark hair was long and much in need of combing. The dress no longer fit her, and it had obviously been some time since it had been washed. The child herself was not too clean, but there was beauty there, just waiting to be bathed—and nourished with more than apples.

"Don't tell anyone," she said to the kitten. She looked around as though some spy might catch her removing a can of milk from the bottom of her bag. She put the apples back inside the bag and set it on the floor beside the couch. "I know I shouldn't steal, Mews," she said, "but you have to have something to eat don't you? Let's go find a bowl."

In the kitchen, she took down a bowl from the nearly empty cabinet. Opening the can of milk, she stirred a small amount of it

15

together with water, and placed the bowl on the floor. Mews sniffed the mixture, looked up at her, and began "crying" softly.

"What's the matter kitty? Don't cry. Drink your milk. It's good for you. Oh, what can I do? You'll starve if you don't eat."

"That kitten's too small to drink from a bowl," an adult voice said from behind her.

Startled, the girl turned around to see a woman standing in the doorway of the kitchen. She looked old. Her mussed, dark hair showed a bit of gray, and her clothes obviously lacked recent care. She wasn't smiling, but there was a hint of kindness in her brown eyes. "What are you doing in my house?" the girl demanded.

"Now how could a deserted old house belong to a small child like you?" the lady asked.

"Because I was here first; and I'm not a small child. I'm gonna be eight next month." The girl grabbed the kitten and held it tightly, protecting it from this unexpected inquisition. Mews began to cry, so she loosened her hold on him, and petted him gently. Warily, she glanced up at the woman, wondering what would happen next.

The woman's face softened. "There's no need to be afraid of old Bodacious, child. Most of the time I'm just as scared as you are right now."

"Bodacious? That's your name? It's a really weird name." Her childish curiosity had overcome her fear for the moment.

"Well, my name is actually Evelyn Johnston, but my husband called me Bodacious for nearly twenty years, God rest his soul. He thought I was the most remarkable woman he had ever met. Remarkable. That's what the word means, you know. It seems strange to think about all of that now, after living for twelve years without him…"

A soft light had come into the weary eyes as she spoke, easing the last of the girl's fear. She looked down at the kitten. "Can you help?" She asked. "He won't eat. I don't want him to die. He's the

16

only friend I have." Tears came as she bent her head into the soft fur.

The lady was almost moved to tears herself at that revelation. "No problem," she said gently. "You just have to learn to improvise."

"How can I do that?" the girl asked as she sniffed and wiped away her tears.

"Well, since you can't feed him the normal way, we'll just have to find a way to do it differently. If we think hard enough, we'll think of something. Come on."

They headed back into the living room and sat down on the couch together.

"You know my name," Bodacious said, smiling at the child, "but I don't know yours. You do have one, don't you?" she laughed.

The girl looked down at the floor and said nothing.

"Is there some reason you can't tell me your name?" she asked, puzzled.

The response was a small nod of the head. Still, she continued looking down, and made no verbal reply.

"Where's your mother, dear? Will she be coming here for you?"

This was met with stoic silence. The little girl was obviously living on her own, and hadn't been faring too well, judging from her thin little body.

Bodacious had an idea. "Where'd you get the kitten?" she asked in as gentle a voice as she could manage.

The girl looked at her then, and shook her head quickly. Dark eyes brimmed with more tears. "I didn't steal it, honest. I found it in a little alley behind the store on the highway. The dogs were chasing it, and it had hidden behind some garbage cans. I scared the dogs away and rescued it, so it's mine now. No one can take it away. It's mine!"

"That sounds reasonable to me. Tell you what. I think I'll just call you Miss Ally, because you're the wonderful heroine who rescued her kitten from the alley. What do you think of that?"

The newly dubbed "Miss Ally" giggled. "That's a funny name. I like it," she said breathing a sigh of relief that she hadn't had to tell her the name she hated.

"Dear, do you know if there is an eye dropper or maybe a doll's baby bottle around here? I think your kitten could drink from either of those."

The dark eyes brightened, and the girl jumped up and headed down the hall. "I know where there's a doll's baby bottle. Oh, I hope it works! Wait right there, Mews. I'll be able to feed you in just a minute, poor, hungry baby."

Poor, hungry baby indeed. She's not quite eight years old, and she must be nearly starved to death herself.

Oh, dear. You'd better be careful, Bodacious. You don't want to get too involved. You're letting some light back into your heart. You'll just get hurt again. Something has to be done about Miss Ally, though. Someone has to help her, and there doesn't seem to be anyone around except you. Oh, why did you have to choose this house in which to pass a few hours? Now you could be stuck here for a while.

She didn't want to admit it, but the idea wasn't exactly displeasing to her. The longing for a home and loved ones, is strong in most people. *In spite of my past hurts,* she admitted to herself, *I can't help thinking of how wonderful it would be to have a real house and a little girl to go with it.*

A happy cry of "I found it!" from the bedroom interrupted her musings. This was followed by hurried footsteps and the child plopping herself down on the couch. "Will this work? Please say it will work," begged Miss Ally.

"This should do just fine. Let's go to the kitchen. We'll wash it out and put the milk in it. You can do that yourself, right?"

"Sure. I'm not a little kid, you know."

"Oh, I can see that you're quite grown up. Come on, Mews, dinner is served."

Miss Ally laughed at that. "Dinner is served, Mews," she repeated. She cocked her head to one side as she made her way to the kitchen.

Oh, my, thought her new friend as she slowly followed the intriguing child. *How could I have gotten myself into this? I've known her for less than an hour, and she's already gone and stolen my heart.*

As she entered the kitchen, she found Ally standing at the sink rinsing the bottle with water poured from a gallon jug. Mews stood on the counter, taking in all of the activity as though he knew it was going to lead to dinner for him. They were so cute together that Bodacious simply shook her head and resigned herself to the idea of taking care of them. Life is full of hurts anyway. One more wouldn't kill her.

Okay, my dear. It's you, me and Mews. For whatever it's worth, I'll do what I can for you. I surely can't leave you like this. She paused for a moment, and then added rather sadly. *It's not as though I really had any place else to go.*

Watching the little girl wash the bottle, she wondered where the water had come from. The electricity was off, and there was no running water. At least they had a roof over their heads. "Dear, where did you get the water?" she asked.

"Outside," responded Ally absently. She was engrossed in the care of her kitten.

Bodacious sighed and decided not to press the issue. She was just glad to know that the water for their use must not be far away. Details could wait until the kitten had eaten. It was mewing rather loudly now, and was obviously very hungry. Knowing that new kittens need to eat frequently, she moved over to the counter to help make this feeding possible.

"I think that's probably enough washing. Let's see if we can get some milk into this little guy, okay?"

"I want to feed him, though—can I?"

19

"Of course. He's your responsibility. When he wakes up three times during the night, you'll get to feed him again and again."

"Will he do that?" The dark eyes were wide with wonder. "Won't he sleep all night long, just like I do?"

"Well, not for a couple of weeks, possibly. We don't really know how old he is, but he looks pretty young. I'd say that you have a few sleepless nights ahead of you. You're very grown up, though. You can handle it, can't you?"

"Sure. I-I can handle it...I want Mews to live."

"Well, I might be persuaded to help out a bit, if you get too tired, but he's your kitten, and he'll mostly be looking to you to take care of him." The graying head nodded sagely, and the small dark one nodded with it.

"Okay, Mr. Mews, let's feed you some milk," his small mistress proposed. She picked him up and carried him back to the sofa.

Bodacious followed, carrying the half-filled bottle. She gave it to the girl as they sat down.

"Let's see how he does," she said. "I'll bet he's so hungry that he could almost figure out how to drink from that bowl by this time."

Ally gently placed the tip of the tiny bottle into the kitten's mouth, squeezed out a few drops of milk, and held her breath. Sure enough, he immediately began lapping at the nipple, and in just a few minutes had emptied the bottle. He looked up at his mistress and mewed.

"Boy, he really was hungry. Did you see how fast he drank that milk? Now he wants more. Should I let him have it? I don't want him to get sick."

He won't take more than he needs. You'd better fix him a little more and see how it goes."

Another half-bottle later, Mews was looking very full and very sleepy. "I think it's time to find a box and some rags to put in it. This kitten needs a nap. Do you know where we can find those things?"

"Yes, ma'am. There are some boxes of old clothes in the bathroom closet." She ran off down the hall, and a moment later, was back with a medium-sized box and a large sweatshirt. They arranged the shirt in the box and laid the tired kitten on it. He quickly fell asleep, and then it was time to feed two very hungry human females.

"I have a bit of cheese and some bread. I guess that will have to do us for supper," Bodacious said. "Tomorrow, we'll need to do something about groceries. Thankfully, we have water." She moved over to the front door to recover her bag which lay where she had dropped it on the floor.

"I have some apples someone had tossed out behind the store," her newly acquired charge called after her. "They weren't in the garbage. They were by themselves. We'll have a good supper, right?" she asked.

"That sounds great to me. Let's go into the kitchen where we can eat at that small table. It's been many a month since I've sat down to eat with a friend. I don't know where the owners might be, but we can surely make use of their house until they come along, right?"

Ally replied with a mysterious smile. Bodacious didn't quite know what to make of it, so she simply began putting the meager meal together. The child went outside and returned with more water, then got the apples from her canvass bag. She carefully washed them, cut away the bad spots, and divided the pieces onto two plates. With cheese and bread on the plates next to the apples, and two glasses of cool water to complete the meal, they sat down and began eating eagerly.

It certainly wasn't a feast, but when they had finished they were both filled and feeling a bit festive. They were enjoying each other's company, for neither had had anyone to really talk to for a long time.

"I just can't believe that someone would go off and leave things behind in a deserted house," Bo said as she took her dish to the sink. "It is lucky for us, though isn't it? We could stay here for quite a while and put together a fairly nice home. I noticed that the roof didn't leak during the storm. None of the windows is broken. The porch needs repair, but it isn't too bad. The grass needs cutting. Maybe there's a lawn mower somewhere."

"I know who lives here," Ally said very quietly, as if she didn't want to be heard.

"I'm sorry. I didn't hear you."

"It's me," she said a little more loudly. "I live here with my mama. We have lived her all my life."

Bo looked around at the sparse furnishings—the neglect—the obvious poverty. More than a little startled at the girl's revelation, she exclaimed, " Why, goodness gracious, dear! Where's your mother now?"

"She left a lot of weeks ago. I don't remember when. It's been a long time. It was after Valentine's Day. I know, 'cause she got mad when Kevin, her boyfriend, didn't give her candy. Then a few weeks later, she said she had some business to do. She just walked off down the road in that direction," she said, pointing toward the west. "She never came back. I guess she's dead," she added matter-of-factly.

"Why were you left here alone, for mercy's sake? She should have taken you with her, wherever she needed to go."

"Oh, she didn't take me anywhere. She left me here, even when I was real little. I used to get scared, but not any more."

"Valentine's Day was more than three months ago. Are you saying you've been all alone for more than two months? How have you survived? What have you been eating? Child, you're so young!"

"I-I can take care of myself okay. There was a lot of food when Mama left. I was careful not to eat too much. It just ran out a few weeks ago. I find food that gets tossed behind that store on the highway. We had some nuts left from last year, and berries are out now, too. If I eat enough of those I don't get too hungry."

Bo was very distressed to think that someone so small had been fending for herself for so long. Finally, she said, "Well, at least you had the canned milk left over."

Stark fear clouded the child's face. She started crying, and her new friend was at a loss to know what to do. "Dear, what did I say? I certainly didn't mean to upset you."

"You're gonna hate me if I tell you."

"Of course I won't hate you. Whatever is the matter?" She was aghast that such a little girl could be so frightened. "Just tell me," she urged.

"I stole the milk today. I had to feed Mews. I'm sorry..." The tears began anew.

There was silence for a long moment.

"Are you mad at me?" The tiny voice brought Bodacious back, and she felt ashamed that she had given the child cause to fear again.

"Mercy no, my dear, I'm just so sad that you have had to go through all of this. Losing your mother must have been hard enough, let alone..."

"I'm glad Mama's gone," She said quietly.

"This time I did hear what you said. Tell me about it. You'll feel a lot better when someone older than you knows about your problems."

The dark eyes brimmed with tears. "I don't like her very much. She never did anything nice for me. I wish my mama was like you. You make me feel happy. She makes me feel like nobody loves me. Nobody!"

She was crying softly now. Her new friend simply took her in her arms and held her until she raised her head and began to sniffle.

"Let's see if we can find some tissue for that nose," she said at last. Ally nodded her head, but she didn't let go.

"You're like the ladies in my books. They always hug their little girls. I never had a hug before. I like to hug you," she said as she nestled close.

At that moment, Bodacious completely lost her heart to little Miss Ally. She knew that there was no way she would ever let her be alone again, no matter the chance that she would likely end up with a broken heart herself.

"I have tons of hugs," she said. "You may have all of the hugs you can ever want. What do you think of that?"

The response was a wonderful smile, a giant bear hug, and a glad proclamation. "Hey! You can be my grandma. I've never had one. There are grandmas in my books, but I never saw one before. Will you be my very own grandma? Oh, please say you will…"

"I think I could do that. Let's see—how would you like to call me 'Grandma Bo'—short for Bodacious?"

"I love that! Grandma Bo—my own Grandma Bo!" There were more hugs and tears, but suddenly the girl stopped talking, and a look of fear crossed her small face.

"Oh, no! You have some place else to go, don't you? You aren't going to leave are you? You won't leave me here. You can't, or I would be all alone again. Please don't leave me alone."

"I promise that I will never leave you alone. Now put the smile back on your sweet face and go find that tissue. Then we'll sit in the living room and try to decide how we should handle our problems. Okay?"

The smile reappeared. "Okay, Grandma Bo," she said, dashing down the hall and quickly back to the couch to join her.

"Now, first of all," Bo said, "we have to do something about money, I don't have any, and you obviously don't either, so we'll have to earn some. Do you have any ideas?"

The child shook her head, so she continued. "Is it possible that your mother might have left some money here for you—in a

24

drawer in her room, perhaps? That would get us something to eat until I can get a job."

"I don't think so. She used to get a check in the mail, but it quit coming. Then the electricity was turned off. The heater wouldn't go, and it got real cold. The pump wouldn't work without electricity either, so we didn't have water in the house. That really made her mad. We had to start using the old hand pump outside. She made me bring in buckets of water for the bathroom and kitchen. She just stayed mad at me all of the time after that. I was trying to be good, but she always said I was worthless. Finally, she started selling the furniture when she wanted money. I don't think she even had any money when she left here, so she couldn't have left me any." She paused and looked up. "I can't go into her room to look, though," she added. "That makes her really, really mad!"

Bo very much wished she had that woman there for just a few moments. She would give her a piece of her mind! She took a deep breath and said, "Well, it doesn't sound like she left you anything. We'll have to work this out another way. Who are your friends? We need to talk to someone who knows you."

"I don't have any friends," was the quiet reply. "Mama doesn't want me around people. She's ashamed of me. She doesn't let me talk to anyone, except Kevin."

Bodacious was so moved by this revelation that she couldn't speak for a few moments. She was beginning to worry that the mother might not be quite normal. Finally, she asked, "Kevin is the boy friend you mentioned before, right? Do you think he would know if you have relatives nearby?"

"No, he wouldn't know. She started bringing him here a few months ago. I don't know where he lives."

"Well, don't you know someone in town that we might talk to in order to find out where your relatives are? No—I guess not, if you never got to see anyone."

"You're my Grandma Bo, aren't you? You know I'm me."

25

"Yes, but I don't know who your relatives are," she responded.

Bo knew she needed to make a hard decision. She would have to go into town and ask her deceased husband's best friend, Jeffrey, for help. Maybe there was still some money in her bank account, but probably not, after twelve long years. She would get money somehow, though. She definitely needed a lawyer, and Jeffrey was one of the best.

Swallowing her fears she said, "There's someone in town I used to know. I think he might help us. We couldn't go into town looking like this, of course. I'm afraid that we look a bit like vagabonds right now. We can clean up easily enough, but we need decent clothes. Your Mama doesn't happen to be about my size, does she?"

"I don't know. Some of her clothes are probably in her closet. She didn't take a suitcase with her. You could look to see if there is something you could wear. If she gets mad at you, you could just say that you didn't know she would care."

"Let's do that. If the dresses look fairly nice, I can sew one to make it fit me. I could cut one up and make a dress for you too. We only need one dress each to get us back into town. I hope there are scissors, a needle and some thread. Come along. Let's go see what we can find in her room."

A look of panic came over the young face once again. "I don't think I'd better go in there," she murmured.

"Honey, I'm not going to let anything happen to you. Your mother may never come back. If she does, she's going to have to answer some pretty hard questions. It's against the law to desert your children. You don't want to spend the rest of your life being afraid of someone you might never even see again. Let's go find the things we need, okay?"

"Okay, but I hope she doesn't find out," Ally said, shivering. "Can you really make me a new dress?" she asked as she bounced down the hall with "Grandma" in tow. The adventure of the moment had caused her to forget her fears.

It didn't take long to find the scissors and other things in a dresser drawer. Then, from among the few dresses hanging in the closet, Bo chose a medium blue one. It was nondescript, but with a couple of simple, quick changes it looked, and fit, much better. The sun was setting and it was getting dark in the house before Bo could start cutting out Ally's dress. Her choice had been a bright pink, and the color went perfectly with her dark hair. Seeing Grandma Bo squinting in the dimming light as she began cutting, Ally disappeared into the kitchen. She came back with a candle which had been set into hot wax at the bottom of a glass. The wax had hardened, and now held the candle in place. She also brought two more candles and a box of matches. Bo smiled at her, thanking her for her help.

Ally watched while her new dress took shape, leaving only to go and feed her kitten. A dim light appeared at the end of the hall, as she lit the candle which she kept in her room. She was gone for a while, and came back smiling.

The two sat side-by-side as the night hours progressed. The happy little girl tried valiantly to stay awake, but finally lost the battle. Bo picked her up and carried her to her room. She didn't even stir as she was gently laid in her bed.

Back on the couch, the newly dubbed "grandma" smiled contentedly as she sewed. She couldn't remember when she had been so happy.

Some time later Bo's candle began flickering. Seeing that it was about to die out, she took it from the glass and quickly removed the wax that had held it. Lighting a second candle with the first one, she then blew out the used one. Letting more hot wax drip into the glass, she set the new candle in it. Before returning to her sewing, she stood, stretched lazily, and breathed a contented sigh.

I ought not to feel so good, since all of this came about because someone possibly died, Bo thought. *Of course I care that Ally's mother is gone, but it seems that she no longer has need of these things. I do wish she had left some money. That would certainly help me take care of her child. She is so dear—acts a bit young for her age, but she is doing pretty well, considering all she must have been through. Making the dress causes me to think of my own dear daughter, though. We had so many good times together. Well, I must not let myself dwell on the past. It will only make me feel sad again.*

For five hours she sewed, interrupted only by a nocturnal kitten feeding. Since she was already awake, there wasn't any need to awaken the child. Settling back on the couch she picked up her needle and thread and continued sewing. She wished there were oil for the lamp. It was difficult to see by candlelight, but she was determined to finish the dress quickly. The sooner they got answers to some questions, the sooner they could start thinking of the future.

Her eyelids were drooping, and she kept nodding off to sleep, but finally she set up straight and sighed. "There. It's all done." She held the small pink dress up for inspection. It truly was adorable, with ruffles and bows. Memories of her own daughter pressed in again, and tears came to her eyes. How many pretty dresses had she made for her dear girl? There had been too many to count.

"Oh, just stop it," she scolded herself. "You'd better be off to bed. Tomorrow will be a very busy day, and you have to make yourself look respectable once more. Let me see," she considered, "I guess I should trim my hair some. I suppose there is shampoo and such. Thank Heaven for nearby water. Electricity would be nice. These candles made sewing at night rather difficult. But, then, my life has been a great deal worse than this during the past years, hasn't it?"

She stood up and stretched for a moment. Then, picking up the matches, the new dress, and the glass with the candle, she started off down the hall. She held the candle high in order to see better, and entered the child's nearly empty room.

That woman! She fumed silently. *She must have sold her child's bedroom furniture instead of her own. Oh, I wish I could just get my hands on her...*

In the closet, she found a hanger. She hung the dress on the doorknob as she closed the closet door. She wanted it to be the first thing Ally saw in the morning. Looking over at the bed, she smiled at the picture of the child, her hand hanging down into the box where her kitten was also fast asleep.

"Little girl," she whispered, "you have totally stolen Old Bodacious' heart."

With a final smile at the sleeping pair, she left the room and crossed the hall. Glancing at her dime store watch, she saw that it was after one o'clock. As she put the watch and the burning candle down on the bedside table, she saw that the bed was now covered in sheets. She was puzzled for a moment, and then she realized that, in spite of her fear of being in this room, Ally must have made the bed for her when she went to feed the kitten. *How incredibly sweet,* she thought. *She is the dearest child!* She sighed happily. Many questions were still unanswered, but those could wait. She had a real bed in which to sleep, and she intended to take full advantage of that. She changed into her one nightgown, and then wound her watch and laid it back on the table. Breathing another contented sigh, she crawled between the sheets, relaxed, and quickly drifted off to sleep.

Chapter Two

Anna Benski sat in her large living room staring out of the picture window. It was a good-sized window, which looked out on a pleasant tree-lined street. Her whole house was comfortable and spacious, and suited her well. Behind where she was sitting, an arched doorway led into the dining room, and from there a door opened into the kitchen at the back of the house. A laundry room and a walk-in pantry were accessed from the kitchen. On the other side of the house a hall gave entry to three bedrooms. Across the hall from these was a bathroom, and beside that a small study.

The picture window through which Anna was staring was framed with pale blue drapes. These captured the shade of blue that was in the flowers on the wall paper. Anna loved her home, and usually enjoyed just being there, and caring for it. Today her mind was on other things, however—painful things.

She sat there, unmoving, her long dark hair falling over her shoulders and down her back. Her brown eyes were full of un-shed tears. For the first time in several years she was struggling with a terrible memory. It was tearing at her heart, and she was puzzled, trying to understand why she was remembering every detail so vividly this day. All she could think about was this anniversary of the loss of their two-year old daughter. On her lap was a current calendar. The date, May 29, was circled in red.

Tony Benski walked quietly around the room, knowing that his wife was trying hard not to cry. He, too, was trying to understand Anna's regression. During those first years they had both wept enough tears to fill an ocean, but she had been doing really well for a long time now. *What is causing this sudden change in Anna?* he wondered. He folded his nearly six foot form onto the couch near his wife, and ran his hand through his sandy hair.

Anna sat perfectly still, the tears now staining her lovely face.

Worried, Tony put his arms around her, and held her as she wept. Love for her overwhelmed him.

There is no way to change what happened that day, he thought. *I hate seeing her suffering like this again.* He felt helpless in the face of the tears.

"Honey, I love you, you know," he said aloud.

"Oh, yes, I know that. You're my whole life. I don't know what's wrong with me." She moved away slightly and looked into his face. "Oh, Tony, don't you remember how happy we were?"

"I can never forget life with our Megan," he answered. "She made us a family. She made life a joy. But sweetheart, it's been seven years. What's caused you to feel the terrible hurt so strongly again today?"

Pain drenched Anna's face, and he repented that he had dared to say anything. "Come here," he said, drawing her closer. He kissed her gently on the lips, but she felt a bit stiff in his arms.

There had been no more children after Megan. Tony often wished that it had been different. Other children might have helped them to forget. They would certainly have made life busier. Anna had seemed okay with things as they were, however, and life had continued with just the two of them.

"If only we could relive that day, I wouldn't go to the grocery store. I'd keep her inside with all of the doors locked!" Anna said through her sobs.

She was torturing herself, the way she had that first year. Tony shook his head as she continued.

"I simply turned my back for a moment," she said. "I was just going to pick up a roast. She was only a few feet away from me. If only that young woman hadn't asked me to help her choose a cut of meat, I might have heard a noise—or seen movement out of the corner of my eye when she was taken."

"Is there never to be an end to this agony?" Tony murmured.

Anna looked up, startled. "I'm so sorry, darling. I keep forgetting that you hurt too. I don't know what's wrong with me. I just keep remembering everything today. I feel so guilty. What kind of mother was I to let someone snatch my precious child?"

"Anna, please stop, darling. You aren't to blame. It was not your fault."

Weeping softly, she went back into his open arms. All he could do was hold her. Some of her mood settled over him. It was true that there could be no real closure. There wasn't a lot of doubt that Megan was no longer living, but not knowing exactly what had happened to her was so hard to bear.

Minutes passed as they sat quietly on the couch together. The hum of the attic fan as it pulled cooler air in through slightly raised windows was the only noise.

Suddenly, the sound of the doorbell jangled rudely against their raw nerves. Neither made a move to respond, but the bell rang again.

"I guess we'd better answer it," Tony said. "It doesn't look like they're going to go away." He got up and moved toward the door.

"Good morning!" a cheery female voice greeted him as he opened the door. "Isn't it a beautiful day? My, it just makes you want to sing, doesn't it? I'm Lynn. I wonder if I might have a few moments of your time. I'm from the Anchor Baptist Church down the road. I'm just out inviting our neighbors to come to the revival services we are having. Do you and your family have a church home?"

Tony stared blankly at the young woman. He shook his head, but said nothing. Vaguely, he noticed that she had long blond hair and blue eyes, and the brightest smile he had every seen. Seeing her joy made him wish, again, that they could just get back to normal—to forget the sadness.

"Well, then," Lynn continued, "I would like to invite you to visit with us. I can promise you that you will find a group of people who love God and worship him with all of their hearts. Would you come?"

Still Tony stared at her. He needed to get back to his wife.

"Do you have any children? We ha—"

Slam! The door closed in her face, and Lynn bit her lower lip to keep from crying. Slowly, she took a small piece of paper from her purse—a tract—a small printed message that told the story of Jesus. It said that he came to earth to die for the sins of all men. All they had to do was to believe on him. It told of the great love that motivated the Father to send his only begotten Son to the earth, to die, and urged the reader to accept the wonderful gift of salvation. She wrote her phone number at the bottom with a note, "Please call me, if I can ever be of any help." Tucking the tract into the screen door, she then turned to move on to the next house. Her smile was a bit less bright, but she had work to do, and she carried on.

At the house next door a young woman was working outside in her yard. She had obviously heard what had happened. Her face showed concern, and Lynn steeled herself for an awkward encounter.

"Don't take it to heart, dear," the woman said, looking up from her weeding. "I talked with Mrs. Benski this morning. She's having a hard time. Seven years ago today, their tiny daughter was kidnapped right out from under her nose, less than a month before her second birthday. She would be turning nine in June. There has never been a clue as to what happened to her. For some reason, it all came back full-force for her mommy today."

"Oh, no! I asked him if they had any children. No wonder he slammed the door in my face. What should I do?"

"I don't think anyone can do anything. There doesn't seem to be an answer for this terrible problem. It just has to be endured. There haven't been any more children, either. If there had been more, perhaps their life would be easier. God knows best, though."

At the mention of God, Lynn brightened. "You're a Christian?"

"Oh, yes, for fifteen years now. I was only seven years old when I accepted Christ." Her hazel eyes were alive with the memory. Her dark, auburn hair matched the sprinkle of freckles across her nose. She seemed very kind, and Lynn relaxed. "I was ten when I trusted Jesus," she related. "That was eight years ago, and there's never been anything in my life to equal knowing him. I'm sure it's that way for you too…"

The woman smiled, and nodded. Of course she felt the same way. Having God in her life was her constant joy.

"I guess I'd better be on my way," Lynn said. "I feel really bad about what I did. But is does seem that the best thing I can do for them right now is to leave them alone."

"I'm afraid so. By the way, I'm Phyllis."

"My name is Lynn. We would love to have you come to the revival. Even if you attend another church you could worship with us during our special meeting."

"I'll definitely be there. I love revivals." she said, accepting the mimeographed announcement that Lynn held out to her. "Goodbye."

Inside the Benski's house, Tony was shaking his head. "I can't believe I behaved so badly. That poor girl had no idea what is going on in here. How could I have been so cruel? Did you see me? I actually slammed the door in her face. Now what can I do to make up for that?"

"What did she want, honey? Did she say?"

"Oh, a church down the street is having a revival meeting. She wanted us to attend." A sudden thought came to his mind as he spoke, and he asked, "Do you suppose we should go? I could apologize to her."

35

"Well, I'm not sure if..." Anna looked into his stricken face. "Oh, of course we can do that. What could it hurt to take one evening out of our lives? It's not as though we have a full schedule. If you want to, we'll go."

"I'd really feel better if I apologize, honey. I was so rude."

"It's settled, then."

Phyllis Turner continued puttering in the yard for another two hours, weeding the flowerbeds and trimming the hedges.

"There, it's all finished," she exclaimed, wiping her damp brow. She walked out to the street and turned to survey her work. "Nice." At the back of the house, she cleaned her tools and put them away, washing her hands at the spigot by the rear door. She went into the house and turned to hook the screen. Knowing that there would be a better breeze from the attic fan if she closed the door, she did that, too. Going to the fridge she poured herself a glass of cold tea, and added ice. Glass in hand, she moved into the living room for a well-deserved rest.

"It always comes down to this, Tom," she said aloud, as she seated herself in the chair by the window." No matter what I do during the day, when evening comes, I'm still alone. I'm not sure that I'll ever get used to these empty nights. It's not hard to understand why the Benskis can't forget their Megan. How do you ever forget someone you love? I'm really good at giving advice, but if your absence were permanent, I don't know how I would handle this loneliness. I'll be so glad when you get back home to me."

Tom's boss had sent him to South Korea to oversee the closing of their business interests there. The company officials were feeling wary because of disputes between North and South Korea. Government officials, there, had issued no warnings yet, but Russia was now befriending North Korea. The U.N. had begun sending supplies and equipment to South Korea. Tom's bosses decided to go ahead and close their operations and bring their people home. The company had felt that the situation might

36

become too unstable for Tom to take his wife with him, so Phyllis had stayed home, assuming that he would only be gone a few weeks. The weeks had turned to months, however, and she was beginning to worry about what might happen to Tom if the situation in South Korea became serious.

Not wanting to think about that, she got up and began pacing the floor, ending at the fireplace mantel. She picked up the picture of herself and her husband and stood, staring at it, for several long moments. Finally, she kissed it and set it back in its place.

Heavenly Father, forgive me. I'm feeling sorry for myself again. I guess it was the Benskis' problem that brought this on. That, and the visit from that young girl. I know how much Tom loves going to the revivals. I couldn't help thinking how excited he would be over this one. Well, I'll attend it for him. Then, I'll write and tell him all about it. For you—I will do my best to take the Benskis with me to the service. That should bring me out of this bout of self-pity, right?

Nodding to herself, she walked back to her chair and sat down to finish her iced tea. She stayed there, looking out of the window as darkness settled over the city. She didn't feel sad or depressed like the Benskis, just lonely.

Suddenly, she realized she had been so busy with the yard that she had forgotten to get the mail. She got up and moved to the front door. Opening it, she stepped out onto the dark porch and reached into the box that was hanging by the door. There was only one envelope, and she felt let down. The mail gave her a break in her empty days, even if she only received circulars.

She turned on the lamp as she stepped back into the living room. Glancing down at the envelope in her hands, her disappointment gave way to gladness when she saw her husband's handwriting. Rushing back to her chair, she sat down and tore open the envelope.

My darling, it began. *I have good news today. Things have finally started moving here. In a couple of days, I'll be sending everyone else back to the States. It looks like I'll be home sometime during the first week of July. That's just a month away! I can't wait to see you. It seems like years since I last held you in my arms.*

Phyllis wept as she read those words. The long separation was almost over. She turned back to the letter, anxious to read every word. A smile formed on her lips as she read, and a prayer of "thanks" bubbled up in her heart. Tom was coming home to her.

Lying in bed later that night, Phyllis couldn't get her mind off of the Benski's problem. How could any parents ever bear the pain of losing their baby—never knowing what had happened? *I have to make a point of spending more time with Anna,* she decided. *My loneliness helps me understand what she is going through somewhat. I think she probably needs me. Help me be a better friend to my neighbor, Father,* she prayed. *Help me teach her of your great love for her, and to introduce her to your dear Son, Jesus.*

Chapter Three

"Mew! Mew! Mew!"

Bodacious turned over in bed and tried to shut out the noise.

"Mew! Mew! Mew!"

"Oh, kitty, you're hungry, aren't you? I'll get your bottle. You wait here," Bo heard Ally say from the room across the hall. The sound of little feet padded down the hall toward the dark kitchen.

The tired lady moaned a bit, and opened her eyes. The kitten was crying in earnest now, and there was no stopping that sound. She waited a moment and then realized that the child would need to light a candle. She got out of bed and lit the candle on the table beside her; then headed for the kitchen, lighted candle in hand.

"Well," she said as she encountered Ally's small form in the dark kitchen. "It seems that you have a very hungry kitten on your hands. Do you need any help?" she asked, setting her candle on the counter.

"Yes, please," the child said sleepily. "I can't find the candles, the milk, or the bottle. I guess I'm not a very good person to take care of a little kitten."

"Well, now, everybody has to learn how to do something before they are able to do a good job. You can't just automatically know how to take care of a kitten. But Grandma Bo knows how to teach you. Come on over to the sink. We'll light another candle so that we can see things better. There you go. The bottle is in the sink. You can rinse it out and fill it for him. I'll hold the candle up high so it will give more light. That's the way!" she encouraged, as Ally filled the bottle with milk. "Now, we'll go see if we can put a stop to that hungry noise. What do you say?"

"Thank you, Grandma Bo. Am I doing good? Am I learning?"

"You surely are. You're doing really great."

The next morning came much too soon. The kitten was mewing again, but Ally had already rushed to the kitchen to fill the bottle. Bo stayed where she was for a few minutes longer. She felt terribly tired, which worried her. She was also having some nausea and a vague pain, which she couldn't define. It wasn't like her. *This would be a bad time to get sick,* she thought, as she closed her eyes and drifted off to sleep again.

The sun was shining brightly when she awakened for the second time, and she realized that it was late in the morning. She swung her feet over the side of the bed and sat up.

I'm feeling much better, she thought. *That's good. I really can't get sick right now. I have a family to care for. Speaking of my family, I wonder why there isn't any noise.*

Dressing quickly, she walked across the hall to the other bedroom. It was empty. Ally and the kitten were both gone. The pink dress was spread out lovingly on the bed. *What if they have left?* She couldn't lose them now! She was beginning to feel like a real person again for the first time in many years. Glancing in the mirror as she passed it, she saw that she wasn't looking quite so old, now that she had had some good rest. That realization brought back feelings that she had forgotten existed. She could look nice— like a "grandma."

But where was the "granddaughter?"

Moving down the hall to the living room, she hoped to find them sitting on the couch, but there was no little girl there. There was no kitten. The kitchen was equally empty. Bodacious ran to the back door hoping that she would find them playing outside. How could she have slept so late?

"You don't deserve a sweet little girl to care for," she chided herself as she stepped outside.

"Grandma Bo, come and see! We can eat this!"

40

Ally stood quite a distance away from the house in the middle of a large patch of weeds. Bo breathed a sigh of relief and rushed over to see what the child wanted to show her. She was surprised to see okra plants. They were all but hidden among the tall grasses, but since okra is very sturdy, the weeds were of no consequence to them. The plants were loaded with small, hardy vegetables, just ready to be picked.

"This is okra," Ally said. "Mama planted lot of seeds before she left. It has to be cooked. Mama won't let me use the stove 'cause I might burn her house down. But you can use it. Now we have something to eat, right? Are you glad?"

"It's wonderful, Ally! Okra is edible, but more importantly, we can sell it. This is very fresh and tender. People will be glad to get it. I wonder if there are any more miracles among these weeds. Let's look around."

Bo began searching for anything else the mother might have planted before she left. Ally moved to a new spot and called, "Grandma Bo, there's some tomatoes over here. She planted these plants before she left, too."

Bo walked over, and pushed the weeds aside. There were dozens of ripe, red tomatoes.

"But why haven't you been eating these, Ally? Look, some of them have just dropped to the ground and rotted."

"Oh, no! Mama would be real mad if I touched her garden, but she won't yell at you." Fear showed again in Ally's dark eyes, and Bo cringed at the thought of what this child must have endured.

"This is very good. I can't believe what I'm seeing," she said, changing the subject. "We can fry some okra, and have fresh tomatoes for breakfast. Then we can sell the rest. With the money we get for the vegetables, we can buy a few things that we really need. I am so proud of you! You did a good job."

The little girl beamed at the praise. It was obvious that no one had given her much of it during her short lifetime. Her "grandma" felt a pang of sadness for the lost years, and determined to make it up to her, somehow.

"Let's get a few of those veggies and go fix us some breakfast, okay?"

In the kitchen they went through the cabinets looking for corn meal and shortening. When they found that they had both, they were as excited as if it were Christmas morning. Slicing the tops and the tips from the okra, they then cut it into small circles and rolled it in the cornmeal. Since the stove ran on butane they were able to fry it, their mouths watering as the wonderful smell of "real" food filled the kitchen.

"I think I'll also make fried cornbread, Louisiana style," Bo said. She put water on to boil, and poured more of the cornmeal into a bowl. Adding salt, she stirred it into the cornmeal, then poured boiling water into the bowl and began stirring again. When the mixture was just soft enough, she took shallow hands-full of it, and made small oval cakes. When these had been fried, the two had a new supply of delicious cornbread.

They happily dished okra onto their plates, alongside of the red-ripe tomatoes, and added the fried cornbread. They could hardly wait to sit down to their unusual breakfast. They chatted like old friends as they ate, lingering over the pleasant meal, reluctant to let it end.

When cleanup was over and the kitten was fed once more, Bo and Ally spent some time in the garden picking the vegetables and getting them ready for market. They might not bring in much money, but it would be more that they had now. The question was—where to go to sell them?

"It's good that we're near the highway," Bo ventured. "Perhaps we could just sit beside the road and sell the produce. We'd make more money that way."

"Should we go over there now?" Ally asked.

"I think so… yes, of course…"

Seeing the child's reaction to her hesitation, she decided she had better explain.

"I used to live in Johnston," she began. "I'm not quite ready to see the people I knew when I was here before. I'm a little worried that some of them might pass down that highway, and it makes me feel uneasy."

Ally's confused look vanished, but the look that replaced it said that this little girl would give anything to be able to see and talk with other people. This caused Bo to remember her promise to go into town to see Jeffrey about Ally's legal matters. She knew that she had to put her own trepidations behind her if she were to help this little girl.

"Don't worry," she said. "We'll go out and sell the vegetables on the highway. We'll also go into town to see my friend Mr. Lawrence—soon, I promise."

"Could I go to school? I've never been to school. Mama taught me to read, and brought me books so I would read and not bother her. But if you let me go to school I could actually play with other kids, like in my books. Oh, that would be so much fun!"

"You definitely will be going to school, one way or another, little darling. Your days as a recluse are over. We both need friends. We're going to live like real people from now on. I just need to figure out a few things."

The child said nothing. She just went up to Bo and hugged her with all of her might. There were tears in her little eyes, and this brought tears to her newly adopted "grandma's" eyes, as well.

"Okay," she said, trying to cover up the intense emotions they were feeling. "Let's get these vegetables packed up and ready to sell. Are there any paper bags around here?"

"There are a lot grocery bags. I'll get them," Ally replied, and off she ran to fetch them.

Moments later the two began putting the fresh okra into various sizes of the brown paper bags. Then they carefully placed the tomatoes into bags to keep them from being bruised. When they had put all they could carry into a small rusty wagon, which had been sitting near the pump house, they went back inside. With a broken crayon, they printed a sign on one of the larger bags. They would display this with their vegetables. The leftover fried corn bread, the remaining cheese, and a tomato apiece went into a bag for their lunch. They also took a bottle of water, a couple of glasses, and some milk for Mews. Then off they went to sell their wares.

"These tomatoes are beautiful, and so fresh," the lady said. She had stopped just after they had displayed their sign. She smiled as she paid for her purchase, then went back to her car and drove away. A few other cars stopped as the day progressed, and most of the people bought some of the vegetables.

Bo and Ally took time between customers to consume their sparse lunch. Ally fed Mews, and they both kept a watchful eye on the road, hoping for more customers.

Just as they were finishing their food, another lady drove up and stopped. Seeing that there weren't many vegetables left, she said, "Oh, I'm glad I got here before everything was gone. I want three tomatoes and some okra. You say that you just picked these a couple of hours ago?"

"That's right," Bo answered, accepting the coins she handed her. "Thank you so much. Enjoy your vegetables." The lady picked up her purchase, smiled goodbye, and got back into her car and drove away.

"Look, Ally. That was almost the last of it. Can you believe how much money we have taken in? There's about three dollars here. We aren't broke any more."

Some time passed before another car stopped beside the road. A man got out and started walking over to them.

"Maybe he'll buy the rest," Ally whispered.

Sure enough, the man was so happy to find such fresh vegetables that he bought all that remained for his wife. He handed Bo two dollars and said, "Keep the change."

She was grateful for the generosity, and responded with a happy "thank you."

Ally could hardly contain herself until the car had left. Then she let out a little squeal of delight. "That's five whole dollars, Grandma Bo. We're rich!"

There was no need to dampen her spirits with the truth. The money would be enough for a few days, but something more permanent had to be done soon. She must look for a job.

"Let's go to the store and get some food. What do you say?" Bo asked. "Where's the little store you mentioned yesterday?"

"It's not far from here. I saw it when Mama and I went walking sometimes. She never let me go in, but I went over there after she left. I was looking for food in the trashcans. That's where I found Mews. But could I stay outside? I don't want to go in."

"You don't have to go in, if it bothers you. You really didn't get to leave the house very often, did you?"

"We went walking sometimes, but Mama didn't let me go where people were. I embarrassed her, she said."

"Can't you tell me what name she called you? She did call you by name, didn't she? It might help us find your relatives."

It took so long for the child to answer the question that Bo stooped down to her height and took her in her arms.

"It's okay, Honey. You don't have to tell me your name. It isn't important right now."

"Grandma Bo," she sobbed. "I don't have a pretty name. Mama named me 'Misfit.' When I learned to read, I found out what it means. I asked her why she named me that. She said, 'you don't belong *anywhere*.' I-don't-think-my-Mama-likes-me-at-all…"

Bo took a long breath, trying to think of the best way to respond to this news. She was on the verge of angry tears, herself. How could a mother be so cruel? This precious little girl must have suffered a lot of emotional abuse, if nothing worse. She let the child cry until she began wiping her little eyes. She gave Ally another quick hug, promising herself that she would see to it that no one ever hurt her again.

"Well," she said at last, "you have a nice name now. You're my Ally. You just give me a little time, and I'll see to it that you get a 'for real' name—not just a first name, either. You're going to have a middle one and a last one as well—all three. What do you think of that?"

The dark eyes were wide with wonder. "Oh, Grandma Bo! Can you *really* do that?"

"Of course. I'm bodacious, remember?"

"Yes. Remarkable. I remember." Ally smiled through her tears. "I'm so glad you came, Grandma Bo."

"So am I, Ally. So am I. Now, let's go find something to eat. I'm starved."

The trip to the store didn't take long. They were both very hungry and anxious to get home so they could eat. The first thing they did when they got back was to check the gage on the butane tank. They didn't want to run out of gas in the middle of cooking their meal. They found that the gage was still registering one-fourth full, so there was plenty of gas for their cooking needs.

Less than two hours after the sale of the last vegetables an early supper was on the small kitchen table. They hungrily consumed pork chops, cooked to a perfect golden brown, a mound of mashed potatoes, with milk gravy and, of course, fried okra and tomatoes. Fresh bread and butter rounded out the meal, with milk for a beverage and "store-bought" molasses cookies for dessert. Neither spoke as they ate. They were both badly in need of a nourishing meal, and they were thoroughly enjoying this one.

As they talked over dessert Bo was struggling with her feelings. Now that she was convinced that Ally's mother had abused her, she knew that she, herself, must give her up. Relatives, or an adoptive family, would have to be found.

The little girl would go to live with them. Even if the woman returned, she must not have her daughter back again. She was an unfit mother.

It's going to be so hard for me to let her go, she thought. *I don't know how I could have come to love her so in such a short time. Perhaps her new family will let me visit her once in awhile.*

"Did you hear me, Grandma Bo?"

"I'm sorry, child. I was off in another world, I guess. What did you say?"

"I was wondering what names you would give me."

Bo hadn't considered speaking about her plans just yet, but she could see that Ally had to know what she intended to do. She took a deep breath and tried to make sure her thoughts were all in order before she spoke.

"Honey, there's something we need to try to figure out. It's a grown-up thing. Can you try to help me?"

"Yes, I'm almost eight. Don't you remember?"

"All right, then, I need your help. You must try to remember everything you can about the past. Do you have any memory of anyone except your mother and her boyfriend—a relative perhaps, or even a friend? Try to remember when you were very little. Isn't there anyone?"

"No, ma'am. I never got to see anyone but Mama and Kevin, except in my books. I have a lot of friends in my books. Mama likes for me to read. She says I can travel all over the world in books, and then I won't need to go running around everywhere."

"You and your mother may have lived in some other place before you came here. Do you remember any other house at all? Can you remember anything that would give us a clue about your identity— your mother's parents, perhaps, or an aunt?"

47

"No. I don't remember anyone. Do you think I may have people I belong to?" I never had relatives. I would love that!"

"I'm sure there must be someone. We will ask my friend to see if he can find out anything. If we can't find relatives, I'm sure we can find a family to adopt you."

"It sounds like my dream of having a family is coming true." Ally laughed aloud with the joy of it.

"Grandma Bo" blinked back tears. They were tears of joy for Ally and of sadness for herself. She had opened herself up to heartache, just as she had feared. She was going to lose another little girl.

"Let's get this kitchen cleaned up," she said. "It's been a very long day for us. I'm a bit weary. Tomorrow we'll go into town and find that lawyer so we can begin our search."

"Can I wear my beautiful new pink dress? I love it so much."

"You surely may, and I'll wear the blue one. I may even trim this hair and see if I can look a bit more presentable. I haven't worried about that for many years," she said quietly.

"I love you, Grandma Bo." Ally grabbed her in the now familiar "bear hug," and then started clearing the table.

They spent the rest of the afternoon just talking and getting to know each other. The feeling of belonging to someone was incredibly special for both of them.

As dusk settled over the quiet seclusion of the ramshackle house, Bo, the child and the kitten all started yawning. Ally fed her kitten again, and put him to bed. After a bedtime snack of molasses cookies, and "not very cold" milk, the child snuggled up on the couch with her new "grandma", and was soon fast asleep. Bodacious knew that she had better sleep while she could. The kitten would be hungry again in a few hours. She would not let Ally wander about the dark house alone. She had been alone enough. They would care for the kitten together. She picked up the sleeping child and carried her to bed, then went to her room across the hall.

As she lay down on the soft bed, she wondered where she would be tomorrow night. Her new "granddaughter" might be taken from her and she, herself, might be forbidden the use of this house. No matter. If Ally has an aunt or a grandmother out there they should be reunited—and soon.

Chapter Four

Anna woke with a violent headache. The tension of the past few days was affecting her health. She couldn't get her mind off of her terrible loss. She struggled against accepting the thing she most feared—that her little girl had been murdered. It was as though her accepting it would make it true; yet, it most likely already was.

Suffering the return of these strong emotions after so many years was driving her to distraction. Why had it all come back full-force like this? Not knowing what had happened to her child was unbearable, of course, but that had been so from the beginning.

"Oh, what's wrong with me?" she moaned. The tears started again, and the headache became worse. Anna put her head under the pillow and held it tightly against her temples. She was beginning to feel nauseous. This had been happening more and more frequently lately.

I must get myself under control. My poor husband doesn't deserve this. She remembered Tony's *stricken face as he kissed her goodbye that morning. I have to do something. These headaches could be migraines. That would explain the nausea and the moods. I guess I'd better get an appointment with my doctor. I'll do that today,* she decided, as she drifted back to sleep.

When she awoke again, two hours later, the headache was better and the nausea was gone. She got up, showered, dressed, and went into the kitchen for breakfast. After eating, she went to the phone and called her doctor's office. She was given an appointment for the next week. With that settled, she was able to think of other things. She knew she had let her housework go for much too long, so she got the vacuum cleaner out and went to work, making things neat for her husband.

The ringing of the phone finally reached Anna's ears above the noise of the vacuum cleaner. Turning off that machine, she ran to the hall to see who was calling. The receptionist from her doctor's office was on the line.

"We've had a cancellation, Mrs. Benski. Would you like to come in this afternoon at 2:30?"

"Oh? I guess so. It isn't anything urgent, but I might as well go ahead and get it checked out. I'll be there."

Returning to her cleaning, Anna found herself considering the possibility of illness. Could something be really wrong with her? How would she cope with that? No, she must not be sick. Of course it was nothing serious…

She put the vacuum cleaner away and began dusting. She had always taken pleasure in making her furniture look shiny and new. They had been blessed and were able to own nice things. They could have had someone come in to help with the cleaning, but Anna liked doing her own housework. Her house had always sparkled with the look of a well-loved home. She took a moment to look over everything. It all looked great, and she felt the warm satisfaction of a job well-done.

কপ্ত-পপ্ত-পপ্ত

"It's been awhile, Mrs. Benski," said the smiling receptionist. "I hope that means you have been enjoying good health."

"I'm doing well, Joy. I've just been having a few headaches and some nausea. We've just passed the anniversary of Megan's disappearance again. For some reason, it's been more traumatic for me this year. I think my physical problems are connected to that, but decided I'd get it checked out so it doesn't become something bothersome."

"Nerves can really make you sick, I know. Well, I'm sure Dr. Williams will have you feeling better in no time. Just have a seat, and we'll be right with you."

Anna smiled at the girl and took a seat next to an older woman. She was soon engaged in one of those, "I see. Oh, dear, that must have been difficult," conversations. She was glad when the nurse called her name and she could excuse herself gracefully. She knew the dear lady needed someone to talk to, but the timing was bad for Anna.

She left the office an hour later, after extensive tests, blood work and a complete physical.

I feel really foolish going through all of that for a bit of nausea and a headache, she thought. *I should have just ignored it. It would have gone away. It always does. Well, the thing is done now, and Tony will be glad.*

On the drive home, she felt less stressed. She did feel better for having committed her health problems to her doctor. It was good to get back home, though, and she breathed a sigh of relief as she pulled into the driveway. She looked up to see her neighbor heading her way.

"Hi, Phyllis. What's up?"

"Hi! I was just making plans to go to that revival tonight. Come with me."

"Well, Tony did say he wanted to go, so he could apologize to the young girl who came by to invite us. She came on a bad day."

"I know. I talked to her. She felt terrible about what she did. Of course, she had no way of knowing what you were going through. How about it? Do you think you might go with me tonight? I do hate to go alone."

"Sure, if Tony hasn't made other plans. I'm not really interested, but we should get this apology out of the way."

"Shall we go in my car or yours?"

"Let's take ours this time."

"Will 6:45 be okay? It starts at 7:00."

"That sounds about right. Come on over when you're ready."

"Will do. See you in a little while."

53

"Bye."

Boy! I'm getting a lot done today. I'm proud of me. Anna was smiling as she went in to prepare a quick dinner for her husband.

৯৶৯৶৯৶

"Hi, honey, I'm home!" Tony was dreading finding his wife still in a weepy state. She was really suffering. He often thought of their daughter, too, but when there is nothing you can do, you have to get on with your life. He was wishing he could think of something that might cheer Anna up when she came bustling through the kitchen door.

"Hi, darling. We have to hurry with dinner. I've obligated us to going to that revival you wanted to attend. I hope that's okay. Phyllis will be here at 6:45 to go with us." She went into his arms for her kiss and looked up into his face. She was smiling.

Tony was taken by surprise. There she was all dressed up, with every hair in place. She even had a pretty apron tied around her slender waist—and the house sparkled. She was energetic. She was his Anna again. Sure, he would go. He'd do anything that would bring this about.

"That sounds good, sweetheart. What's for dinner?" he asked casually, trying not to show his surprise.

"It's just a casserole and a salad. I hope that's okay."

"Of course. Shall 1 go wash up now?"

"It's ready whenever you are. I'll go put it on the table." She left him standing there, wondering at the sudden change in her.

৯৶৯৶৯৶

"You look really nice, Phyllis. I wasn't sure what to wear. Is this okay?" Anna turned around a couple of times, the cream-colored dress flaring out a bit as she did so. The pearls at her neck made the dress special, and her dark hair complemented the light color.

"It's perfect. Churchgoers don't usually criticize other people's clothing, though they do prefer that it be modest. That's one of the nicest things about church. The people know how to love. Most are kind and caring."

"I read that little paper the girl left behind," Anna said as they walked over to the car. "It says God sent his son to die for the world. That would be incredible love. It's too much to believe, of course. Why would God do that? Nobody would do such a thing."

Tony opened the car door for them, and Anna scooted over to sit in the middle. Phyllis got in beside her. Tony closed the door and walked around to the driver's side.

"You're forgetting that God is not a human," Phyllis continued the conversation as they drove. "He is God. We can't understand his love, we just have to believe in it and accept it."

"Phyllis, you have to excuse me if that seems too fantastic to be true. I could never believe in such a fantasy. What would happen to little children? What about Megan, is she isn't …" Anna bit her lip, and then continued. "Well, if she isn't alive. She was too young to have understood such a thing."

"Never say never, dear friend. As for Megan, the Bible makes it plain that small children go to be with God when they die."

"Well, here we are at the church—for better or worse," Anna said, changing the subject.

"It's a great building. It always looks so neat and well kept," Tony said.

"Maybe we'll hear some good singing, at least," Anna ventured absently as they approached the building. "There sure are a lot of people here."

"Look. There's that nice young girl who came by inviting us to the service. Lynn was her name, I think," Phyllis said.

Tony headed for the young woman. "She's the reason I came," he said. "I guess I'd better get this apology over with."

Anna turned to Phyllis and said, "Tony really feels bad about slamming the door in that poor girl's face. I'm glad he can tell her

55

so. He would have just kept worrying about it. Thanks for inviting us. I doubt that we would have ever come on our own."

"Well, as I said, I do hate to have to go places alone. Ever since Tom left for Korea, I have rather withdrawn. He was always so involved in everything. It was always 'us'. Now there is only 'me'. If only we had chil...oh, here comes the evangelist. His name is Brother Glenn. Doesn't he look kind?"

"He does look kind. He's almost here. What should we do?"

"Just talk to him for a minute. There are so many people, he won't have long to talk to us."

"Good evening, ladies. How nice that you could come. I am Brother Glenn."

Anna was surprised. Somehow she had expected an older man. This one was quite young.

"I'm Phyllis Turner," she hears her friend say. "This is my neighbor, Anna Benski. We live down the street. A young woman named Lynn invited us to come."

"Oh, yes. She has spent a lot of time in the neighborhood inviting people these past two weeks. She's a fine girl. Well, I hope you get a blessing from the service. Come back any time you can."

"Thank you."

"Yes, thanks."

Tony returned, smiling. A load had obviously been lifted from him. "What a nice girl," he said. "She isn't mad at me at all. I'm glad we came, honey—and Phyllis, thanks for inviting us. Shall we find a seat?"

Most of the back seats had been taken, so the three had to move on toward the front of the building. They finally found empty spaces on the fourth pew from the front and sat down. A smiling, teenaged boy came over and handed them hymnals. He was followed by a tall, dignified looking man, about thirty-five. He identified himself as Brother Alexander, and said that he was the pastor of the church. Just as he turned to leave, his wife, Susan, came up and introduced herself. After that, several others also came by to welcome them.

"This is a really friendly group." Anna was pleased that the people were accepting them so well. She had had vague thoughts of sitting quietly in the back of the building and leaving without talking to anyone except the young woman they had come to find. She could tell that her husband was equally impressed, and Phyllis was talking with one person after another.

The pianist and organist began playing. The choir entered the choir loft and took their places as a young man stood up and faced the audience.

"Good evening, ladies and gentlemen. Welcome! We're so glad to see all of you, and we want to extend a special welcome to our visitors. Please worship God with us as we sing praises to his glorious name. All stand please."

An incredible peace settled over Anna as everyone in the auditorium burst into song. A gentle breeze from the open windows stirred her hair, and she smiled. Looking down at her hymnal, she joined the congregation in singing "Nothing but the Blood of Jesus," with a strange feeling of joy and wonder.

Jesus. The blood of Jesus, she thought. *Maybe I should pay more attention to this church thing. What if there is something to it?*

Tony was lost in a wonder of his own. *What kind of people are these that they sing with so much joy? What is this feeling in my heart? Is there something to the things Phyllis was saying in the car?* He opened his mouth and sang with an excitement that he did not understand. Phyllis, standing beside them, smiled, and sent a "thank you" prayer heavenward.

All too soon, the singing ended, and the choir special was over. Lynn joined the young man who had led the singing, and together they sang a beautiful hymn about Jesus.

The pastor stood, then, and introduced the evangelist. The congregation was asked to stand for the reading of God's Word.

Brother Glenn gave the scripture text, John 3:16-18, and began reading in a mellow voice: "For God so loved the world that he gave his only begotten son, that whosoever believeth in him should not perish, but have everlasting life. For God sent not his son into the world to condemn the world, but that the world through him might be saved. He that believeth on him is not condemned, but he that believeth not—is condemned already, because he hath not believed in the name of the only begotten son of God."

As the congregation settled back into their seats, Anna was a bit stunned by what they had just heard. *Condemned? Already? But I'm a good person*, she was thinking. *And Tony just came and apologized to Lynn. He's a good person, too. He's a really good person."*

Tony fidgeted in his seat. *That's pretty strong,* he thought. *How could God condemn someone who tries to do the best he can? Isn't he a God of love?*

"You see, dear people," brother Glenn was saying, "even though God is a God of love, he is also a God of judgment and justice."

Tony started at that. *Does this guy read minds?*

"He is perfect," the preacher continued.

Now Tony's attention was riveted on him.

"Adam sinned, as it says in Romans 5:12. And because we are all descended from him, we are born with his nature to sin. That means that we are like him and so all of us sin. Could anyone here tonight stand to their feet and declare to me that they have never committed one sin?" He waited. No one stood. Some were squirming in their seats.

"No, of course not. That's because, 'all have sinned and come short of the glory of God.' This is in Romans 3:23, if you want to look it up. 'There is none righteous, no not one', is found in Romans 3:10, and 'the wages of sin is death', God tells us, in Romans 6:23.

"Face it! By your own admission in not standing just now, you have declared that you are a sinner. The penalty for your sin is death—not only physical death, dear friend—you also deserve eternal death in hell. Don't you see? You are a sinner and you have no hope of saving yourself. I repeat: *you have no hope of saving yourself from the wrath of God!* You sit here tonight, condemned already. But, you need not despair. Why? Because, as we have just read, God loves you! He loves you so much that he sent his only begotten son, Jesus Christ, down here to the earth to suffer death in your place. As Jesus agonized there on the cross with your sins on him, His Father turned his back on him. In agony, he cried out, 'My God! My God! Why hast thou forsaken me?' He not only bore *your* sins, but the sins of everyone who ever lived, or would live after him. We cannot even begin to imagine the horrors he suffered in our place. Because he lived a perfectly sinless life as a human, he was counted worthy to suffer the penalty for the sins of all humans. Jesus was able to be the perfect sacrifice before God, but it cost him dearly. He was God, but he was also man. Do you see the very human emotions mixed with the perfection of God? But Jesus did not stay dead. In three days, he rose from the dead, and now he is back in heaven with his Father. Oh, how he loves you! Only God is capable of such love.

"God does not say that you are condemned just because you are a sinner. He says that the reason you are condemned is that, although you are a sinner, you have not chosen to believe on the name of his only begotten son. God has provided the way of escape for you. You do not have to continue under condemnation. The words of our text in John chapter three were spoken to a man named Nicodemus. Jesus told him, 'You must be born again'. We can't be born again as tiny babies. This new birth is a spiritual one. What a gift God is offering you! Complete forgiveness of all you sins— past, present, and future. Eternal life in his heaven at the end of your physical life assured. All you have to do is accept his gift. Imagine how he feels if you reject it. Imagine how he feels if you try to somehow earn it, when he is offering it to you as a gift. 'How shall we escape if we neglect so great a salvation?' the apostle Paul asks.

Both of the Benskis were deep in thought as the preacher continued, and did not hear much of the rest of the sermon. As the piano began playing, they turned their attention back to the man behind the pulpit.

"Jesus gave his life in your place," he was saying. "God the father accepted his sacrifice—and that sacrifice still stands good today. My friends, I have just shown you in God's word that you are condemned already. Won't you let go of your stubborn pride and trust Jesus to cover you in his precious blood? You need never wonder about eternity again. You need never fear death again, because death for a child of God is really only the beginning of his eternal life."

Extending his hands toward the audience, Brother Glenn asked once more. "Won't you let him save you, tonight? He's waiting. Come on down and tell us about it. Stand, as we sing, please."

The pianist began playing a hymn. The congregation stood and began singing the beautiful words: "Just as I am, without one plea, but that thy blood was shed for me…"

Tony looked down at his wife, and found her weeping, unaware of him, or anything else. Her eyes were glued on the man standing in front of the pulpit, inviting people to trust Jesus as their savior.

"Come and tell us about it, and let us rejoice with you," he was saying as the pianist continued playing softly. "Or, if you still don't understand, come on down and let us help you understand. Oh, my dear friend, don't go home tonight without taking care of this eternal matter. Jesus died for you. The least you can do is to try to make sure that the decision you are making at this very moment is the one you really want to make. As God's Spirit calls you, won't you answer 'yes' with your whole heart?"

A movement beside her startled Anna, as Tony stepped out into the aisle. He turned around and looked at her with a question in his eyes. She smiled a joyful smile and reached for his hand. With tears streaming down their faces, they walked down the aisle together. Moments later, the pastor was telling the congregation that Anna and Tony Benski had just accepted Christ as their savior, and wanted to be baptized into the church. There wasn't a dry eye in the building, as a great chorus of "amen's" was lifted up to heaven.

"Perhaps there is someone else who needs to respond to the urging of God's Spirit. Maybe it is for salvation, or perhaps for baptism or church membership. Won't you come as we sing one last verse?"

Brother Glenn held out his hand toward the congregation, and Phyllis walked down the aisle uniting with the church on promise of a letter from a church in a nearby small town.

They remained at the front after the service so that everyone could file by and welcome them into the church. When Lynn passed by, there were hugs all around. All three thanked her for inviting them. "God bless you for being a faithful servant, Lynn," Phyllis said. With tears in her eyes, Lynn hugged them each again and moved along.

It was late when the trio, as last, arrived home. Saying "goodnight" to Phyllis, Anna and Tony watched her until she was safely inside her house, and then went into their own home.

"What a night!" Tony exclaimed when they were inside. "I doubt if I'll sleep a wink tonight. I'm so excited! Just think, a few hours ago we were on our way to hell, and didn't even know it," he said. "Can you believe the danger we were in? We would have spent eternity in that horrible place."

"It is all so incredible," she answered. "Just that one decision to attend church tonight has changed everything. We must always remember how important it is to invite people to church, even if they don't want to be bothered. I shudder to think of what would have become of us if Lynn hadn't come by yesterday, and if Phyllis hadn't invited us to go to church with her tonight. What if there had been no meeting at all? Oh, Tony, I'm so happy!"

Tony took his precious wife into his arms and they stood, embracing each other for a long time. Anna's head was on her husband's shoulder and a smile was on her lips.

Suddenly the phone rang. Puzzled by the late call, Anna reluctantly moved out of her husband's embrace and went to pick up the receiver.

"Mrs. Benski, this is Dr. William's nurse," said the voice on the other end of the line. "I called earlier, but you were out. The doctor asked that I call you and have you come back in tomorrow afternoon with your husband. Say, at 5:00 if possible?"

"Oh? Well, of course. We'll be there. Thanks for calling."

"You're welcome. See you tomorrow."

The line went dead then, and Anna stood there, a bit stunned. What could be wrong? Here they were, so happy, and now this. *Dear God, please…don't let it be serious. Oh, please*, she prayed.

"Honey, what is it?" Tony's face showed his concern.

"I went to the doctor this afternoon, like you told me to. That was his nurse. She says the doctor wants to talk with both of us together tomorrow afternoon at 5:00. I wonder what…"

"Honey, don't worry. It's probably something simple."

"Probably, but…"

"Come on. Let's go to bed. It's getting late."

"Okay. I'm pretty tired. I'm still really happy though."

"Me too. I love you, Mrs. Benski."

"I love you too, Mr. Benski."

Chapter Five

The next morning at the run-down house began with big bowls of oatmeal mixed with sugar and canned milk. There was also bread, butter, and apple juice. The juice wasn't cold, of course, but it tasted good. How wonderful it was to wake up in the morning and know the there was something to eat.

After they had cleaned up the breakfast dishes it was time for haircuts. Bo tried not to cut very much off, as she hadn't ever cut hair before. She wanted to leave enough length so that it would be fixable if she messed it up. They both looked pretty good, however; so after heating water on the stove, they shampooed their hair. Then they had warm baths and put on the new dresses. Ally twirled around the living room in hers, singing and laughing.

"You look beautiful, darling. With that dark hair and dark eyes, pink is certainly your color. Now, we need to find some shoes that fit you. You really shouldn't go to town barefooted."

Ally swirled around the room, her newly shampooed hair shinning as she tossed her pretty head. Bo could only smile a sad smile and be glad for her. She hoped that it wouldn't take long to find her a family. She was becoming too attached to this vivacious little girl.

"Mama bought me stuff sometimes," she said as she swirled to a stop in front of Grandma Bo. "It always looked like someone had been using the things before I got them, though. I have some white shoes that used to be too big for me. I haven't tried them on for a long time," she said, and ran off down the hall to get them.

Feeling that she must look her best if she were to get results in town, Evelyn carefully dressed and arranged her hair. She thought she could count on Jeffrey to help, but how could she bear to see him after such a long time? He would have so many questions.

63

In the end, she realized that he was the only way to help Ally, so she put her feelings aside and made plans to see him.

Checking her appearance in the cracked mirror, she was surprised to actually see more than a shadow of her former self looking back at her. With her hair neatly trimmed and shampooed, and the blue dress sewn to fit her just so, she looked much younger—pretty even. "Yes, very presentable indeed," she said aloud as she nodded at her reflection. Now, she had to find some shoes. There wasn't much chance that the woman's shoes she had seen in the bottom of the closet would fit. She just hoped they would be nearly enough her size that she could make do with them.

Oh, I need a purse, too, she remembered. *Even if I have nothing to put into it, I want to look like I do. I have the remaining money and a few of my own things. I do still have my identifications,* she mused. *My driver's license is long out of date, but there is the social security card. I need to be ready, in case there are legal matters. I'll do whatever I have to do to get a real family for that precious child. The things that seemed so important to me two days ago simply aren't important any more. Nothing matters except Ally.*

"Look, Grandma Bo. Will these be okay?" Ally was holding up a nearly new pair of white, patent leather shoes. Obviously, they had come from a used clothing sale. A tag with the price of 15¢ was still attached to them. They went well with the pink dress. Now if they would only fit…

Ally put them on, and thankfully they did fit nicely. Her mother had obviously bought used clothing whenever she could find it, and put things up for the future. Bo sent the little girl to look for socks to go with her "new" shoes while she went in search of shoes and a purse for herself.

She found a purse in the top of the closet and took it down to put her things inside. It contained some of the woman's personal things. There was an expired driver's license with the name

Georgia Stephens, and Bo had a moment of doubt. She knew that the woman would probably never need the things again, but still it felt like an invasion of privacy. As she sat on the bed removing the items one by one, she suddenly realized that these things might give a clue to Ally's identity—and even lead them to her relatives. She put everything back, adding her few personal things, and closed the purse with a brisk snap.

She sighed, and shook her head. The effort of actually going back into Johnstown was taking all of her emotional strength. She determined that she must do it, however, and reached into her well worn bag for a pair of nylon hose. She located them at the bottom of the bag, along with her garter belt, and finished dressing. She had found a pair of shoes in the closet. They were about a half-size too large, but she stuffed tissue into the toes and put them on. Then she went back to the hall mirror to straighten the seams of the hose. After a final glance in the mirror she announced that she was ready to go.

"You did feed Mews, didn't you?" Bo asked. "He will have to stay here in his box until we get back, I'm afraid."

"Oh, no, Grandma Bo! Don't make him stay here all alone. Can't we take him with us? He might get hungry, or scared, like I used to."

"Honey, where could we put him once we get to town? We don't have friends there. We can't take him into the lawyer's office. He'll be all right. I promise."

"Okay, but I don't want to."

"I know, but it's the best thing for him, too. He would get really tired." She smiled at the brooding of the child. She was so cute with a bit of a pout on her pretty little face. "Well, if you're ready, let's be on our way," she said, trying to sound confident.

It was early afternoon as they closed the door behind them and began walking toward town.

Since Bo had skirted the town when she arrived, she didn't really know what to expect there. As they reached its outskirts, she was glad to see that nothing had changed much, though it had grown some during her twelve-year absence. She saw a couple of new buildings and on some of the streets the white seashells were gone, and new blacktop was now in their place. It was the old things, however, that affected her most. The old drug store was still there, although it was wearing a fresh coat of paint. Long ago high school memories of sitting at its counter, with a five-cent glass of cherry coke and two straws, evoked memories of her John. Down the street, the library looked the same. *Liz's Dress Shop,* where she worked as a teen, was still there. Main Street sported new street lights, but basically the small town was just as she left it. Waves of nostalgia washed over her as she passed the familiar sights. Longings for her former life were so strong that she was afraid that she might not be able to do this thing she had set out to do. Jeffrey Lawrence had been her husband's lawyer. They had all been friends since high school. He was the best hope she had of finding the missing relatives, or an adoptive family; but it would mean opening herself to the questions and the memories.

"Grandma Bo, you look funny. Are you okay? Are you sick?" Ally's face showed her concern.

Bo looked down at the small girl at her side. She stopped for a moment, wiped her brow, and said, "I'm fine, dear. I just have to find the lawyer's office, that's all."

"I'm kinda scared. What if the man doesn't like me?"

The new "grandma" hadn't thought of things like that. Of course, Ally would have misgivings. Until two days ago, the child had had no contact with people other than her mother and Kevin. She had not been brought into town during all these many years. Having known only the two people, how could she know what to expect from other humans?

"He's a wonderful man," she encouraged the child. "The three of us—he, my husband and I—all went to the same high school together. He will think you are very special. He'll find you some parents, too. I'm sure of it."

"I was just worried. I'm sorry."

"No, dear, I'm sorry. I should have explained things to you better."

"How come your face looks funny, Grandma Bo?" she asked, looking up at her anxiously.

"It just seems to be warmer this afternoon that I had anticipated," she responded. "It's a long walk from your house."

"Are you getting too tired? We could sit on the grass and rest for awhile."

"I'll be okay. Don't worry. I surely could use a glass of water, though. I should have thought to bring some…oh, dear…"

Bodacious stopped walking. The world spun around her. She was nauseous, and the vague pain had returned—only stronger this time. Suddenly she realized that she was going to faint, and she moved nearer to the grass, hoping she would make it there before…

Her feet touched the edge of the grass. She leaned toward it, and then everything went black as she fell.

"She'll be all right, I think, young lady. It's a warm day. Have you walked very far?"

The deep voice of a man penetrated Bo's conscience. She had the vague feeling that he was standing over her.

"Yes, sir. Is Grandma Bo going to die?" Ally little face was pinched with fear.

"No, of course not," the man spoke again. "She has just fainted. There, you see, she's blinking her eyes at us."

Bo turned over and looked up into the face of a young man she had never seen before. His wavy brown hair and blue eyes filled her with a sort of hope. He was smiling kindly, and it gave her a happy feeling in spite of her predicament. She moaned softly, and tried to sit up. He put a strong hand behind her back and helped her.

"There you are. Are you feeling better?"

"Yes. Oh, dear, what a foolish thing to do, falling like that. I'm so embarrassed."

"No need for that. I'm Brother Glenn. I like helping people who need a bit of an assist. I'm here in Johnston preaching a revival at a church down the street. If you look closely, you can just see the corner of the building. Do you see?"

She strained to see, and finally found the place to which he referred. She nodded her head, which sent it spinning again.

"Oh, my," she gasped. She put her hand to her mouth to try to control the nausea, but then she felt herself sinking toward the grass again. "You don't happen to have water with you, do you?" she asked him weakly. "I don't ...I don't...feel too well..."

"No," he answered, "but that's not a problem. Just give me a moment. I'll see if anyone is at home over there." And off he bounded toward the nearest house.

"Oh, he shouldn't have done that," Bo moaned. "What will people think?"

"Don't die Grandma Bo! I need you. Please don't die..."

"Dear child, I'm just a bit too warm. Tomorrow is the first day of June, you know. I promise you, I will be all right as soon as I get some water. Look, there comes the preacher and a lady with a pitcher now. I'll be just fine."

"She does look pale. It's too warm to be walking any distance today," the lady was saying as they approached. Then she bent down with a pitcher and poured a glass full of something cold.

"Here you go, ma'am. I've brought you some nice fresh lemonade. It will perk you up. You'll feel better right away. You just wait and see."

"Thank you, so much. This looks really good."

The woman poured a glass for Ally, too. It was just what they needed, and Bo rallied quickly. Soon she was standing up and, after thanking the lady for coming to her rescue, she was about to go on her way. The preacher, however, had other ideas.

"I think it will be better if I drive you to your destination," he said, taking her by the elbow and leading her toward his car.

"Young lady would you open the door for us?" he asked Ally.

"How do I get it open?" she wondered, pulling on the handle to no avail.

He reached to open the door. "Haven't you ever ridden in this kind of car?" he asked casually, as he held the seat forward so she could get in the back.

"No, sir. I haven't ever ridden in any car," she responded.

He returned the seat to its original position and then helped Bo settle into the front. Closing the door, he walked around to the other side of the car. As he got into the driver's seat, Bo could see that he wanted to ask about Ally's remark. She decided to open up to him.

"What she said is true. I guess since you are a preacher it won't hurt to explain."

Being aware that Ally could overhear, she was careful of what she said. She began to tell Brother Glenn her story, from the moment she discovered the deserted-looking house and met the little girl. When she told him about the mother, he nodded his head and responded kindly.

"It does sound like there was a real problem there. What can I do to help?"

"Getting me to my lawyer helps a great deal. You might add a few prayers to aid our research, too."

"I certainly can do that, dear lady. Would you like me to ask the people at church to pray, too?"

"I suppose that couldn't hurt anything. Thank you, Brother Glenn."

They reached the lawyer's office as she finished speaking. The young preacher stopped at the curb and got out of the car to open the door for her and Ally.

"I'll be on my way now," he said. "I would like to invite you to attend the revival services, though. Do you think you might?"

"We'll try," she said distractedly, then turned toward Ally. *There must be a million thoughts flying around in her small head right now*, she thought. She knew that she must put the child's needs ahead of her own, of course, but the realization of what she was about to do was overwhelming. How could she just go in there, after the long years of unexplained absence, and ask Jeffrey for help? What would he think? How would he react?

I can't do this! She started to tell Ally, but the look on her small face stopped her at once. She would have to go through with it. She told Brother Glenn "thank you" again, and waved as he drove off toward the church. Bo steeled herself for the coming interview. Opening the door, she took Ally's hand and they walked together into the lawyer's building.

Forcing herself to go over to the secretary's desk, she gave her name and asked to see Mr. Lawrence. The secretary disappeared into Jeffrey Lawrence's office to ask if he could see someone named Evelyn Johnston. The two frightened females stood perfectly still, not speaking a word.

I can't do this. I can't. I just cannot... Bo's head was spinning again. She was desperately looking around for a place to sit, when her deceased husband's dearest friend stepped through the office door.

"Evelyn? Can this be true? Are you really here?" Jeffrey Lawrence walked over to her and took both of her hands in his. Neither spoke. They simply stood there, looking at each other. She fought the tears, but they came anyway. His eyes began to mist as well, and he took her in his arms and let her weep.

"Oh, lady, it is so good to see you!" he said at last.

She moved back slightly, so that she could see his face. He was smiling, and shaking his head; then he embraced her again.

"Thank God you're all right. I was afraid you were dead. Do you know it's been twelve years?"

"Oh, yes, I do know that." She smiled wearily.

"What were you thinking? Didn't you know we would all be crazy with worry? Didn't you care at all about that? My word, Bo!" he said, crushing her in his arms, as one would embrace a treasured friend he had thought was forever lost.

She wept again, and he led her gently into his office to a chair. "Come along, child. I didn't mean to ignore you," he said to Ally. "Come on in," he repeated as she hesitated. "Close the door, please."

She obeyed, but remained beside the door.

"Please sit down, little sweetheart," he said, motioning her to a chair. "I'm sorry if I frightened you. I'm really a very nice guy," he said smiling.

She moved cautiously to the chair and sat on the edge of the seat.

"Who is this pretty lady, Evelyn? Is she your child?"

"No, I haven't remarried. This is Ally. She's the reason I'm here."

"She's my Grandma Bo," Ally said, a bit defensively.

"Bodacious. Yes, we always called her that," he said, smiling. "It's so good to see you sitting there, Bo." He was shaking his head in disbelief. "You're going to have to tell me everything, you know. The little girl can't be your granddaughter, so who—?"

"Actually, she can't, but she sort of is. Oh, right now everything seems so insane. Why did I ever leave Johnston? I have lost twelve years out of my life, and to what end? I don't know where to begin I don't know if I can talk about it yet, Jeffrey. I'm afraid I haven't been very wise."

She took a deep breath and let it out. After hesitating for a moment, she began again. "When the money I took with me ran out, I had to start working in the dime stores just to survive. I had

71

no money, no friends—nothing in my life that mattered. That is, until I met Ally two days ago. She gave me a reason to live again. We've rather adopted each other. That's why we're here."

"You've been living near poverty? I can't believe that. Why? There was plenty of money in your bank account."

"Well, the reasons for all of those decisions seem a little ridiculous now, but that isn't why we are here. I came back to Johnston because I had an overpowering urge to return. I didn't know why—I just had to come. I was a couple of hundred miles away, in a really small town in northern Louisiana. I walked most of the last ten miles, because my money ran out. Finally, two days ago I made it back here. I skirted around the town and at last wandered into a narrow lane..."

When she finished telling him everything, Jeffrey shook his head sympathetically, got up and walked over to Ally, kneeling beside her chair. "You've had quite a difficult life, haven't you, little one? Well, you've come to the right place for help. I promise you we'll get you a real name—and a real family. Will you trust me?"

"With a real daddy? I've never had a daddy before." Ally was loosening up, letting go of her fear, as excitement began taking over. She looked over at Grandma Bo, and smiled through her tears. "You said he was a nice man, Grandma. You were right."

Both adults smiled at that, and the tension was relieved somewhat.

"I'm not sure what my financial status is," Bo began, "but if I still have any money..."

"Well you don't have to worry about that," Jeffrey responded. "John left you everything. It is still intact. In fact, it has been drawing interest through the years. As time passed and you didn't return, I thought I should invest it for you. You have enough to be very comfortable for the rest of your life. You will have to give your renters thirty days notice, though, so you will need a place to stay for a little while."

72

"Renters? You mean my house is still mine? I can go home?" Tears came into her eyes, and she fought them back.

"I'm so sorry. I didn't mean to upset you. You seem to have been through some pretty rough times. You know I'm here for you Bo."

"I do know. Thank you, so much. Actually, I've come for help for Ally. We need to find any relatives she might have. Would you help us find them?"

"I'll use my detectives for that. You just concentrate on settling in and putting your life back in order. I'll get Miss Black to call about a suite at the Johnston Hotel for you. You obviously can't stay in that house you mentioned. Just wait here for a few moments."

Totally exhausted, mentally and physically, she simply did as she was told and leaned back to rest. Ally slipped out of her chair and moved over to put her arms around her. "I love you, Grandma Bo. I'm sorry you cried. Did Mr. Jeffrey hurt your feelings?"

"Oh, no, darling. I was crying about things that happened a long time ago—before you were even born. We'll talk about it soon. Right now, I seem to be very tired. Just hold my hand, will you?"

When Jeffrey came back into the room, he found them like that. Their emotions were so intense that he determined that they must never be completely separated. Whatever arrangements he made for Ally's future, Evelyn must be included in them.

"Well, it's all settled," he told them as he came back into his office. "You have a two bedroom suite at the hotel. It overlooks the woods at the back of the park, so it should be pleasant. Miss Black has gone to put together some things for you. You can go on over now, if you like."

"Mews!" Ally said suddenly. "We have to go get him. He'll starve out there."

"Of course, dear. Don't worry. We won't leave him there alone. Actually, Jeffrey, I would like to go back to the house for tonight. Would that be all right with you Ally?"

"I'd like that," she responded, looking cautiously at Jeffrey.

73

"Of course. I'll take you wherever you need to go—to the bank first, maybe?"

"I can't believe I still have a bank account. You're a good friend, Jeff. I was so foolish, feeling afraid to come here. Thank you."

"Afraid of me? Whatever did I do to deserve that?"

They both laughed, and Ally joined in, although she had no idea why they were laughing.

A few minutes later, they left the office. Bo Johnston was back in town! Suddenly, with that realization, the all-too-familiar "sinking feeling" was in her chest again, choking her. But she was determined not to let anything interfere with her helping Miss Ally. So she straightened her back and walked briskly to hide her emotions as Jeffrey ushered them into his shiny new Oldsmobile.

At the bank, she was shocked to learn her account balance. She would never have to worry about working for forty-cents an hour again. Accepting the temporary checkbook, and some cash that would permit her to begin making use of the legacy her husband had left her, she realized that she wasn't afraid any more. She could take care of Ally now. She could move back into her beloved house. She was a real person again. She belonged back here in Johnston. It felt so good to be home.

A short time later, they arrived in front of the run-down house. Jeffrey helped the ladies out of the car and inside. He looked around at the dingy, sparse furnishings, and cringed at the thought of leaving them alone in this place for even one more night. Ally came up and "introduced" him to Mews, and he sat down on the dirty couch to watch as she fed him. The kitten was quite hungry, after such a long time, and it took a one and a half bottles of milk to satisfy him.

The three of them were quickly making inroads into Jeffrey's heart. He was feeling very protective of them—wanting to make sure that they never suffered anything again.

"Thanks for everything, Jeff. Just this morning we hardly knew where our next meal might come from." Bo stood, looking at him, and he at her. "Seeing you brings back long ago, happy memories," she said quietly.

"I know. If only John could...I'm sorry. That was thoughtless."

"Not at all. I was thinking the same thing. It's good to be home." She whispered.

"Grandma Bo, is it okay to say I'm hungry?" Ally was standing there looking very vulnerable. Both adults turned, and smiled down at her. Jeffrey announced that they would be his guests for an early supper at the best restaurant in town!

Ally's eyes got big at that news. "A 'for real' restaurant? Like in my books?"

"Just like that," he replied, smiling.

This child is going to be experiencing an incredible number of new things all at once, Jeff realized. *She might simply delight in seeing and learning all of the things she's been missing, but I think I'd better keep an eye on her,* he decided.

"Are we ready then, ladies?" he asked.

"Jeffrey, we don't want to interfere with your family. Won't they be expecting you?" Bo was concerned about causing distress for his loved ones.

"I'm still a confirmed bachelor. No problem there."

"Well, then, I think I may be almost as hungry as a certain little girl," she said happily. "I'm ready. How about you, Ally?"

"I sure am, Mr. Jeffrey. I never saw a restaurant before."

He reached for her hand, and motioned Bo to precede them. They went out to the car for the drive back into the city.

అలాఅలాఅలా

The dream came again that night. Bo had been sleeping restlessly, but had at last fallen into a very deep sleep. Even in sleep, though, her body had shuddered as the too-familiar memories wove themselves once more into the dreaded dream.

She saw John, so handsome and strong, sitting beside her in the car as they drove through the low hills not too far from their home. The car was new, and she had wanted to drive it, so they had gone for a short trip in the cool of the evening. They had been so happy together that day, laughing and even singing silly songs as they drove. Now, once again, she could see him so clearly. He was talking to her. She was turning her head to respond to some funny remark...

No! Her subconscious mind screamed as she slept. *I don't want to see this again....*

The dream did not stop, however. As though in slow motion, she saw John lunging toward her, knocking her hands from the steering wheel. He was taking control of the car, turning it sharply to the left. She was glancing up just in time to see a car coming straight at them—and their car was now turned so that the impact would be on John's side. Before she could even scream, they were being hit broadside with such force that they were being pushed over into the ditch on the other side of the road. They were skidding in a half-circle and slamming into a telephone pole—once again hitting on John's side. She was being thrown from the car by the impact. She was waking up in the hospital... the dream was becoming fuzzy...

Bo struggled to awaken, knowing what she would have to endure if the dream continued. She sat up straight in the bed. "No! John!" she said aloud. "John?"

Wide awake now, she wept. The dream was over, but the memories lingered. Sitting in the bed, she trembled in the slight chill of the early morning. Her John was not there with her. He would never be with her again. She got out of bed and walked over to the window.

She stood there, remembering snatches of the days that followed—of being dressed in black with a small black hat on her head, a short veil shutting out some of her pain from the rest of the world. People were all around. Everyone was weeping.

She had left him there in the cemetery. Turning to stare out of the limo window, she had watched the little patch of earth until it was gone, at last, from her vision. She was more alone that she had ever been in her life.

Now, memories she had long ago hidden in the back reaches of her mind began to press themselves into her consciousness. She resisted, but she could not shut them out. She remembered the hateful words. "How could you have let this happen? You killed him! You killed him…"

"No, you don't understand," she had tried desperately to explain. "He knocked my hands away…" But the person had not listened. Evelyn had been left standing in the middle of the living room. Alone.

Staring vacantly out of the window of the borrowed house, she wept. "My only answer was to leave Johnston," she whispered into the darkness. "What else could I have done?" Silently, then, she began going over it all in her mind. *I took care of all of the business matters that followed his death. I waited for five weeks, but nothing changed. I realized that the problem was not going to work out. I could not stand living like that. I had to leave. I should have taken more that a thousand dollars though. That money and only a few clothes and personal items—it certainly wasn't enough to last me twelve years.*

How hard it was to lock up my house for the last time, and just walk away with a bus ticket to a far distant town. The train took me even farther away. I didn't want any one to find me. Well, they didn't. I covered all evidence of my destination. I simply disappeared for all of those long years. Now I'm back, and the dream has returned with me. I'll never escape it…

The sobs caught in her throat. Remembering where she was, Bo thought of the child in the other room. She mustn't frighten her. She willed herself to be calm. Still shivering, she wrapped her arms around her body as tightly as possible, and bit her lower lip to keep form crying out. The tears continued for long moments, but she made no noise. The painful memory was too intense for anything but silence.

Needing the warmth, she crawled back into the bed. Sitting against the pillows, still as a statue, she waited for the dawn.

Chapter Six

Ally awakened early the next morning. The kitten was crying his hungry cry, and the busy day was underway. Passing by Bo's door, the child peeked in so see if her "grandma" was awake. Seeing her sitting up in bed, she bounded in and jumped onto the bed with her. "It's morning, Grandma Bo. We have to get up. Mr. Jeffrey is coming—remember?"

"I have a vague memory of that," Bo smiled. "You get Mews fed, and I'll be with you as soon as I can get dressed. Okay?"

"Okay. Let's hurry, though. We have to move to our new hotel."

"I think the rooms will wait for us, but I'll hurry," she laughed. Surprised that she could feel happy after last night's terrible nightmare, she got up and began dressing. She could hear Ally talking to Mews in the kitchen. Then the mewing stopped, and she knew he was getting his breakfast. She must hurry and get something for the two of them to eat, too.

The few things they could call their own were packed and ready to go, long before Jeffrey Lawrence arrived at 9:00. They loaded their belonging into the back seat, and Ally got in beside them. Mews settled into her lap, and Bo slid into the passenger's seat in front. Jeff then placed locks on both doors of the house until the property could be taken care of legally. The purse was in his office safe. The three of them had removed everything from it and the secretary had made notes of the contents before returning them, so that there could be no problems with possible relatives.

"Are you all right?" Jeffrey asked as he got into the driver's seat. He felt concerned by the strain that was showing in her face. "Can I do something to help?"

"I'm a bit weary. No problem, I just didn't sleep well. Too excited, I guess." Quickly changing the subject, she questioned, "Did the wallet give you any clues? Do you know who Ally's mother was?"

"Let's get you settled at the hotel, and then we'll talk at my office," he cautioned, glancing at the little girl who was sitting behind them.

"Yes, that probably would be best. Thank you for everything, Jeffrey. John would so appreciate your helping me."

"I would do anything for you. You know that. You and John were really good friends to me. I still miss him a lot."

"I will always miss him. He was my whole life."

"You were wonderful together. Everyone said so. The town has missed you, Evelyn."

"Oh, I doubt that anyone ever thinks of me after all of these years." The memory of the dream lingered. She struggled to keep her mind on what was being said. She hesitated for a moment, desperately wanting to hear all of the news, yet not wanting to get close enough to get hurt.

He placed a hand on her arm. "Bo, you're missing out on a lot of happiness by avoiding people who love you."

Not responding to this possibility, Evelyn Johnston sat very still in the lovely car. Nice things had always been a part of her life. Sitting now in the luxurious car, the years of living hand-to-mouth were already fading.

The suite was spacious, and nicely furnished. There were two bedrooms, a bathroom, and a living room. In a corner of the living room was a small bookshelf which Miss Black had loaded down with "goodies". An ice bucket, filled with ice was on the top shelf. A large bay window looked out over the nearby woods. The window was open, letting in a slight breeze. Evelyn was glad to see the woods, for Ally had always lived near trees. She thought that this might make her feel more comfortable in her new environment.

"I'll be going, if you don't need my help with anything at the moment," Jeffrey said, once they seemed to be settling in. "I imagine you would like to start putting your life together. There must be a million things to take care of at this point. You can call down to the desk, and they will have a taxi ready for you whenever you want one."

"Oh, yes, of course. You must go." She turned from her thoughts to face him. "I know you have a busy schedule. We do so appreciate all you have done. Thank you, dear friend. Will you let me know when we can talk?"

"Sure, I'll be in touch with you later today. Don't hesitate to call me if something comes up. I do mean that." With a final good-bye, he was gone, and she turned her attention to the rooms.

Miss Black had seen to everything. There was even a doll on Ally's bed, and a few toys in the closet. The secretary had apparently made a mental note of their approximate sizes, and had hung a new dress in each of their closets. There were also a few toiletries, make-up, and other necessary things in the dresser drawers. Evelyn breathed a long sigh, and sank down on the comfortable couch. It was so good to be home. *If only I hadn't...*

Well, I can't do anything to change my past, but maybe I can make Ally's future a lot brighter than her past has been. These thoughts drew her attention over to the child sitting by the open bay window with her kitten. A softly padded bench followed the angles of the window, making it an ideal place for just enjoying whatever you might choose to do at the moment. Ally was a truly lovely child, now that she was all cleaned up and her hair was nicely combed. *She must have a real hair-trim, though,* Bo decided. *I need the attention of a beautician, too. I wonder if mine is still in business. No, that not a good idea. It's too soon. I'm not ready to see people from the past yet. It's best to go to the shop in the hotel.*

Phoning down to see if it were possible to have hair cuts right away, she received an affirmative answer. Calling Ally to come, they headed for the elevator and were soon smiling at each other as they sat side by side in the beauty shop. Before long they were all cut and curled, and ready to leave. After paying, they admired each other's new hairdos, and left the shop.

Back upstairs, Ally ran to check on Mews, and Evelyn went into her bedroom. She opened the closet and fingered the fine fabric of the new dress Miss Black had put there. She breathed a heavy sigh as memories invaded her thoughts once again. The dress was her favorite shade of mauve. John loved to see her wearing mauve…

"Grandma Bo! Grandma Bo!" An excited Ally came running into the room, looking for her.

"I'm here. Is something wrong?"

"No, but guess what Mews just did. Guess!"

"My, I don't know. Did he climb out of his box?"

"No, that's not it. Guess again."

"Oh, well, is he playing with your new ball?"

"No," she said, giggling because the ball was very big. "He drank out of his bowl all by himself. I won't have to feed him at night any more. He's growing up fast, isn't he?"

"He surely is. So are you, Miss Ally. And you're about to have a birthday, I think."

"I know," she said quietly, her head bowed toward the floor.

"We must have a really grand birthday party—if that's all right with you, that is," Bo said, teasing.

Ally raised her head and looked into Grandma Bo's face, wondering if she were serious. "A real party? You mean for *me*?— with kids, and everything? I haven't ever had a birthday party. Oh, if I could have kids that would be so wonderful…"

"We will definitely have kids," Bo replied, trying not to show her emotion. The anger she had so often felt against Ally's mother during the last few days was about to overwhelm her. She reached for the child and gave her a hug. "What would you like to provide for entertainment for your guests? Would you like to take them to the zoo?" she asked.

"I could go to a *real zoo*, Grandma Bo?" The dark eyes were wide with amazement. "With animals, like in my books?"

"Oh, my dear child there is so much that you have missed. It will be wonderful fun showing you everything, but how sad that you are this old and have been completely kept away from life. Come here."

The child complied, and they shared another long hug that ended with a gentle kiss on the top of the little head. Tears formed in Evelyn's eyes as she thought again of Ally's lost years. She determined anew to do everything in her power to settle this child with a family. She would buy her new clothes and things she needed, and get her ready in case Jeff found her family soon. This made her remember that they needed to do some shopping. She sent Ally to put on the new dress Miss Black had bought for her, and then she called down for a taxi. Changing into the mauve dress, she quickly checked her hair and make up, and soon they were ready for their shopping trip.

They had a wonderful time in the stores. Bo had been poor for so long that she had forgotten how much fun it was to go shopping. Ally had never even been in a store, so everything was marvelously new to her. Her very favorites were the dime stores, with their marvelous array of small toys. Of course they purchased a few things to add to her sparse collection. At lunch time they sat at the counter in the S.H. Kress dime store, ending their meal with ice cream. Incredibly, the child had never had any. Again and again, she would be in awe of something new—things she had read about in her books, and had longed to see for herself. Watching her, Bo fought back the tears.

Back at the hotel, they spread their new treasures out on Bo's bed so they could look at everything together. They opened soft drinks with the bottle opener which was lying on the small table, and poured their drinks into the glasses that were sitting beside the ice bucket. Some of the ice was still frozen, and they added that to the drinks. They spent most of an hour trying on the new clothes and checking out everything they had bought. When the phone rang, it was Miss Black, asking if they could be at the office at 4:30. That was only thirty minutes away, but Evelyn said they would be there. She sent Ally off to make sure Mews had water and milk, while she called down to ask for a taxi. Putting on the new shoes they had just bought, and picking up their new purses, they were ready to go.

When they arrived Miss Black took charge of Ally, offering her cookies and milk. Evelyn and Jeff went into his office so they could talk privately. She could tell by the look on his face that the news wasn't good.

"You might as well just go ahead and tell me," she said. "It won't get any easier. What did you learn?" "Well, we did find out who she was—or is. Her name is Georgia Stephens. It's a miracle that Ally is all right. That woman was a mental case. I mean that literally. She escaped some eight years ago from the maximum security section of the state institute for the criminally insane. They never found her, as there was no reason for them to have looked for her here in Johnston, and so the years have passed."

"What about her relatives? Have you found them yet?"

"So far we haven't. She lived with her grandmother after her parents both perished in a plane crash. She was attending college in Dallas at the time. We checked the records at the college. She was a fairly good student during her first year, but after her parents' deaths her grades plummeted. She never returned for her second year. She remained in Dallas with her grandmother for awhile, but she began stealing things from her. Before long she got deep into drugs, and moved out. She was finally apprehended by the police after she almost killed someone while she was high on the drugs. She had really overdosed, and when her head finally cleared her mind was not the same. She was put on probation. Later she got mixed up with a group of thieves, and was apprehended by the police during a major robbery attempt. She was judged to be incompetent to stand trial because of her mental state. That's when she was placed in the prison facility for the mentally ill."

Bo sat staring into space for several minutes. Jeff respected her silence, but watched cautiously as the tears fell and she began to tremble. Her love for Ally was so intense that learning of the terrible life she must have had to live was over-whelming. She finally looked up and saw her friend looking at her with concern. Wiping her eyes, she nodded her head. "I'm okay," she said. "This just confirms the fears I have had all along. Ally's mother isn't just an unfit mother, she's mentally ill. What normal person would keep their child completely away from everything all of her life? She must never get that precious little girl back."

"I have already filed a report with the police concerning desertion of a minor child. She will never be permitted custody again," he told her, smiling.

Evelyn's face blanched upon hearing that the police were now involved. They would take her precious girl from her and put her into a foster home—or more likely, give her to the great-grandmother.

Seeing the intensity of Bo's reaction, Jeff realized what he had done. He quickly advised her that he had submitted a request for the child to remain where she was for the present. He had convinced the authorities that this would be in the child's best interest. After hearing the details of the situation they had agreed to hold off on enforcing some of the rules temporarily.

"Georgia's grandmother died five years ago, so she isn't around to take custody," the lawyer continued. "I have detectives looking for the father and other relatives. For the time being she is legally in your custody."

Bo closed her eyes, drew a deep breath and exhaled.

Jeff continued, "We have checked the health facilities here in town, looking for Ally's birth record. We haven't found it yet. Georgia may have given birth someplace else, perhaps in another state—or even at home. We haven't found any record of a marriage either. We talked with the director at the state facility. There was a custodian named Wesley who showed her special attention. It seems that there was a romance of sorts. She escaped the facility several months before Ally was born. The time frame is right, so it's possible that this guy was the father. He died of pneumonia a couple of years ago, so only Georgia would know for sure."

"It sounds like everyone she knows dies," said Evelyn. "You don't suppose…?"

"All of the deaths seem to have been from natural causes. Let's not borrow more trouble," he advised. "Do you have any questions?"

"No. I was just thinking that maybe the circumstances of the birth might have been the reason she kept Ally away from people. Maybe she was ashamed and resented Ally because of it," she ventured.

"That sounds plausible, considering her mental state. I'm just thankful that you came along and rescued that child out of such a terrible situation. Let's get her in here and see if she knows anything that might help us in this."

Motioning to Ally from the door of the office, Jeff invited her to come in. She entered, and sat down. Obviously uncomfortable with having to talk to him about her mother, she fidgeted in her chair and stared at the floor.

After asking the child a few basic questions, the lawyer was sure that she didn't know anything that would help them find her relatives. He decided to just make sure that she had not been physically harmed.

"Honey, did your mother ever hurt you in any way? I mean physically?" He asked.

Ally kept her eyes averted. "No sir. She never said she loved me, though, like Grandma Bo does. She never let me see people, but she didn't hurt me. She brought me clothes sometimes. I never got many toys, though—and I never got to go to the zoo," she said as an after-thought.

Jeffrey turned his head to one side to hide the smile that this revelation brought on. "Well, every little girl should have regular trips to the zoo. We'll have to see to it that you get to go very soon."

"Grandma Bo is giving me a birthday party at the zoo!" Ally became animated as she thought about her party. "I never had a birthday party. We're gonna have kids, too. I never had kids..."

"Well, it sounds like you were very lucky that you mama didn't harm you, and you were also extremely lucky that a nice 'Grandma Bo' found you. I guess we'll just have to be happy with that, and make sure that now you get to enjoy all of the things you have missed."

There was a long silence. Finally, Ally blurted out, "I like living with my Grandma Bo. I don't want to go live with someone else."

Bo was startled, and for just a moment wanted to say, "me, too!" She pushed the thought aside and said, instead, "If we find your relatives, they are most likely going to want you to live with them, darling."'

"Then, don't look for them, Mr. Jeffrey. I want to stay with Grandma Bo!"

Knowing that the authorities could place Ally in foster care, Evelyn hugged her and said, "For now let's just enjoy being with each other. We don't know what the future holds, do we? Remember, I promised you a whole family. You can stay with me while all of this is going on, though. Mr. Jeffrey has already taken care of that. Are you ready to go back to the hotel now? Mews is probably missing you."

Big, dark eyes glistened as she looked up, and slowly nodded her head. She had understood that there was a chance that she could lose her Grandma Bo completely.

Evelyn was just as upset as the little girl at her side. *Oh, child,* she thought. *You don't begin to know how much I would love to just keep you to myself. That would be very wrong, though. Maybe we'll be lucky and they won't be able to find any relatives.* Such a great love had formed between the two lonely people that she knew it would always be a part of their lives—even if they had to live far apart and never got to see each other again.

"Well, we have a birthday party to plan, Jeffrey," she said as she stood. "May I use a phone to call the taxi?"

He simply buzzed Miss Black, and told her to call a cab for Mrs. Johnston. She responded in the affirmative.

"We'll be on our way, then," Evelyn said. "Do let us know if you find out anything."

"You know I will. By the way, do you need anything? I was wondering about a driver's license and a car."

"I surely do need to be able to drive again. I haven't driven since the wreck. I admit I'm a little nervous about it, but, yes—as soon as you have the time. I know you're busy, and we have taken a lot of your time already."

"If you can manage until next week, we'll go Monday afternoon—say 2:00. You can be thinking about what kind of car you want."

"I feel like a kid at Christmas! Thanks, so much. I can't believe I'll have a car again. It's been a very long time."

"It's settled, then. Once more, it's really good to have you back in town."

"It's good to be home. Goodbye for now."

"Goodbye. Bye, Ally. Have fun planning that birthday party."

"I will, Mr. Jeffrey."

"Oh, Evelyn, I talked with Brother Glenn this morning. He came by to ask how you are. He invited us all to attend the revival meeting tonight. Do you want to go?"

Evelyn tensed. There might be people she knew at that revival. "Not tonight, Jeff," she said. She looked up at him, and he was eyeing her with concern.

"I…well, how about Friday night? I could probably make it then," she conceded.

"Okay. I'll just wait and go then."

"Good. I'll see you later. All right, young lady," she said, turning to the child. "Let's go tell Mews all about the party."

"Yeah! He's gonna love the zoo. He's an animal too."

"I think he thinks he's a people, don't you?" Evelyn said, trying to look serious.

Ally giggled all the way to the taxi.

Chapter Seven

It had been a long day for both Anna and Tony, so they were glad when he finally arrived home to take her to the doctor's office. He had left work early in order to go with her for the appointment. They ate a quick snack, and then started out.

"I wonder what can be wrong," Anna worried as they drove away from home. "I really don't feel that bad. The headache is gone today. I've been nauseous, but stress could cause that."

"Don't try to guess about it, honey. We'll know soon enough now. I'm sure it isn't serious."

Anna did not respond to that, so they rode the rest of the way in silence, arriving at 4:50 at the doctor's office. Tony got out and opened her door for her and they went in together."

"Hi, Joy, I'm back already. It looks like you can't get rid of me."

"Mrs. Benski? Oh, I didn't know you had another appointment. Let me check."

"I didn't have an appointment. The doctor just wanted to see us for a moment. It may not be on the books. Ask his nurse."

"Sure. Just take a seat and I'll see what's up."

Tony was determined not to let his wife know he was worried. They sat down, and he leaned back a bit so that she couldn't see his face. Sighing deeply, he closed his eyes in urgent prayer. Hearing him sigh, Anna turned to look at him, but Joy returned just at that moment and distracted her.

"The doctor will be with you in just a few minutes," she said. Tony picked up a magazine and tried to stay calm. It was a relief when the nurse stepped through the door and called Anna's name.

As they entered the office, Tony greeted the doctor. "Good to see you, Doc."

"It's good to see you, Tony. It's about time for your annual physical. Don't put it off too long. You look like the picture of health, but it's always best to be sure," the doctor said.

Anna's nerves were raw. She had to know..."Doctor?" she questioned.

"I'm sorry, Anna. I should have realized that you would be concerned. Sit down, both of you. I have good news, but there is a possible problem, so I wanted to talk to you in person."

"What's wrong, Doc?" Tony was trying not to be overly concerned, but...

"Well, first of all, let me congratulate you both. You are going to have a baby."

"A baby? Oh, no!" Anna said. "Someone will steal it from me!"

"Honey, it'll be okay," her husband soothed. "Don't let yourself think like that."

"Tony, I can't help thinking like that. Megan—"

He turned to speak to the physician. "Doc, you said there's a problem. What's wrong?"

"The tests show that there is a *possible* problem," the doctor responded. "If what I suspect is true, there could be a miscarriage before long. I want to send her to a larger facility, where they can do more tests to see if I'm right. If I am, perhaps they could do something to prevent the miscarriage."

"I might lose the baby?" Anna was frightened now.

"Yes, you might," her doctor said gently.

She burst into tears, and Tony was helpless to do anything more than hold her until the tears subsided.

"I have called the hospital in Houston. They will have a room for you tomorrow morning if you agree to go. It is urgent that you get this checked out as soon as possible. You shouldn't be there for more than two days."

"We'll go tomorrow morning. Just give us our instructions," Tony responded.

92

Anna looked at him, wanting to refuse to go, but how could she? She had come to the doctor when she didn't really think she needed to. It seemed that God might have gotten her there early enough to possibly save the baby. She would have to see it through.

They asked a few more questions about the headaches, the nausea and the intense mood swings. He assured them that these things were normal, and they left the office feeling better about that. They didn't say much as they drove, but Tony kept his arm around her, comforting her.

"Well," he ventured at last, "now we know why you have been so emotional, and thinking about Megan. Your hormones are adjusting to the new life inside you. It's normal. Everything is going to be okay, honey. It will, you'll see. Would you like to go to the revival tonight?" he asked. "We need it."

She surprised him by agreeing. They rushed inside for a quick supper, and then hurried to get dressed. They arrived a few minutes late, and found a place toward the back where they could sit down quietly without disturbing anyone. Someone handed them a hymnal, and they shared it as they joined in singing "The Old Rugged Cross."

The evening message was precious to their hearts. At the close of the service Tony asked for prayer for Anna and the child she was carrying. By now, everyone knew that the Benskis were the couple whose little girl had been abducted. Lynn had asked prayer for them the night after she had talked with Phyllis. Everyone's heart went out to the young couple as they shared this new trial. The pastor called for prayer, to hold them up before the Lord. Several prayed for them, and the pastor finished with a loving request for God's grace and mercy on them. They went home encouraged, thanking God for the privilege of actually talking to Him. Somewhat haltingly, they prayed together for the first time that night, placing Anna and the baby in his hands. They also added little Megan's disappearance to the list and felt incredibly comforted that God would give them closure at last—perhaps with the joy of the new baby.

The next day was Friday. As they left for the hospital, they felt a kind of peace they had never known before. Their new Christian brothers and sisters would be praying for them.

᠙᠙᠙᠙᠙᠙

Attendance for the revival service on Friday was the best of the week. The building was already packed when Evelyn, Ally, and Jeffrey arrived. An usher found seats for them, and Brother Glenn came over to say a few words to them. He was obviously very glad they were there. He teased Ally a bit before passing on to the people in the pew behind them. The little girl was in awe of all of the new things she was seeing. She had never been to a church service, of course, and had never been around so many people. Evelyn and Jeffrey were glad to see that she didn't appear to be intimidated by it all. She had such a wonderfully outgoing personality, that she seemed to be thrilled by everything.

Brother Alexander also came over to meet them. He had obviously been told about their situation by the evangelist. He asked about Evelyn's health, and how the investigation was going.

Seeing all of the children, Ally was so excited that she could hardly contain herself. "Grandma Bo," she whispered, "can some of these kids come to my birthday party? That would be the very most wonderful birthday party any kid could ever have."

Bo looked at the beaming face of the child, and simply whispered back, "They surely may, my dear. After the service we will see if it is possible for some of them to come." How could she not grant such a simple request? She loved the child to distraction.

When the singing started, Evelyn was taken back through the years to her childhood. She had attended church when she was in grade school. Hearing the old hymns again recalled good memories. She joined in the singing, and her new "granddaughter" was enraptured with the music and followed along remarkably well. Jeffrey tried to

94

sing the once familiar hymns, but it was difficult for him. Somehow, there was a lump in his throat. *I've been out of church for much too long,* he admitted to himself.

When the pastor introduced Brother Glenn, Ally was so excited that she almost said something aloud to Jeffrey. Evelyn was able to quiet her, and they all settled back to listen.

"We're going to talk tonight about a truly sinful woman," the evangelist began. "She had committed a great many sins. She was an outcast in the city of Samaria in which she lived. Open your Bibles to the book of John, chapter four, verses one through thirty-nine. Please stand for the reading of God's Word."

As the evangelist read the story of the Samaritan woman who met Jesus beside the city well, Jeffrey remembered having heard it many times as a child. He was filled with remorse over the years that had passed since he had even been in God's house. His heart thrilled as he listened to the familiar account of the sinful woman to whom Jesus freely offered salvation and forgiveness. He remembered the glad morning when he had trusted Christ. And just like the woman, had his sins covered by the blood of Jesus. As the crowd settled back into their seats, he was deep in thought.

"It's easy to look at someone else and talk about their sins, isn't it?" Bro. Glenn asked. "You may be feeling a little superior to the woman in this example right now. Why, she was a real bad sinner, wasn't she? You're pretty good, in comparison to her, right?" Brother Glenn asked. "But dear friends, God's Word tells us that you may be a good person, or a very sinful one. You may be old, or just a child. All of us are sinners and we are all in need of a savior, if we want to escape the fires of hell." His eyes swept across the people in the packed auditorium, resting for a moment on the pew where Evelyn, Jeffrey, and Ally were sitting.

"You can't do anything to save yourself, any more than this woman could save herself," he said. "Jesus loves you just as much as he loved her. Jesus died in your place, so that you might be able to go

95

to heaven when you die." His eyes moved on to another part of the auditorium, but Ally never took her eyes off of him.

Brother Glenn continued. "Let's look at the exact moment in which the woman believed this wonderful truth. Verse twenty-five says, 'the woman saith unto Him, I know that Messias cometh which is called Christ. When he is come, he will tell us all things. Jesus saith unto her, I that speak unto thee am he.' She believed him! Verse twenty-eight says, 'the woman then left her water pot and went her way into the city, and saith to the men, come and see a man, which told me all things that ever I did: is not this the Christ?'"

As the evangelist's eyes passed over their section again, Ally began wiggling.

"The long awaited Messiah had come! The woman not only believed the wonderful truth for herself," the evangelist continued, "but here she is telling others already. They went with her to see the person she had met, and verse thirty-nine tells us that 'many of the Samaritans of that city believed on him for the saying of the woman, which testified, he told me all that ever I did.' She met Jesus, dear people. She believed that he was the Messiah—the one who would bring salvation—the promised one. She gladly told everyone who would listen that she had met the Christ. Today, right this moment, that lady is in heaven with her Savior. This evening, I am telling you that I also have 'met' him, and he is very real. I stand here before you, forgiven of all of my sins. My eternity is settled, for Jesus truly was—and is—the Christ, promised by the Father thousands of years ago. He came to this earth to die for you, dear friend. All you have to do is accept his gift. Open your heart to see that he offers you eternal life with him in heaven.

"Won't you make the decision to do that right now, and come on down and let us know? We would love to rejoice with you. Please stand. Come, as we sing…"

"Grandma Bo, Brother Glenn said Jesus died for me," Ally whispered. "He died for my sins, Grandma Bo. I want to go down there and tell everyone that I believe Jesus died for me. Okay?"

"Oh, dear. I don't know. You're so young. How do I know that you understand what you're doing?"

"Will it hurt anything?"

"Well, no, I don't suppose it will. If you feel that you need to go down, you may go."

"Oh, yes! I just have to tell everybody that I believe Jesus died for me. Thank you, Grandma Bo." She paused for a moment to turn and ask, "Do you want to go, too? He said that Jesus died for everyone. That means you, too, doesn't it?"

"I need to think about it some more, but you go along."

"Okay. I love you." Ally literally ran down the aisle. As she approached the evangelist, she called out, "Brother Glenn, I believe Jesus died for my sins. I'm gonna go to heaven like you said!" She was weeping and laughing at the same time. "I wish I hadn't ever sinned," she sobbed. "Then Jesus wouldn't have had to die."

"I'm afraid there are a lot of us here who would still have needed a savior, sweetheart. Jesus died for everyone who will believe."

"Then I'll just be glad that he loves me."

Everyone smiled at the childish faith. Many eyes filled with tears, and Brother Glenn took her into his loving arms and wept with her. As the congregation filed by to hug the adorable child with the light of Christ on her face, Evelyn Johnston stood at the back of the auditorium, struggling with the very real conviction of her sin. She was the reason Jesus had died. Her sins had nailed him to the cross. The words of that night's special song came back to her. *What can wash away my sin? Nothing but the blood of Jesus.* She struggled to shut out the conviction that weighed so heavily on her heart and was relieved when Ally came running back down the aisle to her. The relief was short-lived, however, for she immediately began talking about Jesus' having saved her. She was so joyful, that Evelyn could not ignore the fact that something very real had just taken place in the heart of the child. She wondered at it, yet resisted it. She knew that she, too, was a sinner. The hurt and anger that she had harbored for all of these years was sin. If she trusted Christ as her savior, she would have to let go of the anger, and even the hurt.

No, she wasn't ready to do that. If she did, she would have to finally accept what had happened twelve years ago. And although her heart yearned for her former life, she could not risk the heartache that might come from that acceptance. So, she closed her mind to the gospel and, taking the hand of the beloved child, she walked away from the church with pain in her heart.

Jeffrey was very quiet on the way home, and told them good-bye with hardly another word. He had trusted Christ many years before, but had not even been going to church during the last two decades. How could he have forgotten how much he owed God for the salvation he had provided for Him?

❧ ❧ ❧ ❧ ❧

Mercilessly, the dream came again that night. Once more, Bo relived the wreck, the funeral, and the pain; then, there she was, standing in her living room. For the first time, her mind opened and she saw the person who had caused her so many years of heartache. Her only daughter was there. It was she who was screaming those hateful words. "You were driving! How could you have let this happen? You *killed* him! You killed my *Daddy*!" In the dream, Evelyn saw her beloved daughter as she turned toward the stairs. She disappeared into her room. It seemed like forever before she re-appeared. Evelyn was still standing where she had left her, struggling to understand. Her head hurt from injuries she had suffered in the wreck. She couldn't think straight. Her daughter descended the staircase with a large suitcase in her hands. She

98

headed for the front door, and opened it. Turning, she looked at her mother. She hesitated for a moment, in indecision, then opened the door and started through it.

As the door was closing, Evelyn's mind registered what was happening. She started toward the door. "Darling, let me explain. Daddy knocked my ha—"

The door slammed with finality, and the distraught mother stood still, trying to understand what had just happened. Then she opened the door and saw her eighteen year old daughter's car driving away. Her head was hurting. Her vision was blurred. Closing the door slowly, she moved toward a chair. Her head was really spinning. She didn't make it to the chair. She passed out, and slumped to the soft carpet.

The dream continued. The weeks following the funeral, and the loss of her daughter, were passing in a whirl of misery. Over and over she called her daughter on the phone. She went by the house where she was staying, but always her daughter refused to even speak to her or have anything to do with her. Evelyn's depression was deepening. It was overwhelming, even in the dream. She was in agony. Her worst nightmare had literally just passed through her mind in her sleep.

"No! No…"

The dream was ending at last, and she was choosing, once more, to disappear from Johnston. In agony, she literally sat up in bed. She was about to make the horrible mistake again…

"No! Don't do it! Don't go…" she awakened herself with the words. She had never done that before, but tonight she had realized just what she had missed by running away. Sitting alone in her bed, she was shaken with that reality; yet, she could not change the past. It was too late.

ॐॐॐॐॐ

The following day Ally remembered that they had not asked any children to attend her birthday party. She begged to return to the

Saturday evening service so that she could do that. Evelyn was still disturbed by the memory of the dream. She was also fighting the need for her salvation. She was in misery, and wanted no part of another service, yet, how could she manage to say "no" without breaking Ally's heart. As it turned out, there was no way, and that evening she found herself being driven up to the door of the church by Jeffrey. Ally kept chattering on and on about Jesus. Oh, how Evelyn hated to walk through those doors. It was only her love for the child that propelled her through them—and worse yet, to a seat near the front. All of the back seats were full.

She joined, half-heartedly, in the singing of the hymns, and listened with half an ear to the announcements and prayer requests until she suddenly heard the name "Anna." This caught her full attention. She sat there, hardly breathing, wondering if they were speaking of her own daughter.

"As you know, Anna and Tony Benski trusted Christ as their savior last Wednesday night," the pastor was saying. "On Thursday, Anna was called back to her doctor, who told them that they were to become parents again. You will remember that we have been praying all week for this couple, because of their renewed agony over their child who was abducted seven years ago. The loss of this two-year old daughter has darkened their lives for years. Now, they are in danger of losing yet another child. Anna possibly has a problem that could cause her to lose the baby during these early weeks. She and Tony are at the hospital in Houston where she will be tested and, if possible, treated. Let us take a moment for special prayer for the Benskis."

Again, several prayers went up in their behalf, and the pastor concluded with prayer before the singing of the special song.

Evelyn had to know. She looked at Jeffrey. He simply nodded his head. Yes, they were talking about her Anna.

Seven years ago? Anna went through something like that, and I wasn't here to help her? Her heart was broken with love for her daughter, and the last reason for resisting Christ was swept away. She trusted him to take care of her sins in that moment. She did not hear the rest of the sermon that night. She was talking with God. *...and please give me a chance to make up for the lost years, dear Lord. I have been so incredibly stupid*, she concluded.

When the invitation was given, she walked down the aisle as the first notes were being sung, and acknowledged Jesus Christ as her Lord. Jeffrey followed on the next verse, and joined the church. Later, a few words to Brother Alexander put the birthday party in motion, and Bo, Ally and Jeff all went home with great joy in their hearts.

సౌసౌసౌ

"It's hard to believe this is over so soon," Anna said. She was resting in her seat in the car, pillows propped around her as they made their way home early on Sunday morning. "To think that it was all a mistake and I'm fine. More important, our baby is fine," she said.

"The people at the church have been praying for you. God really seems to have answered prayer, don't you think, honey? It's great to be part of a church family, and to know that they will pray with us when we have problems."

Anna smiled a contented smile. "I know, Tony. This is all so wonderfully new. I don't think anyone has ever prayed for me before. It's just so incredible."

"Hey!" Tony said, looking at the clock on the dashboard, "It looks like we're going to make it home in time to get to the morning service. Do you feel up to going? We were supposed to be baptized this morning."

"Oh, yes! I'm so anxious to be baptized. Bro, Alexander said that baptism shows the death, burial, and resurrection of Jesus, and that it shows we are a part of him. It will also make us members of the church. Won't that be wonderful?"

"Very wonderful. Do you feel like our whole life has been changed?"

"Yes, and changed for the better—changed forever."

The rest of the drive was nearly silent, as Anna and Tony contemplated the coming baptism. They arrived home in time to change clothes and make it to the worship service. They walked in and sat near the back just as the congregation was singing the final hymn. The words filled Anna's soul with rejoicing.

Sitting near the front were Ally and Evelyn. The happy little girl was singing her heart out, and her "grandma" sang with real joy. Bo rejoiced in the sermon, and could hardly wait for the moment when they would be baptized, showing that they belonged to Jesus Christ. As the invitation to receive Christ as Lord and Savior began, some people who had been sitting behind Evelyn and Ally moved to the front of the auditorium. This left the two of them exposed

Tony heard his wife gasp and looked down to find that her face was white. Terrified, he grabbed her around the waist, trying to assist her outside to find out what was wrong. She pulled away from him.

"Honey, what is it? Are you okay?" he whispered

"My mother," she whispered back.

"Your mother, what?"

"There—at the front. That's my mother, standing beside that little girl. My *mother*, Tony!" Anna was weeping now, and could hardly control herself. "My mother has come home. Thank God." She had to sit down for a moment, but she did not miss any of the glad scene going on at the front of the auditorium as two more people went down, trusting Christ.

When the invitation closed, the pastor directed all of those who had accepted Christ during the two weeks to go to the changing rooms. After the new Christians had been baptized, they would stand at the front of the auditorium, and all of the members would pass by to offer their love and acceptance to them.

Evelyn and Ally were among the first to step out. As the Benskis were about to make their way down the aisle, Jeffrey came in the door from the foyer. He had been caught up in a legal matter that morning. Thankfully, he had made it in time for the baptism. He grasped Tony's hand in a firm handshake, and then smiled at Anna as she and Tony headed down the aisle.

Evelyn turned as she reached the door of the changing room. She was hoping that Jeffrey had been able to make it in time. As the candidates for baptism came down the aisle, Evelyn suddenly gasped. For the first time in twelve years, she saw her daughter's face. She swayed a little as emotion washed over her and love for her precious daughter overcame her.

Anna opened her arms, and her mother responded. Tears were streaming down their faces as they met in a glad embrace.

"Oh, Mother, I thought I would never see you again. Where have you been?"

"Sh-h, my darling. There will be time for that later. Just know that I love you with all of my heart." The two entered the room together, arms around each other. Both were trembling.

"You've come home early, Tony. Do we have news on the medical problem?" Brother Alexander asked him as they entered their changing room.

"They found nothing wrong with Anna," he responded. "We have a healthy mother and baby. We're certainly thankful for all of the prayers."

As everyone was changing for the baptism, Evelyn introduced Ally to Anna. She shared a bit of the history of their meeting. Anna gave Ally a hug and assured her that she was very glad she was there. The child returned the hug, a little puzzled, wondering who this woman was. She didn't understand that this was Grandma Bo's daughter.

When the time came to baptize the Benskis, Pastor Alexander presented them together with Ally and Evelyn. Tony had told him that Evelyn was Anna's mother. Ally was baptized with Evelyn, and then Tony and Anna were baptized together. When all fifteen had been baptized and changed back into dry clothes, they all stood at the front of the church and the members passed by to welcome them.

It was late when they finally left the church and headed for Anna and Tony's house. They were all excited to be going "home" together. Jeff's client was waiting for him to return, so he had to say his good-byes at church. He left reluctantly, but with plans to pick up Evelyn and Ally later.

Chapter Eight

Lunch was over, and everyone had gathered in the Benski's living room. They were all talking at once. It was a glad day for each of them. The suffering of so many years had been wiped away in one astounding moment.

Ally was uncharacteristically quiet, but in the joy of the moment, the others were not noticing.

Anna's joy was colored with painful memories and recriminations. "I'm still in shock, Mother," she said. "This has to have been the most incredible day of my life—to find you sitting right there in the church after so many years. I had given up hope of ever finding you. When the pain of losing Daddy finally became less intense it was like my mind cleared, and I could think normally again. I was horrified at what I had done to you. I rushed home, but you weren't there...you-w-weren't-there-mother...."

She began crying, and all Evelyn could do was to hold her and weep with her.

"I just knew you had committed suicide or something. Oh, I'm so glad you're home!" The two embraced, and wept again.

"Me too, darling. It's so wonderful to be back where I belong. I'm sorry I left you," Evelyn said. "I don't know if the injuries I suffered in the wreck caused it, or if losing Daddy was just so intense that I wasn't able to think normally, either. I simply couldn't remain here with both of you gone. Once I was far away, my mind played terrible tricks on me for a long time. "Then, one day about a month ago, I suddenly got this terrible longing to come home. When I got here, though, I didn't want anyone to know I was here. What a foolish old lady I have been. It would seem that God just took control and led me home, even though I didn't know him yet."

"I knew that the wreck was an accident, Mother. I was devastated over losing Daddy. I think that, maybe in a weird way, I was trying to protect myself from being hurt again. It was like—if you should die too—like if I were angry with you—then, maybe it wouldn't hurt so much if you weren't here any more. Instead, I lost you by being so stupid. How could I not have realized that you were much more devastated than I was, and were hovering on the brink of an emotional collapse? Oh, I can't believe I said such horrible things to my own lovely mother." Anna was sobbing in earnest and only Ally's voice brought her out of it. She had been deep in her own thoughts and hadn't really been thinking of what was happening around her until this moment.

"You keep calling her mother," Ally said anxiously. "Is Grandma Bo your real mother? For true?" *What will happen if this lady doesn't like me?* She worried. *Will I lose Grandma Bo? Oh, I mustn't lose my Grandma Bo...*

Anna really looked at the little girl beside her for the first time. "My dear," she said. "I'm sorry. This must all be so confusing to you. Yes, she definitely is my mother. Isn't that great?"

"And you are my most precious daughter," Bo joined in. "And as far as forgiving, there is nothing to forgive. I just mourn the lost years. I missed you so much! It was almost unbearable."

"Oh, me too, Mother. I missed you every single day."

The two embraced and wept again. Suddenly they realized that Ally was staring at them.

Mother and daughter looked at each other. Realizing that she must be terribly confused, Evelyn released her daughter, and turned to her little friend. She reached for her, and the child moved quietly into her "grandma's" arms and sat still.

"I'm so sorry. I didn't mean to leave you out. Anna is my daughter. Her daddy was killed in a car wreck many years ago. I was driving when the accident happened. I left town, and we haven't seen each other since, until now."

106

"Do I have to go away now, Grandma Bo?" Ally whispered.

"What? Oh, no darling! You do not have to go away! Why would you think such a thing?"

Ally began weeping, and Evelyn was at loss to know what to do. So many emotions were whirling around her—so many memories. She wasn't "Old Bodacious" anymore. She was Anna's mother. She was Evelyn Johnston again, and Ally was feeling the rather intense emotions that all of this was causing.

"Look at me, sweetheart," Bo said quietly.

Ally looked into her face, and then buried her head on her shoulder.

"You and I are a team, Miss Ally. I am not about to ever give you up. Don't you understand? We belong together, you and I. When we find a family to adopt you, I will still be your 'Grandma Bo,' and we will see each other a lot."

"For true, Grandma Bo?"

"For true, Miss Ally. I love you so very much."

"I love you too, Grandma Bo."

"And don't forget, we have your birthday party all planned. We aren't going to let anything mess that up, are we?"

The child looked up into the beloved face again and saw the smile of love. She returned the smile, and said, "No, Grandma Bo, I can't wait for my party!"

"Then are we back to normal around here Miss Ally, dear?"

The little girl giggled. "Yes, ma'am," she said, smiling.

Anna was smiling too. "Are you having a birthday soon, Ally?" she asked.

"Yes ma'am. I'm gonna be eight. Grandma and me invited some of the kids at church to go to the zoo with me for my birthday." With the attention now on her, Ally was getting back to normal.

"Oh, that sounds like fun! When is your birthday?"

"June 28th. I never had a party before."

Anna was saddened by that statement. It also caused her to remember the dear party she had been planning for her baby. *I wonder if my Megan has ever gotten a birthday party*, she wondered. *Oh, sweet Megan.* She took a deep breath.

"We had planned a party for our little daughter's birthday," she said quietly. "She would have been two years old on the 14th that year. She would be turning nine this month."

Evelyn's heart was broken by the sadness in her daughter's voice. She put her arm around her and said, "I'm so sorry, sweetheart. I can't even imagine what you have suffered. Are you going to be okay?"

"I will. It's just that the memories are pretty hard."

"Do you have a little girl like me?" Ally asked hopefully.

"We did, honey. She is—would be a year older than you are. She isn't with us any more. Would you like to see some photos of her?"

"Yes, ma'am, but wh-"

"We'd love to see the photos," Evelyn intervened quickly, before Ally could complete that question.

Anna stood and quietly walked over to the bookcase to take down a photo album. Going back to the couch, she sat down between Ally and Evelyn. "Shall we look at the pictures together?" she asked. She was trembling as she opened the album, but knew that it was important that she do this.

"This is Megan when she was born," she said. "Wasn't she tiny?"

Ally nodded, smiling. Evelyn stared at the photo of her only grandchild. The emotion was over-whelming.

"Here she is in her high chair. She made a real mess of her face with that cereal, didn't she? And here she is, taking her first step."

"She's real cute. Can I see the next page?"

"Sure." Anna turned the page and then reached for her mother's hand.

What sad moments the two women shared as they looked at some of the pictures of the granddaughter that Evelyn would never get to hold—would never get to see. She looked at Ally, then, and was thankful that she had her to love. She wasn't her own flesh and blood, but she was a very special part of her and always would be.

The next hour passed happily enough. At last, Evelyn stood and yawned. "Well, we need to get on back to the hotel for a nap and a change of clothes before the evening service. Would you two please excuse us?"

"I hate for you to leave, Mother," Anna said. "I don't want us to be separated for even a few hours. Tony will take you, though, if you really need to go."

Tony looked up from his Sunday paper. "Sure," he responded. "I'd love a few moments alone with the lady."

"Well, actually, Jeffrey has made plans to come for me. I'm supposed to call him."

"I'll do that for you Mom," Tony said, and hopped up to go to the phone.

"He is so dear!" Evelyn said. "I can't believe I have a son. I'd never thought about that before. Here he was, all of these years, and I didn't even know it. I love him already," she said smiling.

Anna returned the smile. She was so proud of her husband, and it was good to know that her mother felt this way about him.

"Grandma Bo, is Mews okay?" Ally interrupted. "He's been alone for a long time."

"He's fine, now that he can drink from a bowl. Don't worry, dear," Bo smiled, reassuring her.

"Who is Mews, Ally?" Anna wanted to know.

"He's my kitten. He thinks he's a people," she giggled.

Tony came back into the room just then. "It's all set," he said. "Jeff should be here in just a few minutes."

Evelyn said lingering "goodbyes", as she went back for one more hug from each of her children.

When the door bell rang, Tony went to answer it and ushered Jeffrey in. They all chatted together for a few moments, and then, after making plans to go to the hotel dining room together after church, Jeff, Evelyn and Ally left.

"It's so nice of you to do this," Evelyn said as they drove away.

"Well, I wanted to hear about the reunion, you know. Was it special?" he replied.

She turned toward him. "Oh, Jeffrey, it was really wonderful. I should have listened to you when I first got here. Anna's as precious as she ever was, and Tony is already calling me Mom. I'm so excited, I can hardly contain it! In addition, there is to be the new baby in about six months. Just think—a baby! I haven't held a baby in so many years."

"Can you handle another surprise?" he asked. "It's a good one!"

"If it's anything like the others, I surely can."

"It's about your house. The renters want you to have it back. They've found a new house already. They are going to be moving out tomorrow and Tuesday. You can be back in your own home this week—depending on what you want to do to the house first."

This news left Bo speechless. She sat, unmoving as the glad news sank in.

"I'm sorry. I should have realized that you have already had so many changes. Adjusting must be hard. Do forgive me," he said.

"Oh, no, it isn't that. I was just thinking that the house won't look like it did when I left it. How could it, after so many years?"

"But it will. Anna lived there until she married Tony. Afterward, she realized that the house would deteriorate if it weren't lived in. She packed up every single thing in it, and locked it all in that huge bedroom upstairs. Then she advertised the house for rent, so it wouldn't just sit there and fall into ruin. All we have to do is unpack and return everything to its place—exactly as it was."

"Oh, my! This is much more than I deserve. How wonderful it will be to be home after twelve long years. I'm so glad that I came back."

"So am I, Bodacious Evelyn Johnston. So-am-I!"

110

"Me too," a kid's voice said from the back seat, causing the adults to laugh.

The little girl yawned, then, and lay down in the seat. "Goodnight," she said, and was soon fast asleep. The adults were left with a few minutes alone for a more private conversation.

Their drive took them over an especially lovely hill. It wasn't a tall hill, but it had always been one of Bo's favorite spots, and she was enjoying it immensely. It was like frosting on a cake, after all of the wonderful happenings of the day. They were just rounding a sharp curve near the top, and were having a lively conversation when they saw that a truck was headed straight for them on their side of the road.

Jeffrey honked as he swerved to avoid a collision. The trucker moved back to his side of the road, but it was too late. The car had hit the loose gravel on the side of the road, and Jeff fought to regain control. Ally sat up, terrified!

"Ally, get down on the floor! NOW!" Evelyn screamed.

The frightened child obeyed, and lay there, afraid to move. Time stood still as Jeff struggled to save them. The car went into a skid, sliding down the road, sideways. At last, the skid ended, and the car headed for the rocky hill on the inside lane of the road. It stopped abruptly, just before it would have crashed. Evelyn was thrown into the windshield, headfirst. The glass broke, and everything went black.

Chapter Nine

"The concussion is pretty severe. I have to advise you that there could be some brain damage. If you will just..."

Evelyn drifted back into unconsciousness. Anna was weeping and poor Ally was beyond tears. She had just found a wonderful "grandma," and now she might lose her.

Why did this have to happen? Anna wondered. *We were all so happy.* She stood like a stone in the pleasant hospital room, not moving, not letting herself feel anything. It hurt too much.

"Ally? Are you here? Are you all right?" Bo tried to sit up, so that she could see, but the pain in her head was too intense. Ally moved over to stand by the bed.

"Grandma Bo, I'm here. Does it hurt? Can I help you? Oh, Grandma Bo, don't die. I need you so much."

She began crying, and the nurse stepped forward to take the distraught child from the room. *I knew I shouldn't have let her come in here,* she worried. *I'm going to get into trouble for having broken the rules. I know children aren't allowed in the rooms, but she was so shaken by the wreck, and so distraught. She needed to see for herself that her grandmother is alive. Oh, dear.*

Just as she was about to tell Anna that the little girl would have to leave, Evelyn reached for her "granddaughter."

"Come, darling. Grandma Bo isn't anywhere near dead, yet. You come and give me a hug."

She went into her "grandma's" arms, and they comforted each other.

The nurse stood, watching. She was smiling. *It would seem that I've been vindicated for breaking those rules,* she told herself happily.

Tony stood with his arm around his wife, also watching the pair together. "That child is a marvel, the way she accepts things," he said.

"She does seem to be good for Mrs. Johnston," the nurse said quietly. "What a wonderful child she is."

"She truly is," Anna responded, and then turned to her husband. "Honey, maybe you'd better take Ally to the waiting room before we get this nurse in trouble, though. She was so good to let us break the rules a bit."

"Sure," he said. "Tell 'Grandma Bo' good-bye for now, little one." He took hold of her hand and squeezed it, to let her know that he was there for her.

Miss Ally and Grandma Bo said their goodbyes, and Anna followed the two out into the hall. She watched as her husband and the little girl walked away down the hall, hand in hand. *I like the way that looks,* she thought. *Maybe I was wrong not to have wanted more children. Well, there's one on the way now. I wonder if it'll be a boy...*

For her mother's sake, she brightened as she went back into the room and stepped up to the bed. She put her hand on her Mother's shoulder and smiled down at her.

"Mother, how are you feeling? You gave us quite a scare."

"I think I'm all right. I was wondering what the doctor is saying, though. I thought I heard the word 'concussion" when he was in here."

"It's a pretty severe one. Do you want me to have the doctor paged so you can talk to him?"

"I can wait until he comes around. I just thought you might know. Honey, Ally seems to be all right, but I have to know about Jeffrey. I'm afraid to ask."

"Oh, Mom, please forgive me. This has to have brought back memories of the wreck with Daddy. I was so worried about you, that I forgot to tell you about Jeffrey. Actually, you were the only

114

one injured. The car didn't crash. It stopped abruptly, and your head hit the windshield, breaking it. Ally was on the floor, so she was protected. Jeffrey was able to brace himself using the steering wheel."

"Thank God. I don't know if I could have handled it if Jeffrey hadn't made it. It would have been so much like John."

"Jeff's waiting to hear how you are. I'll go get him."

"I'm here," Jeffrey said from the doorway. He was smiling, and Evelyn responded to the smile.

"I was just telling Anna to bring you to me. I kind of needed to see for myself that there hadn't been a repeat of the accident with John."

"I was afraid you were remembering that. I'm so sorry. I feel bad that you have been hurt, and here I am, not a scratch on me."

"Well, wouldn't it have been worse if we had both been injured?"

"You're right. I wouldn't have been able to take care of you. As it is, I am at your command—anything you need or want."

Sitting in the waiting room, Tony was deep in thought. *My mother-in-law is quite a lady. I'm beginning to see why my Anna is such a special person,* He thought of all of the years he had missed knowing Evelyn. "Thank God she's back, though," he said quietly. "You mean Grandma Bo?" Ally questioned.
She never misses a thing, Tony thought. *Think, before you speak in front of this little girl.* He put his arm around her little shoulders. "Yes, I do mean Grandma Bo," he said, smiling.
Jeff had gone home, and Tony was feeling restless. He didn't want to leave Ally alone in the waiting room, but just sitting there was hard to do. In her room, Evelyn was tired. She was also feeling stressed because she needed to ask Anna a favor and the opportunity to do so hadn't presented itself. Finally she just said, "Anna, honey, I need a favor."'

"What is it, Mother?" Anna asked. "Is there something I can do for you?"

"Yes, dear, but if you can't, please just say so."

"Of course, Mom. What is it?"

"It's Ally. She has no place to go. Would you watch after her until I get out of here? Oh, and there's the kitten. He's at the hotel. The key is in my purse."

"I'd love to take care of her for you. She's a sweet little girl. Don't worry about her—or the kitten. We'll take care of them. You just concentrate on getting well."

"Tony must be getting tired of sitting down there. You should run along. I'll be fine."

"Oh, no, Mom, I'm spending the night with you. I'll go tell Tony to take Ally to the house."

"You just go on to church," her mother said. "How would it look if we were all baptized in the morning and didn't return that night? No, you have to go. I'll be fine until you get back after the service."

After much protesting, the three left, and the nurse came back into the room. She checked her patient and made her comfortable, then quietly left the room.

Alone at last, Bodacious Evelyn Johnston had herself a good cry.

కికికికికి

The nausea struck with a vengeance, and Evelyn jerked awake. She sat up quickly in her hospital bed to reach for the small tub beside her. As she did so, the pain in her right side immobilized her and she tried to subdue the resulting scream.

Nurse Grey was passing by her room and rushed in.

"Mrs. Johnston, what's wrong?" she urged.

"P—ain. In—my—right—side," she managed between gasping breaths.

"Let me check. Can you lie back for a moment? There. I'm just going to press very gently right here to see…"

Evelyn almost passed out with the pain that the slight pressure caused. She was gasping for breath.

116

"I'm going for the doctor," Miss Grey said. "I'll be right back. Hang in there. Okay?"

"Yes, but—do—hurry!"

"I know! I know!"

At the nurses' station she paged Dr. McDermott with an emergency code, and his return call came in almost instantly. "I'm on my way," he said in response to her hurried description of Evelyn's pain. "Stay with her!"

In moments he rushed into Evelyn's room and immediately saw that Nurse Grey's diagnosis of acute appendicitis was correct. "Prepare the patient for emergency surgery," he told her, "and have someone notify the family immediately."

In moments, everything had been set into action, and after signing a release form Evelyn was being wheeled down the hall to surgery. Miss Grey called the local police, told them of the situation, and asked them to send someone to the church and notify the family.

When the policeman stepped into the foyer of the church he quietly asked an usher to bring Mrs. Johnston's daughter to the foyer.

The usher went quietly to the pew in which the Benskis were sitting, and relayed the message gently. The three family members went quickly to the back of the auditorium and into the foyer, closing the swinging doors.

Tony held Anna close as the officer told them of the grave situation. She went to pieces, and only Tony's warning of possible danger to their un-born child helped her to control her emotions. Ally said not a word, but stood like a statue, waiting.

"Grandma Bo will be all right," she said at last. "Isn't God there?"

"Yes, honey, God is there." Anna held her close, and fought to control the tears.

"Tony, is there something that the church needs to be praying about?" The voice coming over the speakers into the foyer startled the three, frightened people.

Tony opened the door to the auditorium. "Yes, there is, Brother Alexander. Anna's mother has been taken to the operating room for an emergency appendectomy. We must leave. Please pray."

Upon hearing this, Jeffrey got up quickly, and moved to join the family.

Brother Alexander was speaking again. "We'll do that right now, Tony. God be with you."

"Thank you, pastor."

The group left quickly, and headed for the hospital. Anna kept saying that she should not have left her. Tony tried to re-assure her. Ally remained silent until they arrived at the hospital.

"Grandma Bo will be all right. God will take care of her," she said as they rushed through the hospital entrance.

"God can do anything. We know that, dear. We'll just trust him," Tony replied.

Anna was wishing that she had the faith of this little child. *Surely God won't let my mother die on the same day we have finally been reunited, will he?* she asked herself.

They rushed up to the empty surgery waiting room. The nurse appeared, and asked Anna to come to the desk to sign papers. Tony went with her, leaving Ally with Jeffrey.

Ally was weeping softly, and the lawyer moved to put his arm around her shoulders.

"We have to put Grandma Bo in God's hands, honey," he said. "He loves her even more than we do."

"He could just make her well if he wanted to, right?"

"Sure. We can ask him to do that, but I think we have to let him do what he knows is best, okay?"

"Do I have to say yes?"

"I think God will allow you time to work it out in your own heart."

"Thank you for talking to me, Mr. Jeffrey. It's so good to have someone to talk to me when I'm scared. Mama never…"

118

"Well, you have plenty of people to talk to now, any time you need to talk. You can count on that. Okay?"

"But if Grandma Bo dies, I'll be all alone again. And there are locks on the doors at my house. I can't get in." Deep sobs shook her small frame, and the man beside her was horrified to see that such a small human being could suffer such incredible agony. Never, ever, would he let that Georgia woman have her child back. He moved to console her, but the crying made it impossible for him to talk to her for long moments.

"Ally, listen to me, okay?" he said at last. "I want to tell you something very important. Can you listen just a moment?"

Raising her head to look at him, she calmed down a little and nodded. The look of trust on her face shook him emotionally. *What must it be like to be so young, and finally have someone who cares enough to simply talk to you—listen to your fears and longings— even your joys?* he asked himself, shaking his head.

"I'm going to make you a promise, Ally. Okay?"

"Yes, sir, I'm listening."

"The promise is this: I will not ever let you be alone again. You know that I'm a lawyer. I represent the law. It is against the law for children to have to live all alone. Do you understand that?"

She nodded, and he continued. "So, when I tell you that you will never have to live all alone again, you should be able to believe that, right?"

Once more, she nodded, but still said nothing.

He took both of her hands, and spoke softly. "I believe that Grandma Bo will be okay. If God *should* choose to take her to live with him in heaven, though, I will still see to it that you have a wonderful family who will adopt you and love you forever and ever. Will you trust me on that?"

"I want to live with my Grandma Bo. I love her so much."

"Honey, this is just in case God takes her to his home in heaven. It does not mean that we're giving up. We're going to keep right on praying and believing that she's going to be fine. I want her to stay here with us, too. She's very special, isn't she?"

"Yes, sir. She knows how to love little girls."

"Okay, the thing to do is to quit thinking that we might lose her, and just pray for her. Deep inside, though, you'll still know that you will always have someone to love you and care for you—no matter what happens. Okay?"

"Yes, but will you always be my friend, too, no matter what? I don't have any friends besides Grandma Bo."

"I will always be your friend, no matter what. That's a promise. And tonight, you and Mews will be going to Mrs. Anna and Mr. Tony's house. You can stay there until your Grandma Bo gets well."

She flew into his arms and he hugged her and then kissed the top of her head. When he did that, she looked up and smiled. "That's what she does. It means 'love', doesn't it?"

"It surely does mean 'love,' Ally. It does, indeed."

They sat quietly together, comforted by each other's presence, until they saw Anna and Tony approaching. Jeff got up as they reached the waiting room, and Ally followed. She put her little hand in his, and he held it tight.

"How does it look?" he asked.

"She's in surgery, of course," Tony responded. "They took her in nearly an hour ago. It's going to be awhile, and the prognosis isn't the best. At this point, no one seems to be able to tell us if the appendix has ruptured or not. A lot of people are praying, though. That's a comfort to us. She must make it. She's too important to too many people. I haven't even had a chance to get to know her yet."

Brother Glenn and Brother Alexander came through the door just then, and Tony repeated what he had told Jeff concerning Evelyn's condition. These men dropped to their knees beside chairs, and the others stood around them as they prayed. It was as though a blanket of peace descended over the group as they talked with the

Heavenly Father. God's Spirit comforted them, and they knew that whatever the outcome, God was in control.

"Honey, we'd better get you something to eat," Tony said to his wife, a little later. "I just realized that you haven't eaten since lunch. Well, none of us have eaten, but you probably need food more than the rest of us."

"Oh, I'm okay. I had a nourishing lunch. I'll get something after Mother gets out of surgery. I don't want to leave."

"Then we'll bring something up here. I'll check with the nurse."

"I don't want to eat in front of everyone else, honey. Let's see if we can get something for all of us. Okay?"

"Okay. I'll ask if they'll permit us to eat here. If it's all right, we can go to that drive-in burger place down the street. It should still be open."

Tony left the waiting room, and went down to the nurses' station. He soon returned with an affirmative answer. Under the circumstances, it would be okay to eat in the waiting room. The two pastors said they would go down for the food. A list was quickly put together, money exchanged hands, and the men left on their errand.

Ally had been quiet for a long time. Finally, she asked, "Mrs. Anna, isn't Grandma Bo through yet? I want to see her."

"Honey, it's going to be a while, I'm afraid. The doctors, have to be very careful. You don't want them to make her worse, do you? Of course you don't. After you have had a hamburger, perhaps you can sleep a little while. When you wake up, she might be out of surgery."

"I don't know. What if I go to sleep and when I wake up she's not alive anymore?"

"We aren't going to think like that. Let's just believe that God will let her get well. Can you do that?"

"Well—but—what if he decides he wants her up in heaven with him? Then I couldn't see her."

"Your going to sleep won't change anything, Ally. Let's talk about it after you eat, okay? I'll tell you what," she added, "I feel a bit tired, too. We'll both take a short nap after we eat. How about that?"

"Okay, Mrs. Anna." She smiled up at her, and added, "I like being with you."

"And I like being with you. You're a special little girl—so grown up." Anna smiled at her as they walked together to a couch and sat down to wait.

After they had eaten, it wasn't hard to get the child to go to sleep. She was exhausted. Jeffrey was dozing, also. The stress of the accident was catching up with them.

All across town, members of the church had stayed up late to pray for Mrs. Johnston and her family. Different people had agreed to pray during certain hours, and the prayer chain would continue throughout the night. The preachers remained with the family. They said they would not think of leaving before Evelyn was out of surgery. Brother Glenn was supposed to leave to go home to Oklahoma early in the morning, but he stayed with them, saying he would delay leaving if necessary. After all, hadn't he rescued that dear lady from her heat stroke? She kind of belonged to him too.

Tony was glad that his wife and Ally could go to sleep after they had eaten. *What a remarkable child*, he thought, as he watched the little girl sleeping, snuggled close to Anna. *I could easily learn to love her.*

Restless, he walked over to Jeffrey, who had just awakened. He had been thinking about something, and wanted to discuss it with the lawyer.

"Jeff, I need to talk with you about Ally while she's asleep—if you're up to it," He said. He was feeling nervous. The stress of the past few days, compounded by the accident, was affecting his emotions. "If you don't feel like discussing it right now, please say so," he continued.

"No, go ahead. It might even take our minds off of this for a while. What is it that has you so restless?"

"It's just that Ally doesn't seem to have any family to go to. For years, I've wanted to adopt a child. Anna has always opposed that, but now, well, if Ally has no one, well…"

"It could be some time before we can make certain that there are no relatives who want to take her. I'll get back on the case first thing tomorrow, if Evelyn is doing okay. I don't really want to be away if she's in any danger."

Tony cocked his head to one side, and really looked at Jeffrey for the first time. *This guy's in love with her*, he realized. *How could I have missed that? He must really be in misery. I know how I would feel if Anna were the one in the operating room.*

"Do you want to talk about it?" he asked gently. "I don't mean to intrude on your private thoughts, but 'love' is written all over your face. This has to be more than a little difficult for you."

"It's that plain, is it?" Jeffrey questioned. "You're right. I don't know when it happened. Maybe it was the moment she walked into my office the other day. I realized just how much I had missed her. She and John were both close friends, but I never thought of Evelyn in any other way—until that day in my office. She doesn't know, of course," he added.

"Don't worry. I would never say anything. I do feel for you. For all of our sakes, I pray that she comes out of this without problems."

Jeffrey let out a sigh and shook his head. "I just hope she comes out of it alive. I don't want to have to live without her. I've lived alone all of these years, and have done okay, but if I lose her now…"

Tony patted him on the back, and nodded his head gravely. He walked over to wait by a window.

Traffic had long since slowed to an occasional carload of teens, out for their last date before the new week began.

123

Dear God, he prayed silently, *I am new at this, but they tell me that I have the right to talk to you, and you will listen. That's a mind boggling privilege. I'm so thankful that you are in control here. We sure would love to have Mother Bo well and healthy again, if that's okay with you. Amen*

Just then, the two preachers came back from their trip to the small prayer chapel downstairs. The four men sat down together and spent some time discussing the Bible. It was a thrill to Tony to hear of the many blessings that go along with being a child of God. Jeff also got involved in the discussion, remembering many things he had been taught so long ago. Talking helped to pass the long night hours more quickly for them, as they waited for news of Evelyn.

Chapter Ten

Sunday had turned to Monday when, at last, the men saw the doctor approaching. They breathed a final prayer for good news, and Tony went over to quietly wake Anna. He was careful not to disturb Ally, knowing that his wife might need a few moments before she could cope with the child's questions.

Dear God, please let her be all right, Tony prayed silently.

They all got up and waited, together, as the doctor came to them. He was smiling, and everybody relaxed a little.

"Well, she got through the surgery just fine," Dr. McDermott said. "The appendix had not burst, but it was right at the point of doing just that. She's a lucky lady. If she hadn't already been in the hospital... Well, anyway, she's in recovery now. She'll stay there for a while. Tomorrow we'll check out the head injury again to be sure that's okay. You may go in, two at a time, to see her, but don't be worried if she doesn't know you are there. She has responded to us, but she's not fully conscious. She's through the worst of it, and I don't anticipate any complications. She just has to get her strength back. Don't stay more than a few minutes. After you've seen her, go on home and get some rest. You can't remain in recovery with her, and she has the very best of care. We will call you again, if there is a problem. Any questions?"

Anna asked if Ally could possibly go in to see that her Grandma Bo was still alive. The doctor said he would leave instructions with the nurse to let her go in for a couple of minutes. After answering a few more questions, he turned to leave. Tony took his wife's arm to lead her in to see her mother. The preachers returned to their seats to wait their turn.

125

Jeff followed the doctor down the hall. "Mike," he called after him. "Can you give me a moment?"

The doctor turned and smiled at his old high school friend. "Sure, Jeff, walk along with me for a little way. What is it?"

"I just have to know how she really is. Will she be all right?"

Mike looked closely at his friend's face and nodded his head knowingly. "That's how it is, is it? I care about her too, Jeff, though maybe not quite like you do," he smiled. "I think you can relax. She's not in the best of health, but she's a fighter. Always has been. After the wreck with John, she was in bad shape. She had a head injury then, too, but we couldn't keep her in the hospital. She had a daughter to look after, she said, and she went home, against all of our advice to the contrary."

"Is this head injury bad? You haven't said much about it."

"Well, like I told her daughter, we have more tests scheduled for tomorrow. I think it's going to be okay, but we need to check it out some more to be really sure."

"Thanks, Mike. I know you'll take good care of her. I just feel so protective of her."

"That's the way it is when you're in love, old friend. Sometimes it hurts."

"I'm finding that out. See you later."

"Life was so wonderful, just yesterday morning," Anna said. "It's hard to understand why this had to happen."

Tony looked at her and smiled. "Life is still wonderful, honey. Your mom's back, the baby is on the way and, most important, we have Jesus as our savior, and a great church full of wonderful people who care about us. Mom is going to get well. Like Ally said, I just know it. And honey, there is also the fact that she was here in the hospital when this attack occurred. What if she had still been far away and alone—or even out in that old house with no one except Ally. The child didn't know where anything is, or even have a friend to ask for help. It seems to me like God is watching over her."

She smiled at him and nodded her head. "Okay, I can see that you have been thinking about this. You're right. I need to just be thankful and stop worrying, right."

"Let's go in and see how's she's doing. Remember, the doctor said she might not be aware of anything yet."

Anna took a deep breath as they entered the room.

"Oh, Tony, she looks so helpless. What can I do?"

"She's just recovering from major surgery, honey."

"Her color is good, isn't it? I just wish she had had more time to build her strength back up. There's no telling what she has been eating all these years, or even if she has been eating very much of anything. She was living on such a small income—all because of me."

She sighed, and walked over and stood by her mother's bed, taking her hand. "Mom," she said. "I love you so much. I don't know if you can hear me, but if you can, would you squeeze my hand? Can you do that?" She waited. A moment passed. "Oh, if only…"

She felt a faint movement on her hand. Looking down, she saw the dear hand move, ever so slightly, and relax.

"You can? You can hear me? Do it again! Oh, Tony, I think she hears me!"

She felt the slight pressure again, and her face broke out in a smile, then the tears came. Silent tears. Tears of joy.

"We need to let her rest, honey. There are other people out there who want to come in for a moment, too."

"You're right. I'm leaving for a while, Mother. I'll be back in with Ally soon. I love you."

"Bye, Mother Bo. I'll be back later this morning. I love you, too," Tony said, smiling broadly at his mother-in-law. He thought he saw the faintest hint of a smile touch her lips.

Jeffrey was the next to go in. He stared down at the silent form, then took her hand and held it.

"You don't know how much you scared me, lady," he said quietly. "I knew that I had always admired you, but incredibly, during these last short days, that admiration has turned to love. If I had lost you, I don't know what I would have done. Do you understand, Evelyn Johnston? I am in love with you. Head-over-heels in love."

The hand he was holding moved slightly.

"You heard me? I can't believe this! If you love me, too, squeeze my hand again."

The hand he was holding moved weakly and was still.

"You love me? You love me! I can't believe this. If you hadn't had this surgery, I wouldn't have had the nerve to tell you, and all the time you loved me, too. There are so many things I want to say to you. Oh, I know I have to go. You shouldn't get too tired. I'll send the preachers in, then Anna and Ally will come in. I love you, my darling."

She squeezed his hand again, slightly, and he left, walking on clouds.

The pastors went in as Jeffrey exited. He stood just outside the door as they went in to have prayer with her. Then he walked with them as far as the waiting room. The pastors said their goodbyes and left the hospital.

Ally was anxious to see for herself that her "grandma Bo" was still alive. She had awakened, and was waiting her turn, none too patiently.

After she and Anna went in, Jeffrey related to Tony the things that had happened in the recovery room. Tony expressed his surprise and delight at such an incredible thing to have happen just after major surgery. The two men shook hands, and Jeff left for a much-needed rest.

In the recovery room, Ally whispered, "Grandma Bo? I'm here to see you. I'm glad you didn't die."

"Mother, we won't stay long," Anna interrupted. She was concerned about having the child in that room so soon after the operation. "Ally just needed to see that you are going to be okay." She put her hand on Evelyn's shoulder, wanting to be close to her—to protect her, somehow.

Ally moved up to the bed and took the limp hand. Slowly, it began to tighten a bit. Bo was trying to say "I love you," to her "granddaughter."

Anna put her hand on the little shoulder, and then spoke to her mother. "We have to go now, but we'll be back later this morning. The doctor said the surgery went great. Now you just have to recover. Try to get some rest, and get well. I love you," she said, and her mother's eyes opened slightly. Her daughter smiled at her, and received a weak smile in return.

Ally squeezed the hand she had been holding. "Me, too," she said. "I love you. Good night. I'm going home with Mrs. Anna and Mr. Tony. They're real nice. We're gonna get Mews, too. I'll see you tomorrow, okay?"

Evelyn smiled weakly once more, and then closed her eyes.

"Let's leave quietly, Ally. Grandma Bo has gone to sleep. She will need a lot of sleep to get well. We'll go get Mews, then go home and fix up a bed for you. Would you like that?"

"Yes, ma'am." She looked up into the eyes of the young woman. "I like being with you and Mr. Tony."

Tears stung Anna's eyes as she wondered if her own lost child was with someone kind. She was determined not to distress Ally, though, so she blinked the tears away.

"Well," she encouraged, "from now on life should be a lot better for you."

Tony saw Anna and Ally holding hands as they walked down the corridor. His heart swelled with excitement. Maybe Anna would be willing to adopt the child. "Please, God," he whispered.

"Mrs. Anna is gonna fix up a bed just for me," the little girl told him as she walked up. Her face was glowing, she was so happy.

"Sure, we will. Tomorrow we'll fix up a whole room just for you," Tony said, smiling.

"It will almost be like I *belong*, won't it?"

Tony felt the sharp stab of pain that occasioned such a statement. Had this child ever felt like she belonged anywhere before "Grandma Bo" entered her life?

The three walked together through the emergency exit, and headed for the car.

Anna felt comforted in knowing that inside the hospital angels were watching over her beloved mother while she slept. It was also comforting to know that people from the church would be sending prayers heavenward on her behalf all through the rest of the night.

The three tired people climbed into the car and headed off to rescue Mews.

৯৬৯৬৯৬

Jeffrey returned to the hospital early. The others hadn't managed to make it back yet, and he congratulated himself, thinking that he would have some time alone with Evelyn. She was awake, and fairly alert. She smiled at him as he entered the recovery room. He returned the smile, and stood there, shaking his head in disbelief of the thing that had happened such a short time before. Walking over to the bedside, he took her hand once more and stood there looking at her. Her face wore a puzzled look.

"What is it, Evelyn? Is there some problem this morning?" He spoke gently, and increased the pressure on her hand a little. She returned the pressure, and smiled a tentative smile.

"I-I'm not sure whether I had a wonderful dream last night, or if you actually said that—"

"Oh, it wasn't a dream, my darling. I am madly in love with you! I want to marry you and spend the rest of my life with you," he said, smiling. She returned his smile, and he bent down to kiss her lips.

They heard the doctor speaking to the woman in the next bed, so Jeff moved away, and they waited for him. The doctor wore a satisfied smile as he greeted them, and informed her that she would be moving to her room within the hour.

"You are one lucky lady, Evelyn Johnston. If you hadn't been in the hospital already when your attack occurred, you might not have made it in time. Hadn't you been experiencing some pain and nausea? It's possible that the accident caused the problem to surface, I suppose, but I don't really think so."

Bo remembered the vague symptoms she'd had at the old house, and later on the sidewalk, when she collapsed. She hadn't connected the incidents with this attack, but now she could compare them, and knew that they had probably been warnings. She related each incident to the doctor, who nodded his head knowingly.

"I thought you must have surely had something. The next time anything that severe happens to you, go to the emergency room. Don't wait for the problem to reach the danger point."

"I'll remember that, Mike," she responded. "What about the concussion? I keep waiting for this headache to go away. It is less intense, but it certainly is making itself known."

"Let's give it a few more hours, and then I want to do some tests. We'll get you settled into a room where things are more normal. That should help you get back on your feet. Do you have any more questions?"

Jeffrey spoke up, voicing the question that was uppermost in *his* mind. "How long before we can take her home, Mike?"

The doctor smiled, knowingly, at him and said, "She'll be out of here in a couple of weeks—maybe less, Jeff. We don't want to rush things too much. It will depend on how quickly she mends."

131

"Just checking. I need her to get well. Thanks for taking such good care of her," he said. "I've waited a long time to find her."

Evelyn blushed, as the doctor grinned at them. There was no hiding their love from their old classmate. He knew them too well. "I'm truly glad for both of you. Don't forget to invite me to the wedding," he said as he turned to go on to the next patient.

The two smiled at each other, somewhat over-whelmed. Their love—the idea of a wedding—it was all so new, that having heard it voiced by someone else made it suddenly seem more real. They looked at each other, truly aware for the first time that this was actually happening to them. How could it all have come to pass in such a short time?

Jeffrey smiled at her, shaking his head in disbelief. "Whew!" he said. "Whew!"

"I know!" she agreed. "I'm having trouble assimilating all of this too."

"You aren't changing your mind, are you?" he asked. "I know you were in a drugged state, but..." The worried look on his face caused her to respond immediately.

"Not a chance," she said, smiling.

"Whew," he said again—this time for a different reason.

"I'm going to have to leave now, sweetheart. I hate to, but the office doesn't take care of itself. I'll be back later, though, I promise. Still love me?" he questioned, just to be sure.

"Oh, yes!" she responded.

He bent to kiss her, told her he loved her, and then moved away. At the door, he turned for one last smile, and was gone.

Oh, how I love that man! Evelyn told herself silently, and then, *I'm so tired...*

She was asleep in an instant.

When Bo's family arrived a couple of hours later, they found her in a regular room. She was sleeping peacefully, so Tony suggested

132

that they leave her for the moment and get some breakfast in the cafeteria.

Getting to go by and pick out her own food was another new experience for Ally. As they passed by the fresh fruit, her face lit up. She looked up at Anna and asked, "Mrs. Anna, may I have an orange? I've always wanted an orange."

"You've never eaten an orange? Ever? Surely you have, dear."

"No ma'am. My mama ate them sometimes, but she said I couldn't have one until I'm twenty."

"That wicked woman! Of course you may have one. You may have *two*!" Anna said, placing them on the tray with an angry thump.

Tony tried to calm her down, though he, too, was furious.

The dark eyes looked up at Anna to see if her anger were directed at her. "I'm sorry," she said. "I didn't mean to make you mad. I don't want an orange. Mama wouldn't like it. I was just teasing." She was on the verge of tears, and the two adults were horrified that their anger had frightened their little guest.

"Oh, Ally, no! We aren't upset with you, dear. We were mad that your mother would tell you such a terrible thing. Please don't cry. We are very glad to get to give you your first oranges. You're going to love them," Tony said. "Don't be afraid. Your mother won't be taking you back to live with her. Not ever again. You don't have to worry about her being angry about anything anymore. You will have a new family who will love you and share with you. There are laws against parents treating children the way your mama has treated you. Parents can't just walk away and leave young children all alone like she did."

"But I'm scared. What if she comes back and just takes me away?"

"Ally, look at me," Tony said. "Look at my eyes."

She did as she was told, and then started crying.

"Don't cry, honey. I didn't want you to be even more afraid. I wanted you to see that I care about you. As long as you're with us,

I'll protect you and keep you from harm. Your mama will not take you back again. I won't let her."

"I'm not crying 'cause I'm scared. I'm crying 'cause your eyes say 'love' to me." She threw her arms around him and sobbed. "I love you, Mr. Tony."

Oblivious to the people around them, the three wept together, and hugged and laughed. It seemed as though the terrible years with her mother were losing some of their power over Ally.

Watching his wife, Tony felt even more encouraged about the prospect of adopting this precious child. Once more, he lifted his petition to his Heavenly Father, and left it in his hands.

Chapter Eleven

Evelyn was awake, and waiting, when her family returned. She greeted them with a smile. "Grandma Bo! You're awake! You're smiling. That means you're gonna be okay, right? I came to see you before, but you were asleep." Ally ran to stand beside the bed, and grabbed Bo's hand.

"You'll have to excuse me for that, Ally." Her voice was still raspy from the tubes she had had in her throat. "I'm afraid that I may be sleepy for awhile because of my medications. It won't be long before I'll be back to normal, though, and we'll be together again. We have something special together, you and I. We found each other, and helped each other when we were so lonely, didn't we? Mews, too. He's a part of us. How is he, by the way?"

"He's at Mrs. Anna's house. I'm staying with them. They let me have my own room. Do they let you eat oranges in here? I had two oranges for breakfast. They were so good."

"I have to be careful about eating right now, because of the ether they gave me during the operation. I'm pretty nauseous. I'll be back to normal soon, though. We'll get oranges when we get home, if you like."

"My birthday party is almost here. Will you be able to eat ice cream?"

"Oh, I may not be able to go to your party this year, honey. I'm not sure I'll be able to walk around the zoo for a while. The party is all planned, though, and the kids from church will be there. I will choose a big present and have Mrs. Anna pick it up for me, if I'm not able to do it. How does that sound?"

"No!"

"Ally, don't be rude, dear," Anna corrected. She was realizing that caring for an older child was a lot different that taking care of her toddler had been.

"I'm sorry."

Bo squeezed the small hand and said gently, "Tell me why you said that, honey. Grandma Bo knows that you didn't mean to be unkind."

"I don't care about the present. I want *you* at my party. Can't we wait until you get well, so you can come too? You're my Grandma Bo…"

Tears came to Bo's eyes, and she smiled at the child she had come to love so very much. "We will do whatever you choose. It's your special day. If you will be happier if we delay it, then that's what we'll do."

"Do I still get the present?" Ally was laughing, and everyone laughed with her.

"I think that can be managed," Bo answered, with a grin.

The nurse came into the room just then, and recognized the signs of fatigue on Evelyn's face. She told the family that visiting hours were over, and to come back during the afternoon visiting hours. They left, after quick, gentle hugs, and Evelyn relaxed.

"That little one is quite a girl, isn't she?" The nurse arranged pillows as she talked. "She is really a beautiful child. Is she your granddaughter?"

"The only one I have at the moment. She's actually an abandoned child. We sort of found each other. The three of us are caring for her while my lawyer searches for any family she might have. I'm afraid we spoil her. My daughter is expecting in a few months, so I'll have two to spoil. Well, that is, if we should get to keep Ally," she concluded with a sad smile.

"It's only natural to spoil children. She seems very mature."

"She is, in a lot of ways. In other ways, she's younger than her age. Her mother kept her completely hidden away. She had never been around other people until we found each other in the old house where her mother had deserted her. She's very special to me." Bo yawned, and breathed an exhausted sigh.

"Well, if you don't need anything, I'm going to let you get some sleep. That's the best way to get well quickly," she advised.

"In that case, I'll sleep a lot. I'm anxious to get on with my life. I've been away for a long time."

"Sleep, then," her nurse said, smiling. "Ring if you need anything." Turning out the light she quietly left the room.

෴෴෴෴

The Benskis stopped at the grocery store on the way home. Ally saw so many products she had never seen before, that she simply wandered up and down the aisles staring.

"Mrs. Anna, look at this!" she said, laughing. "It's a cookie, shaped like a person. Did you ever see such a thing?"

Tears came into Anna's eyes as she smiled back at the little girl. "It's quite wonderful, isn't it, darling? You just look around all you want to. I'll be right over here, and Mr. Tony is in the next aisle."

Ally wandered on, looking at everything, and exclaiming over little treasures. Suddenly she felt that someone was standing very close to her. She shivered. Something was terribly wrong...

"Misfit! What are you doing away from home? And where did you get those fancy clothes? Did you steal them?"

Ally was paralyzed with fear at the sound of her mother's voice. She was standing close behind her—so near, that Ally knew she could grab her at any moment. She thought of running. She wanted to cry. She was more afraid than she had ever been in her life.

Then she remembered the love in Mr. Tony's face. *He won't let anything happen to me.*

"Mr. Tony! Mr. Tony, help!" she screamed. "It's my mama, Mr. Tony. Come quick!"

Almost before she had finished speaking, Tony had her in his arms.

Straitening up, he found himself face-to-face with his old college sweetheart, Georgia Stephens. She wasn't pretty any more. She looked old. And mean.

"Georgia?" He was struggling to keep the anger down. "What? Why? My word, Georgia! How could you be so cruel to your own daughter?"

"That's her, Mr. Tony. That's my mama who abused me. Get her, Mr. Tony!"

"I think we'll leave that to the police, honey," he said, holding Ally tighter. "Georgia you have a lot to answer for. Child abandonment is a serious crime. We're going to have to call the authorities."

"No way, Tony. You don't have any proof that I did anything wrong. Who would listen to a little brat like this one?" It took all of Tony's self restraint to keep from hitting the woman, but Ally was holding onto his neck so tightly, he could hardly help remembering that he had to be an example for her.

He reached out to take Georgia by the arm, but she slipped away from him and headed for the door. He started after her, but Ally tightened her grip on him again, and he stopped.

Anna walked up just in time to see the anger in his face. "Honey, what's wrong?" she questioned "I've never seen you so angry."

"That's Georgia," he growled, pointing toward the door as the woman was making her escape. "You remember her from college, don't you? Well, she's…"

"I don't have to live with you anymore!" Ally yelled after her tormentor, but she didn't loosen her grip on Tony's neck.

"Shut up, Misfit!" Georgia screamed as she pushed her way past the crowd and through the doors.

Anna glared after the woman. "Georgia Stephens? But—in college she seemed so nice."

"Well, she sure isn't nice any more," Tony said angrily. "Did you hear her yell at Ally? She obviously isn't dead, the way we thought. Why in the world didn't she go home to take care of her child?"

"I can't believe any of this," Anna said, trembling. "Honey, let's get the groceries paid for and go home." Anna looked at her husband. She was worried about him. She had never seen him like this before. "Come on, honey," she said, when he didn't move.

"What? Oh, sure, let's pay for the food." He absently started toward the checkout counter, still holding Ally.

"Mr. Tony? I can walk now. I'm okay."

"Ally, I'm sorry, baby. The thought of your being in that kind of danger has me sort of rattled." He put her down, but kept holding her hand.

The groceries paid for, they left the store, and soon they were in the car, headed for home.

Anna was glad that she had picked up some lunchmeat. She quickly prepared a light meal, and they all sat in the living room with sandwiches and soft drinks. No one spoke much for a while. There was a lot to consider.

Tony ate quickly, for he wanted to go to the police station to let them know that Georgia definitely was in town. Maybe they would be able to find her before she could get away. If she were angry with him, though, she might not cooperate in helping them find Ally's relatives. What if they couldn't adopt her after all? He was now sure that Anna would agree to keep her. He could see the love in her eyes.

Ally went over to him and hugged him. With the resilience of a child, she seemed ready to get back to normal. She was happy again, with Mews on her lap.

"Grandma Bo will be out of the hospital soon, Mews," she said. "She'll be glad to see you. She loves you. We'll have my birthday party. You can come, too. You're one of the family, you know."

She broke off a small piece of her sandwich for him, and continued talking to him as though he understood. "I think we're lucky, Mews. We have Mrs. Anna, and Mr. Tony, and Grandma Bo, and Mr. Jeffrey—and I told Mama we don't have to live with her any more."

She stopped talking to Mews and sat quietly, apparently lost in her thoughts. Anna wondered whether they would ever know even half of the things this child had endured. I must not let Georgia have a victory over me either, she admonished herself. Ally's free of her. We have to look forward to our happy future together. She didn't even realize that she had added Ally to her future. It just seemed natural. She put a smile on her face and asked, "Anybody want to go back to see Grandma Bo?"

"Me! I do!" Ally squealed. "Can Mews go, too?"

Tony laughed. "Nope. Mews wouldn't make it past the front door, I'm afraid. You see, we're the only ones who know that he is a people. It's our secret."

"I like secrets, Mr. Tony. I won't tell. Okay, Mews, you'd better stay here. You can see her when she gets home." She put the kitten on the floor, and followed her guardians out of the door.

"I'm meeting Jeffrey at the hospital," Tony said, as they got into the car. "After I see Mom, I'll leave you two there, and we'll go on to the police station. You can come back home in our car, and Jeffrey will drop me off, okay?"

"Sure, honey. Do you need me to go with you to the police station?"

"I can go too," Ally said. "I can tell them that Mama left me all by myself."

"It may come to that, but I think I can handle it for today. A dear lady in the hospital is probably wondering if she has been deserted. I think you had better go visit her, don't you?"

They found Jeffrey sitting in the waiting room when they arrived at the hospital. "She's asleep," he said. "The nurse thought I shouldn't

140

wake her. She says that sleep is a major part of healing, and I want that lady well."

Anna and Tony sat down, but Ally ran to the window to look out at the city. Although they were only three stories up, she could see all over the small town from that height.

Responding to the news of Georgia, Jeff said, "If they catch her, I think they'll put her away for a good long while." He was trying to keep his voice low so Ally wouldn't over hear. "Such abuse of a child is unheard of in these parts. The whole town is angry about it."

Ally turned from the window. True to her nature, she had heard every word. "Mr. Jeffrey, I'm big. I can go tell what she did." She looked very small as she headed toward them. She sat down beside Anna and continued speaking. "Mama was mean to me. She didn't like me. She didn't even hug me. I always wanted someone to hug me and kiss me. All I had was my stuffed animal. I hugged him and kissed him until he got dirty, and she just threw him away."

The adults had to turn their eyes away from the pain. But there were tears all around. Seeing their sympathy, Ally flew into Anna's arms and wept, too. Great sobs shook her small body as she released pent-up emotions. Gradually, she regained control, and looked up at Jeffrey, her eyes brimming with tears.

"I want to help," she said. "I don't want to ever live with her again. If they put her in prison, then I'll feel safe."

"I imagine you'll get you chance to tell what happened to you during those long years, little darling, " Jeff said.

"Can we go see Grandma Bo, now?"

"I'll check with the nurse, honey," Tony replied. "It's been quite awhile. She may be awake. Oh, look. Here comes the nurse now. I'll bet she was just coming for us. What do you think?"

"Yes!" With the elastic spirit of a child, Ally had already dropped the painful subject of her abuse, and was ready to be happy again. She ran to meet Nurse Grey.

"Can I go see her, Miss Grey? Can I?" She was jumping up and down in anticipation.

"You may, but only for a few moments. She's asking for all of you. You may as well go in together. She seems to like it that way, even though it means bending the rules quite a lot." She chuckled as she told them this, and turned to lead the way back down the hall.

"There you all are. I thought you had deserted me." Evelyn was smiling, obviously stronger. Jeffrey breathed a sigh of relief. She was truly going to be okay.

Ally rushed to the bedside, anxious to share her news. "Grandma Bo!" she reported. "Mama tried to get me, but Mr. Tony protected me, just like he said he would. Isn't that great?"

Anna put her hands on Ally's shoulders. "Oh, Ally, maybe Grandma Bo…"

"She's alive, then? Ally, I'm so glad Mr. Tony was there for you! Now I won't worry. I'll get well for sure. Come here, you little bundle of energy."

The two had a special moment that the others could not really share. Evelyn had seen more of what the child had endured. She had been her rescuer, her first real friend. The two hugged and laughed. "I love you, little 'granddaughter.' I'm really glad that you have someone who protects you."

"He was great. Boy, was Mama mad at him! I'm gonna tell the police about her."

"If that isn't too hard for you, I'm very glad. No one knows better than you do, just what she is like. Child abuse is a terrible crime."

"I know, 'cause I was abused."

The adults tried to hide their chuckles at this bit of reasoning. They didn't want her to think there was anything exciting about what had happened.

Bo wisely changed the subject. "Anna, how are you, darling? You've had a lot of stress. Is the baby okay? Should you be resting at home?"

142

"Mother, I'm doing great. Now that I know you're better, I'm fine. The baby is fine, too. I'm taking good care of your grandson. If he is a boy, his name is to be John, you know."

"Do you think it is a boy?"

"I hope so. We both want a 'baby John' to add to our family."

"This is becoming a wonderful day. There's such good news all around."

"Mother Bo, Anna and I have been wondering if you might like to move in and live with us when you leave here—you and Ally, of course." Tony was smiling at his newly found mother-in-law.

She smiled back, and glanced over at Jeffrey. "Somehow, I don't think I'll need to, dear, but what a kind offer. I can see that you're the son I always longed for. I love you, already."

Tony smiled, sheepishly. *Of course she will be married and living with her husband*, he realized. *What if she wants to take Ally to live with them?* He was surprised at the emotion that thought stirred up in him. He definitely did not want to part with that little girl.

"Whoops, I forgot about our lawyer friend here," he replied. "I guess we can settle for frequent visits from you. I love you, too, you know."

Jeffrey was getting impatient. His whole heart longed to be alone with the woman he loved.

Anna came to the rescue. "Well, Mother, we need to be going. I'm glad you're doing so well. I love you so much."

"Bye, Mother Bo. I love you, too." Tony smiled at his mother-in-law. "I'm so glad you have come home."

"Bye, Grandma Bo. I love you more that anybody else does." Ally grinned, and followed the Benskis from the room.

"I'll wait for you in the family area, Jeff," Tony said. "No need to hurry. I want to see Ally and Anna to the car, first."

"What did Tony mean by that?" Evelyn asked when she and Jeffrey were alone. "Are you two planning something?"

"We're going to the police station to let them know that Georgia is in town. Tony wanted his lawyer with him, which is probably wise."

"I see. So I only have you for a few moments?" she pouted, half teasing.

"I thought they'd never leave, didn't you?" Jeffrey was grinning mischievously. He had her hand in his, and noted with joy that her grip was much stronger than it had been the last time he held it. "I'm kidding, of course, but I do so long to be alone with you, and hold you and tell you how much you mean to me. It's strange that I could have known you for so many years and never realized that I could love you like this. If you had not survived our accident, I think my heart would have died within me."

"I know. I thought I would die before they told me you were okay. I finally had to ask. What a blessed relief it was to see you standing there. You know that I loved John with all of my heart, but ours was a love of two young people who grew older together. This is different. I'm certainly old enough now to know what I want, and what to expect. I can't wait until we can be married and start our life together."

"Then let's not wait. Darling, we could be married here in the hospital, and when you are able to leave, I could take you home with me."

Evelyn laughed aloud. "We sound like couple of love-sick teenagers. My, I never expected to have these feelings again, but let's pray about this, Jeffrey. I have no doubts that God has given you to me, but there are others to consider. We have a church family now. Wouldn't you like to be married with all of them present? There are also our own families. Since you have never been married, don't you think your family will want to be present at your wedding?"

"I know you're right. I guess that now that I have found you, I just want you to be mine. It's true that my family would be terribly hurt if they were left out. After all, I am fifty years old. I've been waiting for you all of my life—and so have they."

Evelyn smiled, and drew his hand to her lips to kiss it. He bent to kiss her gently, and then stood there, smiling back at her, his eyes full of love. The nurse found them like that when she entered the room a while later. Jeffrey turned when he heard her come in. "I know. I know. Visiting hours are over. I have to leave. I'll be back this evening, darling. Get some rest." He made his way out, waving good-bye.

Evelyn murmured softly to herself, "Who would have ever thought I would fall in love at fifty?" Her face was glowing with happiness. Nurse Grey walked over to give her a gentle hug. "I'm so thrilled for you, Mrs. Johnston. You certainly deserve some happiness. He's a fine man."

"Yes, he is. God is so good."

"Well, try to get some sleep now."

Evelyn sighed, and snuggled into her pillows. Sleep wrapped its arms around her, and she drifted off.

Chapter Twelve

Jeffrey dropped Tony off, just as Anna and Ally were getting out of the car. They had stopped by the store for some of the groceries that had been forgotten during the episode with Georgia. Together, they all walked to the house. Mews heard the door open and ran to meet his mistress. She scooped him up into her arms as soon as she was inside. "I missed you, too, Mews. You get lonely here all by yourself, don't you? I think you need another kitten to play with." She looked at Tony and Anna with the question in her eyes.

"Now would not be a good time for that, honey. Let's get things settled around here before we even think about another animal to take care of, okay?" Tony patted her on the shoulder and started down the hall to his study. He hadn't had much time to take care of business lately.

"But Mews is lonely now."

He stopped and turned to smile at her. "That may be honey," he said, "but kittens can get pretty rowdy together. We don't have the time to train them right now. Mews is here because he was already family. Just enjoy him, and forget about another kitten for now, please."

"Are you mad at me, Mr. Tony?" The big, dark eyes were brimming with tears again. Tony's heart melted at the sight, but he knew that giving in would not be in her best interest.

"Of course not, sweetheart. It's okay for you to ask for things, but as the head of the house, I have the right to say 'no.' Do you understand? That's what being part of a family is all about. We each have our place."

"I guess I don't know a lot about being part of a family. I'll try to learn, I promise. I love you, Mr. Tony."

"I love you, too, honey. Don't be afraid to talk to me, or ask me for things. Just remember that if I say 'no', it's because I feel that that is the best answer for our family."

"Being a family is really good, isn't it?" she asked. A hint of sadness was in her voice. *It would be so good to belong to a real family*, she thought longingly.

Anna went over and put her arms around the little girl, hugging her for a moment. "It sure is, and we're very happy to have you here with us. The baby is on the way, too. God has been so good to us."

"I love you, Mrs. Anna."

"And I love you. Let's go see what we can do about getting some lunch around here, okay?"

The evening visit to see Bo was over, and the family was back home for the night. Ally had said "goodnight," and was dressed in new pajamas and house slippers that Anna had bought for her. Mews even had a brand new, lined box to sleep in, sitting right beside the bed. He had slept beside her bed ever since that first night, but he had never had such a fancy box as this one. It was pink, to match the bedspread, and even had a small, pink pillow for looks. The doll Jeffrey had bought her was on the bed and was her sleeping companion each night. Anna slipped the doll under the sheets, and then the two of them knelt together beside the bed. Putting her arm around her small charge, Anna began to pray. She had only had a few days' experience at praying, but she wanted to share that new privilege with Ally. It was still unbelievable that she could actually speak with the creator of the universe, and he would want to listen to her.

"Dear heavenly Father," she began, "how can I every thank you for so many blessings? Thank you for your beloved son, Jesus, who was willing to die for me and my family, so that we might go to live in your heaven with your some day. Thank you, for letting him come to earth. What a sacrifice that was on your part, to let him leave your home, and come here to die for us. It has been so lonely

148

for us, without our daughter, so I know a tiny bit of what you must have felt. I'll always miss Megan, but Ally has come to us, and I thank you for that. Thank you for my mother and for my husband and all of the blessings you have given me. Please help me to live for you always. Please forgive the sins I committed today. I love you, Father. Amen."

Ally looked up at her, but Anna's head was still bowed, waiting for Ally's prayer, so she began: "Dear God, thank you for Jesus, and for Mrs. Anna and Mr. Tony, and Grandma Bo, and Mr. Jeffrey, and Brother Glenn, and Brother Alexander and Mews. Please let Mama get caught. Amen. Oh, and thank you for my pretty room. Amen, again."

The two smiled at each other, and shared another hug. Then the happy little girl climbed into her bed and snuggled up to her doll. She put one hand down on Mew's new basket and sighed a great sigh of contentment. "Good night, Mommy. I love you," she said sleepily.

Anna gasped, but managed to say, "Good night, darling. I love you, too. See you in the morning." She turned the light off, and quickly left the room. Glancing up toward the attic, she thought of the dear baby bed Tony had carried up there earlier that day—just until the arrival of the new baby. She stifled a sob and made her way to the couch and sat down, her hand covering her mouth. She knew that Ally hadn't even realized that she had called her "Mommy." Tears came unbidden, as she remembered her own precious daughter. How could she ever accept someone else's child as her own, when Megan...

Just then Tony walked into the room. "What is it, honey? Are you okay? You look like you've seen a ghost."

"She called me 'Mommy'. She didn't even realize it. Oh, Tony, I have already come to love that child, but what about our Megan? How dare I love somebody else's little girl? I don't even know where mine is."

Tony's face lit up with this revelation, and he took his wife in his arms. "Honey, I don't know of any way we can do anything for our Megan, but Ally needs us. I love her too. I want to adopt her. Do you think you could?"

"I want to, but Megan…"

"We won't love our Megan less, honey. Maybe God has sent Ally to us to mend our broken hearts. That child is very special."

"I know. She's so thankful for everything. You should have seen her and that kitten. You'll have to go in and look at them, honey. They are so adorable together. She has her doll in bed with her, and one hand is in Mews' basket. I think she leaves it there all night."

"She is really precious. Come here, my beautiful wife." He held his arms out to her, and she left the couch and went to him. "I can't begin to tell you how dear you are to me. I love you with all of my heart," he said.

"And I love you," she responded. "Could life ever become more wonderful than this?"

"I don't think so, but that's what I thought on our wedding day, and look how much more fantastic our life is now."

"You're right. I can't wait to see what the future holds for us. Honey, you have to come look at Ally and her kitten," she urged. They moved over to the door of Ally's bedroom, and quietly opened it. She was sound asleep. Her hand was still in Mew's box, and the giant doll was snuggled up against her on the other side. The couple shared a smile and turned away, leaving the door open. Together, they went to turn out the living room light, and then headed for their room.

Anna dressed for bed and crawled in. She slid under the light cover and sighed contentedly. Tony soon joined her, and the lights went out.

৯৵৯৵৯৵

The man waited just outside in the darkness for another forty-five minutes, and then left the seclusion of the bushes in which he had been hiding. Hugging the side of the house he crept up to the bedroom windows. He paused in the darkness to listen for possible movement inside. All was quiet, and he checked the windows carefully. He saw that there were new screens, and also locks that secured the windows at a height of about seven inches—just the right height for the attic fan to pull a cool breeze into the house. This was not going to be easy. He almost turned and left, but then he thought about the anger he would face if he failed. Moving on toward the back of the house, he continued checking each window until he came to the laundry room. "Ah-ha!" he said under his breath. "This is more like it." He quickly slit the screen with his knife and removed it; then quietly raised the un-locked window. Using his strong muscles, he lifted himself up to the windowsill and slid across the washing machine to the floor. He landed with a small "thump," and then stood perfectly still, listening for any evidence that he had been heard. All remained quiet, and he moved across to the door.

"I hope this thing is well oiled," he muttered to himself as he carefully turned the doorknob. The door opened silently, and he stepped cautiously into the kitchen. A nightlight was burning, and he moved to turn it off. This made a tiny "click," and he stood still, cringing in the darkness—again waiting for some sign that someone had heard the noise. Hearing nothing but the quiet ticking of a clock somewhere in another part of the house, he took a deep breath and moved across the kitchen. Entering the living room from the dining room, he could see that the bedroom doors were open. He nodded his head and smiled.

Maybe this won't be so hard after all, he thought. He moved quietly toward the middle bedroom door and peeked in.

There she is. He breathed a deep sigh and hesitated…

Tony had stirred in his sleep, and gradually awakened. He looked at the clock and saw that it was 11:30. Needing a drink of water, he got out of bed carefully so that Anna wouldn't be awakened. He threw on a robe, not bothering with slippers, and left the room for the kitchen. He had just stepped into the hall, when he realized that he wasn't alone. He saw the shadowy figure of a man about to enter Ally's room.

Blind fury swept over him, and he charged the man with all of his strength. They fell together onto the floor, but there was no further need for combat. The man had been knocked senseless when his head hit the hardwood floor.

Anna rushed into the hall, eyes filled with terror. "Tony, what is it?" Seeing her husband and the intruder just outside Ally's room, she let out a little scream. She stood, with her hand over her mouth to keep from screaming again. Tony got up from the floor and went to her.

"It's okay, honey. He's out cold. Are you up to calling the police? I should stand guard."

"I sure am. I hope they throw the book at him! How dare he? How *dare* he come at my little girl?"

Anna's sobs broke her husband's heart. All he could do was hold her until she regained control.

Ally came out of her room, rubbing sleepy eyes, and dragging the doll. She spied the man on the floor. He was lying face up, and was still out cold. "Why is Kevin sleeping in the hall?" she asked with a yawn.

"Kevin? You know this creep, honey?" Tony was aghast.

"Sure, that's Mama's boyfriend. He used to come to the house to visit her. She left him with me a few times. We played games. He was nice," she said.

"Ally, this man was about to go into your room in the middle of the night. He is not a nice man." Anna wasn't crying any more.

Turning to her husband, she said. "I'll go do what you told me to do." Then to Ally, "I love you, sweetie—so much."

After she had gone to call the police, Tony knelt down and held his arms out to the sleepy child. She went to him, but didn't take her eyes off the man on the floor.

"Honey," Tony said, "Mrs. Anna has gone to call the police. What Kevin has done is a crime. He will have to go on trial for attempted kidnapping. Do you have any idea what he was up to?"

"Probably doing what Mama told him to do. He always did what she said. I think he is kinda scared of her. Shouldn't you help him wake up? He doesn't look too good."

"I think we'll leave him like that until the police get here, sweetheart. It shouldn't take too long." He turned toward Anna as she came back into the hall. "Is everything all right?" he asked her. "Are they on their way?"

"There was a patrol car in the area. They should be here any moment. There, I hear the sirens. I'll go let them in."

Soon the hallway was filled with officers. They awakened the prostrate man, sat him up, and leaned him against the wall. They then began questioning him. Tony knew that all of them probably had small children, and he could see that they were feeling almost as angry as they would have if this guy had attempted to kidnap someone they loved. They stood him up, preparing to take him off to jail. He moaned as they took his arm.

"Don't hurt Kevin, mister!" Ally pleaded. "He was just doing what Mama told him to do. Please don't hurt him." There were tears in Ally's eyes, and she was biting her lips.

Tony suddenly realized that until Bo had entered her life, Kevin was the only person who had ever treated her with kindness. He knelt down and put his arms around the child and held her close, then looked up at the officers. "Perhaps you should check his arm. He could have injured it in the fall. For Ally's sake," he added.

An officer nodded, and sat the man down in a chair. Sure enough, his arm was swelling and Kevin flinched when the officer touched it.

He looked at Ally and shook his head. "Thanks, little one. I'm sorry I listened to Georgia. You know I would never hurt you, though. You do know that, don't you?"

"It would hurt me if you took me away again, Kevin. I love it here. Why would you do that to me? You said we were friends."

"I'm sorry. All I can do is ask you to forgive me. Will you do that?"

"You mean like God forgave me when I believed in Jesus as my savior?"

"I don't know much about Jesus, but yeah, I guess kinda like that."

"No one ever told you that Jesus died for your sins, so that you could go to heaven when you die?" Ally's eyes opened wide with fear for her friend.

"Aw, I don't go in for that old religious stuff..."

"But..." Ally hung her head, biting her lips. She didn't move.

The man did not reply. The officers got him to his feet and led him toward the door. He was staring straight ahead. As he started through the door, he turned to Tony. "I'm glad you stopped me. I couldn't have lived with myself if I had caused that kid any more pain."

Tony simply nodded and stood there, quietly watching the men pass through the door and into the night. Would problems never end for them? Even as he had that thought the memories of a few hours ago came to mind, and he felt repentant. How could he question God? There stood Ally, perfectly fine, and his wife was uninjured. They were all three together. God was watching over them. "Forgive me, Father," he whispered.

He turned to his wife. "Let's have an ice cream party before we go back to bed. How about it, Mrs. Anna?" he asked.

The three enjoyed their ice cream and soon thereafter, two grateful people stood over a sleeping child, having a moment of prayer together, thanking God for keeping her safe.

Back in their bed, Anna spoke softly. "What would I have done if we had lost her? Tony, I do want to try to adopt her—if it's okay with Mother. I love that child. I don't want to ever give her up."

"Are you sure, honey? It's what I want, but I want you to be happy. Do you have any doubts?'"

"No, I don't have any doubts. I want that precious little girl!"

Tony looked at his wife and shook his head, hardly believing what was happening. How could he have ever resisted going to church, and becoming one of God's children? God was actually answering his prayer.

"Then we'll talk with Mom when she gets a little stronger, honey," he said. "Maybe she'll like the idea of being her grandmother, and not having the responsibility of mothering a young child at her age. If she agrees, I'll go to see Jeff, and get things started. The court will surely rule that Georgia is an unfit mother, and since it seems that there are no other relatives…Anna, why are you laughing?"

"It's just hard to think of mother as 'someone her age,'" she giggled.

"Yes, well…" He looked at her, and gave up. They laughed together until they fell asleep in each other's arms. Their lives were changing. They would never again be quite the same.

Chapter Thirteen

The next days passed quickly, and each day brought improvement in Evelyn's health. She was weary of the hospital, and was longing to go home. The news of Ally's near abduction had really frightened her, and she was feeling protective—wanting to be able to be near her. She also wanted to spend more time with Jeffrey. Surely this would soon be over, and she could start her new life with him. Jeffrey also waited for the time when they could be together in a normal environment. He was just so thankful to God that she had survived the accident and the surgery, though, that he was able to be more patient.

Arriving at the hospital on Saturday afternoon, he pulled into a parking space and got out quickly. He was very much anticipating a few moments alone with the woman he loved. There was a spring in his step as he went through the doors and into the hospital. Today, they would be making some early plans for their wedding.

He found Evelyn sitting up in bed, waiting for him. There was color in her cheeks. Her health had been improving every day, and on this day she looked especially well. They smiled at each other and he kissed her and sat down in the chair beside the bed. "You look wonderful!" he said. "You seem to be getting stronger every day. Soon, this will all be just a distant memory. I know time must seem to drag while you're in here, though."

"It does. I guess it's mostly because I had just come home, and was anxious to get my life back when everything came to a stop. I want to start living again."

"You know, though, if the appendix had burst while you were on that bus, or especially while you were walking to get here...I don't even like to think about it. I'm just so thankful that God was watching over you—keeping you safe for me."

"I know I have a lot to be thankful for. Even when I fainted on the street the day I first came into town, God sent one of his ministers to help me. He has been so good to me."

"And to me! What would I have done if something had happened to you? "

He took her hand, and they sat still for a moment, just happy to be together.

"Well, now," he said at last, "how about those wedding plans? I'm afraid I won't be of much help. I've never been married before, you know. You'll have to tell me everything you want me to do."

"Well, you and I will need to make some decisions about the songs and maybe the colors and such. We could just hire a lot of the work done, but I imagine that my daughter will want a part in this. It could be that Ally will want to get involved as well," she said. They laughed together about that. Ally liked to be in the middle of everything!

"Your mother and sister might want to help, as well. After all, it is your first wedding, and you are their only son and brother. Is your mother still well?"

"She's in great shape. She's sixty-nine, but she still lives alone. She pretty much does all of the things that she has always done. You're right. She will love getting involved. Maybe a big wedding is a good idea. I had thought that it would be nice to just sneak away somewhere for a quiet ceremony. This will be great, though, with all of the people we love surrounding us and having a part in the plans."

"Shall we have our own pastor preside?"

"Yes, of course; and maybe Lynn could sing. She has such a beautiful voice."

158

"That sounds like a wonderful idea. Also, I over-heard someone at church mention that Susan, the pastor's wife, does decorating. Perhaps we could pay her to do that."

"Sounds good. And my sister, Alexandra, plays the harp really beautifully. Would you like harp music?"

"Oh, that would be perfect! Yes, do ask her. What do you think about pink roses for the flowers? I love the pale pink and dark green in these flowers you sent me," she said, looking at the arrangement beside her. "I want this vase somewhere in the decorations too," she continued, "perhaps sitting on the organ." They looked at the vase together—a white one, with a single perfect pink rose lying on a piano keyboard. He nodded. "I can see that it would look good there. Do you want pink roses for all of the flowers?"

"I think so. These are just so pretty!"

He smiled, and took her hand again. They were quiet for a while; then he stood up. "Well," he said, "there never is enough time, is there? We mustn't be impatient, though. God has been so good. By the way, have they given you any idea of when you will be discharged?"

"It looks like it won't be until the middle of next week—probably on Thursday. That seems like a long way off right now," she said, not too happily.

"It can't come too soon for me, but I guess we can manage a few more days. You should probably go to Anna's for a while, don't you think?"

"I will. She has already told me, in no uncertain terms, that that is what I'll do. Tony said so, too. He's such a dear. Ally, of course, will agree. She wants us to all live together."

"She's very special. I've been thinking that it's about time to..."

"Who's very special, Mr. Jeffrey?" a voice from the doorway.

"Why, a certain pretty little girl, my dear," he answered.

159

Ally had her arms around her Grandma Bo before Jeffrey could move out of her way. He chuckled and made room for her.

"Grandma Bo, are you going to Mrs. Anna's house? Mews would like that. He misses you." She slid onto the left side of the bed, beside Evelyn.

"Yes, I am. Anna won't take no for an answer. Besides, it will be nice for us all to be together for a few days. I really miss you, Miss Ally."

Ally smiled, and hugged her "tight."

Evelyn squeezed back, a bit gingerly because of her surgery, and got a great big kiss in return.

"Hey, what about me? I'm going to be part of this too, you know. Don't I get a hug?" Jeffrey feigned a sad look. Ally laughed and got up to give him a big hug and a kiss.

"I love you too, Mr. J," she said.

Jeffrey gave the little girl a fond smile and nodded his head. "It's good to see you so happy, little one. You were pretty sad when I first met you."

"Then I found out about Jesus. He really makes me happy! I love going to church. Do you like to go to church?"

"I sure do! I didn't know what I was missing, not going for so many years. I was sixteen when I trusted Jesus. That was a long time ago."

"Why didn't you tell Grandma Bo about him back then? Didn't you like her?"

"Why, I've never thought about that before. I certainly should have told her—and John too. That's the reason God leaves us here on the earth—to tell others about Jesus. I'm so sorry, my darling," he said to Evelyn. "What a terrible thought. If you hadn't survived that crash…"

"Did your husband know Jesus, Grandma Bo?"

Jeffrey looked at Evelyn. She was smiling.

"He heard about Jesus at work, honey. He tried to tell me, but I wouldn't listen. Then, he was killed in the auto accident. I was very angry with God for letting him die, so I closed my mind to all thoughts of God."

"But—how could you be mad at God, if you didn't even believe in him? That's silly."

"Why, I guess it is! Here I was, not believing in him and his son, yet blaming him for taking my husband. You're quite right. That *is* silly. Anyway, I certainly believe in him now, and my husband is in heaven with him, so you need not worry about that."

"Whew! I'm glad. I would hate to think he was in that other place where the fire is, like Brother Glenn talked about." She eased herself back onto the bed and snuggled up close.

"Me too, sweetheart," Bo said softly, and kissed her on the top of her head.

"Is she talking your leg off, Mom?" Tony asked as he stepped into the room.

Evelyn smiled, and hugged her Ally a little tighter. "She's just been sharing a bit of her heart with us," she answered, and went on to explain.

"A little child shall lead them," Anna said, as she stooped to give her mother a kiss. "That's in the Bible. Phyllis, my neighbor, has been reading the Bible with me. We read that just yesterday."

Evelyn closed her eyes and smiled to herself. *What a wonderful change has come over my daughter*, she thought. *She's not sad or angry any more. Her new life is so full with her family, friends, and church that she seems to always be smiling. I'm smiling too*, she told herself with a chuckle, *for all of the same reasons.*

"Phyllis is quite a good friend to you, isn't she, dear?" she asked her daughter.

"Oh, yes! I just wish I had had sense enough to open up to her years ago. She could have helped make everything bearable. I

161

dearly love her. I just feel so bad for her. Her husband is working in South Korea, and she is really missing him."

"And you, dear mother-in-law are going home very soon, I hear," Tony interrupted—stepping up to the bed and putting his arm around his wife. "I have to admit that I'm anxious to have you around the house. I've heard a lot of stories about you. I can't wait to find out if they're all true."

"And who has been telling these stories?"

"I'll never say," he teased in return. "I sure am glad you have come back to us, though."

"Me too, dear. I'm so glad Anna has had you to love her through all of these difficult years."

"He's been my whole life," Anna said. "He's going to have to share that role now, though."

Her husband smiled at her. "Under the circumstances, I gladly relinquish a bit of my time to these people," he said, his hand sweeping the room to include them all.

"Thanks for including me in that," Jeff said. "I want to be in on everything. I feel like I have just inherited a whole new family."

"Indeed you have, darling. You are one of us. We couldn't do without you." Evelyn was beaming. They were all getting excited about life after the hospital. The patient was feeling well, and it was hard for her to stay down. She put on her robe and very slowly walked through the hospital corridors with the others, remarking how good it felt to be out of that room.

As they started back to the room Tony touched Jeffrey on the arm, and they walked a short distance behind the ladies. The lawyer in Jeff knew that there was some special need. "What is it, Tony? Is there a problem?"

"No, it's just that Anna and I need to talk with Mom about adopting Ally. Could you get Ally to do something with you for a few minutes?"

Jeff nodded his head, and said that he would do that. He had no trouble persuading her to agree to a trip downstairs for an ice cream sandwich. They left the others at the door to Evelyn's room and moved off down the hallway, chatting like two old friends.

In answer to her mother's questioning look, as she settled back into her bed, Anna quickly told her that they had asked for a few minutes alone with her. "We have something important to ask you," she explained.

"It must really be important, dear. You both look so serious. What is it?"

"It's just that we've both fallen in love with Ally. We want to try to adopt her. But, of course, we wouldn't do that if you're planning to adopt her for your own."

Anna held her breath as she waited for a response. Tony was waiting anxiously, too. What would her mother say?

"What a wonderful answer to prayer!" Evelyn was ecstatic. "Oh, dear children, you can't know how happy this makes me. I could just be her real grandmother, and she could be part of a young family. Of course, I give you my blessing. Of course!"

Jeffrey and Ally came through the door just as the conversation was ending. Tony and Anna were both smiling as they prepared to leave with Ally soon afterward. "I can't wait until you finally get to come home, Mother," Anna said.

Her mom smiled and replied, "me either." All three of them hugged her "goodnight", and headed for the door. 'Tell everyone at church "hello" for me tomorrow—and that I thank them for all of the prayers," she said.

Promising to do that, they waved good-bye and left.

As they exited the elevator on the main floor, none of the three noticed the woman sitting in a half-hidden chair in the foyer. As they left the hospital, the woman got up and followed them at a distance. When they reached the parking lot, she kept them in view as she pretended to be headed for her car at the other end of the lot.

Her eyes flashed with anger as she stood by a car and feigned opening the door. "This isn't over yet, Misfit!" she growled. When the young couple drove away with her daughter, she turned and disappeared into nearby trees.

The prospective bridegroom sighed after the last good-byes had been said, and he had Evelyn to himself again. "Just think darling, before long I won't have to say 'good-bye' any more. You'll be my very own."
"That will be wonderful. It seems like far-away dream right now."
"It won't be long, though. Time passes so quickly."
"Yes, but not in here. Everyone has been so nice to me, but I'll be glad to get out of the hospital and start my life."
Jeffrey nodded agreement. "Well, as much as I hate to, I guess I'd better say goodnight for now, and be on my way. I love you, dearest."
"Oh, wait. What do you think of the kids adopting Ally?" she asked.
"More importantly, what do you think, my love?" He was feeling her out, to make sure she was okay with this plan. He had to admit to himself that he had been concerned for Ally. If he and Bo adopted her, they would love her always, but they were fifty years old. He had worried that it might not be good for the child. This new plan sounded great to him, but not if it meant pain for Evelyn.
"I think it's wonderful!" she told him. She was so obviously excited about the idea, that he quickly assured her that it sounded wonderful to him, too. Being a grandpa would be another new experience for him. He would go from being a bachelor, to having a wife, a daughter-in-law, a son-in-law, and a granddaughter—with another grandchild on the way. Wow! He thought. Wow!
They said their good-byes, again, and he turned to leave.
"I love you," she called after him. "Thank you, again, for the beautiful roses."

He turned back around, and smiled at her. "I would like to buy you everything beautiful that you could ever want."

"Just having you is much more than enough. Goodnight, darling."

"Goodnight."

Not long afterward, Miss Grey came in with the evening medications. "Time for meds," she said. Bo took the medicine and chatted with her nurse for a few moments. Soon, she became sleepy. "I'm so sorry," she said. "I can't seem to stay awake."

"It's the medicine," her nurse assured her as she watched her eyes flutter and close as she drifted off to sleep.

What a special lady she is, the nurse thought to herself. *The whole family's such a joy to be around.* Smiling at that thought she quietly moved to the door and started down the hall to the nurses' station.

☙ॐ☙ॐ☙ॐ

Concerns over the possibility of encountering Georgia again receded as the days passed with no sign of her. Thursday, June fifteenth finally arrived, and Tony went to the hospital to check his mother-in-law out and bring her home. Ally spied them coming up the sidewalk from the driveway. "Wait! Wait!" She called. "Mews wants to see Grandma Bo, too." She scrambled from the room and returned with the kitten dangling rather precariously from under one arm. "Now, let her come in. We're all here."

A very happy Evelyn preceded Tony through the door, and reached for the pair. She had to kiss Mews on his head before his mistress would be satisfied that the two had been properly reunited.

"See, Mews, I told you she was coming home. Here she is, just as I said. Grandma Bo, I think he wants you to hold him," she advised, holding the compliant kitten out for her to take.

"Ally, Grandma Bo is just home form the hospital. Let's give her a moment to catch her breath. Mews won't mind waiting awhile," Anna said protectively.

"Are you tired, Grandma Bo? We have your bed all ready. You can take a nap. Mews and me can nap with you so you won't feel lonely."

"I think I'll just sit here and drink in the feeling of being home for a while dear. I will need that nap later."

"Where's Mr. Jeffrey? He's supposed to be here too."

"He has to work, honey. He'll be coming for supper this evening. He's a very busy lawyer, you know. Remember his office and all of the people coming and going? Many people depend on him to help them."

"Like he helped us? Okay. He can come later," she said very seriously.

Anna and Evelyn chuckled at this magnanimous decision, and then settled down on the comfortable couch for a long chat. Ally was soon wedged in between them, with the ever-present Mews on her lap.

"If you ladies don't need help with anything, I'll get on back to work," Tony said. "I'll see you at supper time." Bo and Ally said goodbye, and Anna hopped up to kiss him, and see him to the door. Back in her place on the couch, she resumed their conversation. "There is so much to catch up on. How will we ever get it all said? Oh, Mother, I'm just so glad to know that you are here, and safe, at last. Those twelve years were the longest of my life." There were tears in Anna's eyes. "I wish I could take back…"

Evelyn shushed her daughter and held her close, but she soon began again.

"It's no wonder you didn't want to come home. When I think of you out there with hardly any money—afraid to use what you had here in the bank—I get so scared. So many bad things could have happened to you while you were living like that."

"Baby, please don't think of all of that anymore. Everything is so wonderful now, and we can't change what is past. I was foolish to refuse to come home. I missed your wedding and Megan's birth, and I wasn't here for you during those terrible years of such great loss. You did everything you could to make it right. I was just acting so strangely. Dr. Mike said that the blow to the head that I received when I was thrown from the car was pretty bad. He said that it could have caused me to behave in ways that I wouldn't have usually behaved. By the time my injury began to heal, though, I was far away, and had myself convinced that I had to stay hidden. Normally, *nothing* could have caused me to just walk away and leave you like I did—no matter what you might have said or done. You know that."

"I know, but you would never have left if I hadn't said such horrible things, just when you needed my support the most. I know you are right about our not being able to change the past, but..."

"Anna, darling, God has been so good to us. There is nothing to be gained from mourning over the past. Let's just forgive each other and enjoy our wonderful new life. Okay?"

Quickly changing the subject, she said, "Jeffrey and I have decided to sell both of our homes and buy something that will be ours together. I thought you and I might go over to our old house before it is sold, and just spend some time remembering. I need that, and I thought you might, too. Jeffrey and I will be using some of the furniture and things, but you may have whatever holds special memories for you. I want Ally to have something, also. It will be somewhat bittersweet, going through everything after so long, but I really do want to." Laying her head back against the couch, she sighed.

Anna realized that they had been talking for a long time, and her mother must be very tired. She set about getting everything ready for a quick lunch. After they had eaten she got her settled into the quiet bedroom at the end of the hall. Bo snuggled into the soft comfort of the bed, and quickly drifted off to sleep. Ally and Mews would have to wait for another day to share naptime with her.

"I like having Grandma Bo here, don't you Mrs. Anna?"

"I surely do, sweetheart. She's so special. We love her a lot, don't we? And we're so glad that God answered our prayers and made her well, right?"

"Uh, huh." A sleepy yawn reminded Anna that Ally needed a nap. "How would you like to take a nap with me? Does that sound like a good idea?"

"Oh, boy!" She exulted, scooping Mews up off the floor and heading for the bedroom. "Now that he's trained, can he sleep on the bed with us?" She was begging with such sad eyes that Anna didn't even try to resist. She nodded her head. Off came shoes; a small blanket went onto the bed for Mews, and they all settled in for a refreshing nap.

 howihowihowi

That evening, Phyllis came over with a special dessert for a welcome home surprise. She had seen Evelyn and Jeffrey at church, of course, but there hadn't been much opportunity to really talk with them before the accident. "I hope I'm not intruding," she said wistfully. "I was lonely over there, and also I wanted to get to know you two better."

Jeff and Evelyn both assured her that they had been anxious to get to know her, too. "Anna talks about you all of the time," Evelyn said. "I almost feel like I know you."

"Me too," Jeff assured her. "It's like you're family. Tony says your husband has been working out of the country for a while. South Korea, right?"

"Yes, he's been gone a long time, but he'll be back next month. I can hardly wait!"

"I know you'll be glad to have him home again," Jeff responded. "We'll be looking forward to meeting him."

Anna and Ally had taken Phyllis' gift to the kitchen and now came in with coffee and plates of the nice dessert. Tony and Jeff talked together, and the ladies all chatted while they enjoyed the special treat. Ally ate hers, and then played with Mews on the living room rug while the grown-ups visited. After awhile she curled up with the kitten in her arms, and nodded off.

"Oh, dear," Phyllis said, seeing them asleep. "I didn't realize it was so late. I have to be up early tomorrow. I'd better be on my way. It was so nice getting to know you two better," she said to Evelyn and Jeff. They thanked her for the dessert and Tony walked outside to watch her until she was safely in her house.

"I guess I'd better be on my way, too," Jeffrey said. "I don't want to wear my lady out on her fist day home from the hospital." Bo stood, and they walked to the door together. He kissed her gently. "I'll see you tomorrow," he promised. She smiled, and kissed him once more as he left.

ॐॐॐॐॐ

When Evelyn returned to her suite at the hotel a few days later, it just seemed to be taken for granted that Ally would remain behind at the Benski's. Evelyn began getting back in touch with some of her old friends. As the days passed, she and Jeff came to know Phyllis better, as well. They saw her at church, of course, and when they visited the Benskis she was often there, or out in her yard. They learned to admire the young woman for her faith and strength.

Evelyn was finding special delights every day, as she settled into her new life. It was a great joy to go over to her old house with Anna and Ally. They went through a few things, and then decided to wait until they could all go there together and separate the things they wanted from the things that would be sold.

The day she got her driver's license felt like a holiday to the happy lady. Going to the car dealership afterward to choose her car was wonderful too. Secure in Jeffrey's love, the nightmare of the wreck with John retreated into the past, and she was able to drive her car out of the showroom with much excitement.

169

She also looked up her former hairdresser, which made her feel like she was really home, at last. Life was getting back to normal for Evelyn Johnston.

৯৺৯৺৯৺

Sunday, June twenty-fifth, dawned bright and clear, with no hint of disaster. Jeffrey and Evelyn had plans to take a picnic lunch to the nearby park after church. They drove there, following the service, and found a table near the road. Taking it slow, they made their way over the rough ground to the table. Sitting a short distance away was a group of young people. The older couple was lingering over their lunch when the kids turned on a radio. The music wasn't unpleasant, but it was very loud, which made conversation difficult. Jeff and Evelyn decided to leave. They were just gathering the remains of their lunch when a news bulletin interrupted the music.

"…and the North Korean communist troops have crossed the 38th parallel with tanks and artillery. They are approaching Kaesong…"

"Oh, no! Phyllis!" The two looked at each other in disbelief.

"Let's go," Jeff said, as he scooped up their belongings. Bo reached for the small tablecloth. "Go on ahead and turn the car radio on," she said. "I'll be a little slow."

He nodded, and rushed to the car. Soon, they were driving out of the park.

"Oh, Jeff, I hope we get there before she hears this. It would be harder for her if she hears it over the radio. It has me in shock, and I don't have a husband there. I think Tom has been staying at a hotel in Seoul. That's pretty close to North Korea, isn't it? Oh, my! This is a major trial for someone so young. She's going to have to be really strong."

Jeff's face was grim. He had turned eighteen in 1918, and had been drafted near the end of World War I. He knew personally of the horrors of war. Unless Tom had somehow gotten word in time and had escaped, he would be caught up in all of this. Jeffrey didn't

170

want to think about what might be facing Phyllis' husband during the next months—maybe years—as an American civilian in a foreign war zone.

Turning into Anna's driveway, they spied Phyllis sitting in a lawn chair, reading. She waved happily as they got out of the car.

"Oh, dear, how can we tell her this? Look how happy she is. We have to get Anna before we go over there," Evelyn said.

"She's going to need strength from all of us, for sure, honey. Oh, here comes Anna now. Judging by the look on her face, she has heard the news."

The three exchanged solemn greetings, and headed next door.

"What are you three up to this lovely Sunday afternoon?" Phyllis asked as the trio approached. When she saw their faces, her own expression changed. "Oh, dear, something is wrong. What has happened? Is it Ally? She's been so happy. No, I can see that it isn't Ally. Then who…"

Their faces were full of sympathy, and before they could answer, she knew. "Not Tom," she said at last. "No, he's coming home, you know. In July. He…"

"Phyllis, North Korea has attacked South Korea. They are about to invade Kaesong." Jeff's face was grim, in spite of himself. *The months of waiting have taken their toll on this young wife,* he thought. *To have her excitement over her husband's soon return changed to disappointment would be bad, but what if he were never coming home?*

They had been walking toward the house, and were going up the steps, when Phyllis stumbled. A sob escaped her lips, and she began weeping.

"Dear, we don't have any news of Tom. He may have gotten out safely," Evelyn comforted her. The calm voice had its effect, and she allowed them to help her up the steps and into the living room. Evelyn and Anna sat with her on the couch, and Jeff took a chair facing them. After he had told her everything they had heard on the news, they turned on her radio in hopes of the possibility of good news. The reporter was giving details of the assault. He told of the fighting, and the world response to it. The reports on the advance of the enemy as they moved south were not good.

Jeffrey saw that Phyllis was struggling to keep control. What might be happening to her Tom right this very moment? Where was he?

"Oh, dear Father," Phyllis prayed aloud, "please guard him from danger." The other three remained quiet, as she sat biting her bottom lip, struggling to control her emotions.

"Would you get the encyclopedia, Anna," she asked at last. "I really need to see a map. I'm not sure where Seoul is, in relation to North Korea and Kaesong. Maybe Tom has time to get out of there before they get that far."

Evelyn had gone to the kitchen to make iced tea. She brought it in, passed it around, and sat down. No one spoke as they listened to the frightening news on the radio. It was hard to believe that there was already another war, just five years after the end of World War II.

Sighing, Phyllis picked up the encyclopedia from the coffee table where Anna had laid it. When she found the map of South Korea, and saw how close Seoul was to the fighting, she put her hand to her mouth. She was trying to keep from crying, but it was no use. She broke down in tears again, and wept for long moments. Then she began shaking her head. She looked up at them and said, "I'm so sorry. This isn't like me. It's just such a shock. He's supposed to be home any day."

The tears came again, and Anna held her until she was back in control. Jeff began quietly praying out loud, asking God to give her peace, and to protect Tom. The moment passed, and a gentle calm settled over the little group.

"I know that God is in control," Phyllis said at last. "He'll take care of my Tom. It doesn't matter that I am helpless to do anything—

our Father is there with him. How could I possibly wish for any greater protection for him?"

"I'll see if I can contact Tom's boss," Jeff promised. "He may have had some news."

This comforted the young wife, and she accepted Anna's invitation to spend the night at her house. Jeff and Evelyn left, then, promising to remember Tom in prayer. The two ladies gathered a few things to take over to Anna's house, and they soon left as well.

The news finally settled down, somewhat. Life resumed a more normal pace. Phyllis had gone back to her own home after a couple of days. Jeff had found it to be impossible to get any news of Tom, and even though this had been hard on Phyllis she remained strong. The pastor and the church friends constantly encouraged her, and so she waited.

Evelyn and Jeffrey were together for at least a short time each day, and they attended church services together. Her church had quickly become Evelyn's strength, and she reveled in learning more about her savior. She never ceased to be amazed that God could love her so much that he would actually send his only begotten son to die in her place. She wanted to tell everyone she saw that he had died for them, as well, and she took every opportunity to do just that.

Ally's birthday party had been delayed, so that Evelyn would be able to attend. The little girl waited patiently, but grew more excited every day. She and the Benskis settled into a "family" routine, and were enjoying the summer together. Tony did not forget the very real danger which Georgia, Ally's mother, presented his family, however. He had cautioned Anna to be watchful, but not frightened. This woman was not normal. There was no way to know what she might try next. It was easy to forget the danger, when day followed day without incident, so they developed a plan to remind each other to remember. Each night, as they told each other good-night, they also simply said, "remember." Each morning, as he left for work, they again said, simply, "remember." The summer continued with no sign of Georgia, but they did not forget to be careful.

Chapter Fourteen

The birthday party was like nothing else in Ally's young memory. Needing to delay the party so that "Grandma Bo" could be there, they had finally settled on Saturday, July 8th.

Ally got her wish for children to celebrate with her. They all gathered at the church parking lot to take the small church bus to the zoo. Some were shy, but Ally was so glad to have each one of them, that she quickly made friends with all. By the time the bus arrived at the zoo, everyone was excited, and the fun had already begun.

Anna, Tony, and two couples from the church were on the bus with the children, but Evelyn and Jeffrey had opted to take Tony and Anna's station wagon. That would permit her to leave quietly, if necessary. Three weeks had passed since her release from the hospital. She was feeling stronger, but had not quite fully recovered.

As the children spilled out of the bus, Ally was beside herself with joy. Being together with other kids was a fulfillment of a dream. That, alone, would have made her birthday happy for her. As they began making the rounds at the zoo, she was so excited, that all of the children had fun just showing her things she had never seen.

"Look, Ally!" one would say. "Did you see that?" another would ask. "Hey, Ally!" someone would yell, and so the day went. By lunchtime, they were all tired, but happy.

Tablecloths were spread out on the picnic tables, and the children feasted on a variety of things which all children love—but probably shouldn't have. The cutting of the cake was the highlight of the party. It was three tiers high, covered with little dime-store ceramic kittens of all sizes and in various positions. When the cake was cut, each piece had a kitten placed alongside, so that all of the children had a memento of the party. On top was a larger kitten—white, like Mews. Eight candles surrounded him, and the birthday girl blew them out with much ceremony.

"I never blew out candles before!" she exulted. The children laughed along with her. The adults shed a few tears through their smiles.

The large kitten was put into a box for Ally to take home, and everyone "dug in" to the cake and homemade ice cream.

After the cake had been consumed, the excited birthday girl opened one gift after another, amid many squeals of delight. She waited until last to open the gifts from her "family." For a little girl who had had virtually nothing, it was a fairytale day. The large box from Grandma Bo proved to contain a dollhouse, complete with furniture. There was also a tiny family, and even a kitten that closely resembled Mews. In a little baby bed upstairs, there was a baby. The miniature furniture was examined piece-by-piece. The little girls were almost as excited as Ally, but the boys began looking for something else to do. They soon resorted to playing chase, as the remaining gifts were opened.

The box from Anna and Tony was small, and when Ally looked inside, she found a gold ring. Several miniature pearl birthstones were set in the shape of a solid heart. She squealed with delight, and immediately put it on her finger.

The last gift was from Jeffrey. Ally carefully un-wrapped the box and pulled back the tissue paper. Inside she found a stuffed kangaroo.

"A Kangy! A Kangy!" She cried. "Oh, thank you Mr. J. I love it." Bo thought she saw unshed tears in her eyes.

She made the rounds of her "family," kissing each one, and saying "thank you." Then she thanked the children and gave each of them one of the small gifts that Grandma Bo had provided for them.

"Let's go to the pony rides!" said someone.

"Yes! The pony rides!" they all agreed, and off they went with Anna and Tony and the other parents who had come along as helpers. Evelyn and Jeffrey began gathering everything and preparing to take it to the station wagon. It had been a long, busy day, and she was feeling the effects of it. They sat in lawn chairs which Jeff had brought, talking and resting awhile. She was relieved when she saw the children returning and beginning to gather around the bus in which they had come.

Tony stood at the back of the bus, making sure all of the stragglers were gathered up. He walked out into the trees a short distance to check on some of the children he had seen playing there earlier. Assuring himself that they had all made their way to the bus, he turned to go back to the group. Some movement a little deeper into the vegetation caught his attention, and he went to check. Everything seemed normal, however, and he was headed back the other way, when a female voice called his name.

Surprised, he spun around to find Georgia standing there sneering at him.

"You aren't gonna get rid of me that easily Anthony dear," she said. "You have my kid, and I'm gonna get her back."

"What are you thinking, Georgia?" he questioned, trying to control his temper. "All of the cops in the city are looking for you. You won't ever get Ally back."

"I have my ways. She's my kid, and you are not going to keep her. I promise you that! And her *name* is *Misfit*!"

Tony stepped forward in an effort to apprehend her, but once more she eluded him and disappeared back into the under-brush.

Visibly shaken, he waited a moment trying to calm down before he went back to the bus.

"I think that's all of the kids," he called out as he approached, hoping he sounded normal.

"They're all here," came the reply, and the bus began moving out of the parking lot.

"See you at church Sunday!" Tony called after them.

With everyone on their way home and the gifts neatly packed into the station wagon, along with the remains of the lunch and the cake, it was time to leave. Ally sat in back, between her Grandma Bo and Jeffrey, and chattered all the way home. She had experienced so many new things that, of course, she had to talk about each one.

Anna smiled at Tony, and laid her head on his shoulder. She was just about as happy as Ally. The little girl had been so wonderful with the other children. She had praised each gift, and made each child feel as though he or she had given her something she loved. Anna wondered if Georgia was responsible for this special part of her personality. She couldn't let herself think about any of the terrible things that might have happened to the child during her years with a mad woman. She turned her thoughts away from Georgia, and leaned back in the seat and closed her eyes. Her pregnancy was beginning to wear her down a little. She was in need of a nap and was soon fast asleep.

Tony drove in silence, the stress visible in his face. Bo and Jeff looked at each other, worried, but said nothing.

The next thing Anna knew, Tony was waking her, and Ally was bouncing up and down in anticipation of getting her new toys to her room where she could really enjoy them.

"Hurry, Mommy! I can't wait to play with my stuff!"

Evelyn heard, and was surprised. She looked at Anna, but her daughter was busy and showed no sign that something unusual had happened. There could certainly be no better solution for the problem of Ally's future than this adoption. Anna and Tony would be loving parents, and she would be Ally's real Grandma Bo.

The moment passed, and although no one mentioned Ally's calling Anna "Mommy," Evelyn would definitely not forget it. She could hardly contain her excitement at the thought. She wondered if Jeffrey had made any progress on the adoption process.

"What a great day!" Anna said. Evelyn smiled and agreed. "It's been a great day, indeed, darling."

Anna laughed happily, and then suddenly placed her hand over her stomach. "Oh, my!" She said.

"Honey? What's wrong?" Tony's encounter with Georgia had left him jumpy.

"The baby moved. I just felt the first tiny flutter. Our 'son' is making himself known. Soon Ally will have a playmate."

Tony embraced his wife, shaking his head. What a day of delights and miracles. He would try to forget about Georgia. What could she possible do? She was a fugitive from justice. "Let's go inside," he suggested, and they all headed for the house.

They found a very tired little girl curled up on the couch with her kitten, both of them were fast asleep.

"Happy Birthday, dear one," Anna whispered.

Evelyn reached out for her daughter, and gave her one of Ally's "bear hugs." They spent a long moment just being happy together.

Jeffrey waited until the moment was over, and then said, "I'll be going now. I think my lovely fiancée needs some rest. It's been a memorable day. Thanks so much for including me. Let me help you bring the rest of those things in, Tony." He gave Anna a brief hug, and then turned to Evelyn, and she went into his arms.

"I'm so glad you were here, and the stuffed animal was the perfect idea. She loved it."

"And I love you. I'll see you tomorrow. You must get some rest."

"I will." She lifted her face for his kiss, and then he was gone. She excused herself to her children, and borrowed the guest room for a nap.

Outside, Jeffrey questioned Tony about his mood. "Something happened out there in the woods, didn't it?" he asked.

"She's never gonna let go. She was out there spying on the whole party. I guess I should be glad she didn't grab Ally, but I have to wonder what else she might be up to. Isn't it enough that someone snatched our Megan? Does the same thing have to happen to us again? And Ally—she's so happy with us." He began weeping, trying to control himself, but not finding that easy to do.

Jeff put his hand on his shoulder, and waited. The depth of his agony was hard to watch. The empty years without their daughter combined with this—it was totally devastating.

"Thanks for being here for me," Tony said. "I sure can't talk to Anna about this. I don't want her to get upset because of the baby."

"Of, course. But God sees. He knows what you're going through. And he knows the answer to the problem. Let's talk to Him about it."

The two men prayed together, and the burden lifted. By the time they parted, Tony had determined not to let himself give in to worry. God was in control. How could he not trust Him?

లపలపలపలప

As the summer progressed, the war news became increasingly serious The U.S. had joined the South Koreans in their fight to retain their freedom. Hundreds were already dead. Seoul had fallen to communist control, but Phyllis had not lost the trust she had clung to on that first frightening day. God would take care of her Tom, according to his will.

లపలపలపలప

Anna was enjoying good health. She threw herself into helping her mother prepare for her marriage to Jeffrey. They had all become a real part of the church family and found places of service that used their particular talents. The members of the church were almost as excited about the upcoming wedding as the prospective bride and groom. After each service, the ladies always had to be filled in on the latest developments in the planning. Many of them offered to help.

Evelyn and Jeffrey chose their songs. They then turned that part of the ceremony over to Lynn and the church organist, knowing that the music would be perfect. The harp music was to be a very special part of the ceremony. Jeffrey's sister, Alexandra, would be playing a chosen arrangement just before the exchange of the vows. A verse of "The Love of God" would be played first, followed by parts of two love songs; then the chorus of "The Love of God" would end it.

Susan, the pastor's wife, would be arranging the flowers. She and Evelyn went shopping for all of the things that would be needed to put them together. Susan was a joy to work with. She, Anna, and Evelyn spent many hours in Evelyn's living room at the hotel, planning and laughing together. Ally often brought Mews along and played quietly with him, and the toys Grandma Bo kept around for her.

Jeffrey's mother, Jeannette, spent a lot of time with Evelyn, too. She talked about her son, and rejoiced that she had lived to see him married. She remembered Evelyn from Jeffrey's high school days. John had often dropped by to see his friend, with her on his arm.

The two shopped together for Jeannette's dress, and found a tea length two-piece, of dark pink lace. They had shoes dyed to match. A light pink rose corsage, with dark green leaves would add the finishing touch.

"I don't even feel like I'm sixty-nine," she said happily. "I feel like a young girl. I'm so excited with the new dress and the wedding!" Her face had taken on a special glow, and Evelyn loved seeing her so happy. She missed her own mother so much, that having Jeffrey's mom there to share her thoughts helped a great deal.

Soon, it was time to send the invitations, and several of the ladies volunteered to help address those. Evelyn was enjoying the wonderful friendship of the women who helped. *Every tiny detail is so special, because everything is being done with love*, she thought. Even the young girls helped prepare the rice bags. A great many were needed, so there was plenty for everyone to do.

Susan was so good at organizing details, that everything was moving along beautifully.

There had been no news of Tom, but Phyllis wanted to help too. "I can make the pew bows," she offered. "How would you like pale green candles set among tiny pink roses and dark greenery? I think that the ribbon should be pale green as well."

"Oh, that sounds pretty," Evelyn said smiling. "Roses will be on the podium, and pew bows would make it feel like they were spilling over into the auditorium. Let's do that. It will take some time to make that many, though. Shall we ask a few of the other ladies to help?"

"It would be great if we could get them to do that. The roses could wilt if it takes too long to put everything together," Phyllis responded.

Susan had shown them a picture of a bouquet like the one she wanted to put in the special vase Jeffrey had given Evelyn in the hospital. "It would sit on the organ," she said. "There would be more of the pale pink roses—two dozen of them—nestled among white baby's breath and the dark greenery."

"That's exactly what I wanted. Yes, it's perfect, Susan. Go ahead with that," Evelyn said.

The harp was to be brought from Alexandra's home. It was a golden color, and there would be a single, long-stemmed pink rose in a gold colored bud vase, standing on a small table beside it.

One-by-one, the details were planned. Putting it all together would take the rest of the summer.

❧❧❧❧❧❧❧

One late August morning, Ally, Anna and Evelyn went to the old house to go through things one last time. Jeffrey and Tony had brought everything down from the large bedroom some weeks before, and the five of them had gone through much of it. It had been a bittersweet time for Jeffrey, as much as for the ladies, for he had dearly loved his friend John. In the midst of all of the

182

memories, it was hard for him to think that he was gone. He had made notes of a few things that he would like to have taken to the new home—things that held some special memory of his friend. Now, everything that they hadn't yet sold needed to be disposed of, moved to Anna's, or to the new home.

Arriving at the house on this day, Ally asked, "Can I go play upstairs?" Receiving an affirmative answer, she ran ahead and up the stairs to explore the empty rooms. The two women stood just inside of the open door—arms around each other. The thing that they were about to do meant that they would be putting to rest their happy past, with its sad ending.

"Mommy, Mommy, Help!" Ally suddenly screamed from upstairs. The sound struck terror in the hearts of the two women as they hurried to get to her. The child came flying down the stairs and into Anna's arms before she could even reach the stairs.

"It's her, Mommy! It's her! My mama is out there! She looked at me real mean, and told me to go down there to her. She's out there, Mommy! Don't let her get me!" She held on to Anna with all of her might, and cried as though her heart would break. Anna was too frightened to even move.

Evelyn quickly turned around and closed and locked the door. Her heart was beating fast, as she tried to think of a way to handle this problem. As she moved, she was praying for guidance. Anna looked at her mother, fear in her eyes. This galvanized Evelyn into action, and she said "Anna, get Ally into the bathroom and lock the door. I'm going to confront that woman! Lock this door!"

"No, Mom, don't go out th…" but Evelyn had already shut the door behind her. "Lock it!" she ordered from the other side.

Doing as she was told, the frightened woman locked the front door and ushered Ally into the bathroom. She locked that door as well, and took the trembling child in her arms. "It'll be okay, sweetheart. Don't cry," she consoled her. *I wish I knew that was true*, she thought. *Oh, God, please take care of my Mother. Please help us get out of this situation.*

It seemed like hours had passed when Anna's mother's voice reached her through the closed doors. "Anna, open the door, dear. The police are here. We're safe. They're taking Georgia to jail."

"Don't make me see her, Mommy. Please! She'll get me. I don't want to live with her again. I want to live with you." Ally was hysterical, and clinging so tightly to Anna that it was all she could do to get the bathroom door open and move to open the front door. Evelyn entered with two policemen. Seeing Ally's fear they shut the door and locked it. "It's all right, little one. Your mama's locked in the patrol car. It's okay, really. Don't you remember me from the night Kevin was in your house? I'm going to protect you. Can you believe me?"

Still clinging to Anna, the child sniffled and nodded her head. "Is she out there?" she whispered.

"In the patrol car," he answered. "It's locked. She can't get out. Do you want to see?"

Ally buried her head in Anna's skirt. "No!" she said. "I don't ever want to see her again. I don't want her to get me. I don't want her to get me!" She was sobbing as though her heart would break, and it took all of them to calm her down.

"It looks like we'd better get those cars on out of here," the policeman said at last. "We'll be in contact with you later, Mrs. Benski."

Anna nodded. The stress was obvious in her face. She put her hand protectively over her stomach, and hugged Ally close to herself.

Soon the police cars were gone and the three of them could relax a little. They were all very much shaken by the episode.

"How did you get the police, Mom? I thought we were all alone in this."

"I was praying like I've never prayed before," she replied. "The police car drove by and I stopped it. I told them what was happening. They called for back-up, then got out and started looking for her. She had gone into the shed in back of the house. She put up quite a fight, but there were four policemen. She'll be going back to the facility for the criminally insane."

"Grandma Bo?" Ally had loosened her grip on Anna and was looking with huge eyes at Evelyn.

"What is it, sweetheart?" her Grandma Bo asked, reaching out to her.

She went into the open arms. "Is she really gone?"

"She is really gone. She won't be coming back. She's a very sick woman in her mind. We must pray for her. God loves her, too, you know."

"I don't think so, Grandma Bo. She's mean."

"Well, I think we can give you some time to think about that. You've had a very bad scare today."

"Can we be happy again now, Grandma?"

Evelyn hugged her "granddaughter" tight, and then lifted the little face so that she could see her eyes. "We can be happy again. Right now. Can you give me a smile?' She tickled her a little, and got the beginning of a smile. "It really is okay, honey. God took care of everything, just like he always does."

"Okay, Grandma Bo. I'm happy," Ally said, and smiled a crooked smile to prove it.

It was difficult to get back to their sorting, but after awhile the emotions from the Georgia incident were replaced by the more loving ones that were evoked by the photos.

A picture of the three of them when Anna was a teenager brought tears to their eyes. Evelyn hugged her daughter and quietly reassured her. "No one can ever replace your Dad, sweetheart," she said. "Jeffrey will be my husband, but he won't be replacing Daddy. No one can ever replace another person. My new marriage will just begin a new and different life for me. It's time now, for me to say goodbye to the old one, and put it into a special place in my heart. I don't want you to ever think that I have forgotten John."

"Oh, Mama, I'm so glad that you and Jeffrey have found each other. I think it's so special that he knew and loved Daddy, too. I love him for that. He's just so dear."

Her mother smiled at her and both of them had tears in their eyes again, as they hugged each other.

Anna had taken the old photo albums to her home when she put everything in storage years before, but there were loose photos that needed to be sorted. They were handled with care, because more that anything else in the house, they held the dear past.

Together, Mother and daughter explored their old memories, and set aside those things which would be passed down to future generations. They divided the ceramic figures and wood carvings between them, and a few were set aside for Ally's room.

"Oh, Mom, do you remember this?" Anna held up one of her most special treasures from childhood for inspection. It was a ceramic merry go round. It could be wound with a key, and the miniature horses would turn around, and go up-and-down as the music played a happy tune. "I'll let this reside in Ally's room," she said, "but I'll be 'visiting' it once in awhile." She no longer thought in terms of "if" they could adopt Ally, but "when" they would.

Evelyn found things from her own childhood, which she had long ago wrapped in tissue and placed in strong boxes. Many things would be stored in the attics of their homes; stored, but not forgotten.

"The furniture is all in great condition, honey," Evelyn said to her daughter. "Please choose anything you want of the pieces that are left. We'll just be selling the remaining ones, so feel free to take anything at all. Jeffrey and I have decided that we want to mostly begin fresh, with our own things."

Lunch time came, and Anna volunteered to pick up hamburgers at the local drive in. "Do you want to go with me?" she asked Ally.

Of course she did, so off they went to get the food. After lunch they continued working into the afternoon. Tony and Jeffrey joined them when work was over for the day. With their help, the rest of the sorting went quickly.

"Honey, just leave everything where it is, and Tony and I will pick it up in the morning," Jeff told Evelyn. "I know you must all three be really tired. Right Ally?" he asked, grinning.

She grinned back at him. "Right," she repeated, though she didn't really feel tired at all.

The boxes and furniture for keeping were placed in the living room where the men would pick them up the next morning. The other things were placed in the dining room, and would be sold at auction along with the furniture. A few things were antique, and all were in good condition.

Even Ally was quiet as they drove in silence to a nearby restaurant for dinner. Her bubbly personality soon broke the spell, however, and their talk turned to the expected baby, and the approaching wedding. By the time they left the restaurant, everyone was in a festive mood, and looking forward to the future.

Jeffrey drove Evelyn back to the hotel, and they went into the restaurant for coffee. They both spoke of their love for John, and the blessing he had been to them. Thoughts quickly turned to their coming wedding, however, for they were anxiously waiting for the day that would make them "one."

Anna struggled with her memories during most of the evening. She brought out the photos, and introduced Ally to her father. The child was delighted but felt sad that she had never met him. She was glad that there were pictures, and she could get to know him a little.

"Grandpa Jeffrey is my first grandpa. I knew him first, but I want your daddy to be my Grandpa John. May he? I'll see him in heaven one day, and I'll know who he is, 'cause I've seen his picture."

Anna didn't try to correct the child. She knew that she would know her dad in heaven, but she also knew that he would not look the same as he did on earth. In heaven, all would be perfect...*Oh, Daddy*, she mourned, *I just miss you so much.*

She lay in her husband's arms for a long time that night. The tears simply would not stop. Seeing Ally wanting to know her father had made her think of her precious Megan again. Tony encouraged her to have her cry. "There's something healing about tears," he told her. "They seem to wash away the things that hurt us. Go ahead and cry, darling. Let your heart heal."

Anna had done that, and had finally fallen asleep in the strong arms of the man she loved. Tomorrow, she would be back to normal.

Ally lay awake for awhile, also. She was thinking of Anna's sadness and of how much she missed her daddy. *I don't even have a daddy*, she thought. *I probably won't ever know who he is.* Tears welled up in her eyes. Why did life have to be so sad? Why didn't she have a real family of her own? She remembered Grandma Bo saying that she would find an adoptive family for her—a real mommy and daddy—but nothing had happened. Now, she was afraid that it might. If it did, she would lose Mrs. Anna and Mr. Tony. That would be too terrible! *I won't think about that*, she decided, and fell asleep with Mews snuggled up close for comfort.

Alone in her hotel suite that night, Evelyn chose to put the memories out of her mind. Life with John had been very good, but it was over, and now there was Jeffrey. She would look forward to the future, and be happy. Jeffrey deserved that, and John would have wanted it.

With her mother safely in prison, and the promise from the prison officials that they would be notified immediately if she should ever escape again, Ally felt safe. She spent the remaining summer days playing in a wooden play house Tony had made for her. She had a wonderful time getting to know her new friends at church. She also took plenty of time for Mews. He was growing up so fast that, before she knew it, he was becoming a magnificent adult cat.

ಊಲ‌ಊಲ‌ಊಲ‌ಊಲ

Soon the time came to register Ally for school. She had to go to school to be tested to see what her grade level might be. Never having gone to school, there would likely be many gaps in her education.

"She should be going into the third grade, since she is eight," the principal said to Anna. "She seems to have learned quite a lot from reading so many books, but…well, shall we try her in the third and see how she progresses? If you can work with her at home when we find weak spots, it may turn out to be okay for her to be in that grade."

Leaving the school, Anna took Ally that afternoon to the doctor for her immunizations. There wasn't much doubt that she had never had them. The next day they went shopping and came home with several pretty, new dresses for school. She was thrilled with the whole idea of school, and could hardly wait for the first day.

Classes began at last, and Ally settled in quickly. Soon she was going to school as if she had been doing it all of her life. Mews adored his young mistress, and he waited patiently each day for her to come home. He seemed to know when she was approaching, and was always right there to greet her. She looked for him the first thing through the door, and Anna usually got her hug with a cat between herself and Ally. Baby "John" was also sandwiched in between, and they often laughed when he gave Ally a kick for getting too close.

Working together on her studies each day after school, they soon had her nearly to the level of the other children in her class.

Chapter Fifteen

At last, one perfect early September morning, Evelyn awakened to her wedding day. There was not a single cloud in the indescribably brilliant blue sky. Bright leaves were chasing each other around the yard. The bride-to-be smiled at the scarlet cardinal which had perched in a tree just outside her window.

"What a perfectly glorious day! I couldn't have had a better one for my wedding if I had been able to order it myself," she said aloud.

She called for breakfast to be sent up to her, and then sat down to read the Bible while she waited. Thoughts of John came to her mind unbidden. She realized that they must be dealt with now, so that she could tuck them into that special place in her heart. *I might take them out to treasure them once in a while* she thought, *but my heart will belong to Jeffrey now. I want no ghosts from the past to intrude. John will always be my first beloved, and the father of our daughter, but Jeffrey's is the love that has wiped away the memories of my sad, empty years. I love him so deeply that it almost frightens me.* She paused to thank God that he had given her the love of two incredible men. In a few hours, she would be Jeffrey's wife. Her new life would begin. What joys awaited her? What new treasures would she be storing up in the years to come?

A quiet knock on the door told her that her breakfast had arrived. She received it and tipped the young man who had brought it. Sitting down with her simple meal, she gave thanks for it, and then sat there, deep in thought as she ate. When she had finished, she opened her Bible again, for just a few more moments alone with God. She had been steadily learning more about God's Word during the last months. This morning she found herself drawn back to her study of the book of Ruth. The story had been special to her, because Ruth, too, had lost her husband, and God had given her a wonderful new husband. Her miraculous marriage to Boaz had put her into the linage of Christ. Ruth, a Moabitess, had actually been the great-grandmother of King David. *My! The wonderful things God does for his children,* Evelyn mused.

The wedding ceremony was scheduled for three o'clock that afternoon. It was almost eight a.m. now. People would be coming soon to help her with final details. She smiled at the thought of all of the new friends God had given her. *Four months ago I was a broken down, friendless wanderer,* she thought. *Now, I have an entire church family of friends. I have my own family back. I have Jeffrey. I have Ally. Most of all, I have God. Has anyone ever been so blessed.?*

She lingered awhile over her Bible and her prayer time, not willing to let go of that sweet communion with him. *Oh, Father,* she prayed silently, *please help me to be the kind of wife and mother whom her husband and children will call "blessed." Help me be the kind of friend who will be there for others when needed. More than anything else, help me to be the kind of child who will bring glory to your dear name. Bless this wonderful day when I am to become Jeffrey's wife. Let everything go according to your will. May others be blessed through our happiness and find great joy in their fellowship with you. Dear Father, I love you so much. I hate to end this special time. Please be with me all through this day. Bless the man you have given me. In Jesus' name. Amen.*

The phone rang soon after, and Jeffrey's voice made her heart leap with happiness.

"Darling, I know you are terribly busy, but I just had to hear your voice. How is your day going so far?"

"Wonderfully! I just talked to our heavenly father, and he always makes the day bright. I prayed for you, and for us, especially. It's our day, at last! Can you believe it's finally here? Sometimes I have almost wished I had gone along with your idea of just getting married right away. Now that the day is here, though, I'm so glad we waited. What a glorious day it is—just for us!"

"I know. When I looked outside this morning, I stood there and shook my head in wonder. God has been so good to us. In a few hours, you will be my own. I can hardly believe this is happening. I am so very happy!"

"Me, too. I love you, so much."

"And I love you. I guess I should let you go now, so that you can do the things that brides do on their wedding day. After three o'clock I'll be claiming a lot more of your time for the rest of our lives."

"That sounds good to me, darling. Good-bye for now."

"Good-bye. I can hardly wait."

The smile lingered on Evelyn's face for a long time after she had returned the receiver to its cradle. She straightened the rooms and did last minute packing for her honeymoon. They would be going to Niagara Falls for two weeks, but for tonight, they had reservations in the bridal suite of the hotel. Following the wedding ceremony, a light meal would be served and the cake would be cut. Their family would have a later dinner with them in the hotel dining room before saying their good-byes for two weeks. Tomorrow morning, the newlyweds would be flying to their honeymoon destination. *I wouldn't care where we went,* Evelyn thought. *As long as I'm with him, any place will be wonderful.*

Once the first person knocked on her door, the rest of the morning was a flurry of activity. Flowers were everywhere as the women worked feverishly on the pew bows. As each one was finished, it was placed in a cooler to keep it fresh. When these were finished, the ladies enjoyed the tasty lunch that Evelyn had ordered to be sent up at eleven-thirty. With everything finished at the hotel, Anna said, "Mom, you just stay here and get the bride ready, okay? We'll receive the cake and prepare the punch. We'll make sure that the flowers are perfect, too. Just relax and don't worry about anything except yourself." The rest of the ladies joined in, assuring her that they would take care of everything.

"How can I ever thank all of you for helping me so much? Everything will be so beautiful because of you."

"Tony, Ally and I will be here for you at two o'clock, Mom," Anna assured her. "I can't wait!"

"I can't believe it's finally here," her mother replied. "Okay, everyone, I'll see you there!"

At last it was time to go. Evelyn gathered the remaining things that she needed to take to the church. She would be dressing there, surrounded by those who loved her. When the knock on the door came, her heart gave a glad leap. She opened it to find her family standing there with smiles on their faces.

"Grandma Bo, we came to get you. It's your happy day!" Ally was smiling her happiest smile. "I'm gonna have a grandpa J!" she exulted.

After more hugs all around, the family stood in a circle for a last minute prayer together. The trip to the church was joyful, with Ally talking non-stop.

No one could ever have a happier wedding day than this, Evelyn decided.

At the church, corsages, bouquets and boutonnieres had been delivered and placed. Flowers were everywhere. The entire church auditorium had taken on an atmosphere of joy and expectancy as though it knew that something very special was about to happen there.

Anna was the matron of honor. She had said that she couldn't do it, because of her pregnancy, but her mother had convinced her that she would be beautiful, as indeed she was. Ally was a junior bridesmaid. She would also drop miniature pink roses as she entered just before the bride. The rings were in her basket too, nestled on a small pillow beneath the roses. The pastor's eleven year old son, James, would remove the rings when the time came, and hand them to the best man. Jeffrey had chosen Tony for this honor. The couple had decided not to have more attendants, as it was Evelyn's second marriage. Tony's mother was ushered to her special place. She was radiantly happy to see her beloved son married, at last. She had long prayed that he would find joy, and a family of his own. She had loved being part of the preparations, and had already learned to love Evelyn.

Evelyn dressed carefully in the long, pale pink gown. It was in two pieces—straight and simple—but the fabric was silk. There were seed pearls scattered all over the blouse section, and down the three-quarter length sleeves. The pearls at her neck were a wedding gift from Jeffrey. She wore a tiny headpiece with a bit of veiling, which did not cover her face. Her shoulder-length hair was hanging loose, at Jeffrey's request. She looked every inch a bride, and wore the smile of one as she stood, waiting to follow her daughter and "granddaughter" down the aisle to meet her groom.

Jeffrey stood at the front of the church, watching her come to him. He was handsome in his tuxedo. The small amount of gray at his temples gave him a distinguished look. *I can't believe this is actually happening*, he thought. *I assumed I would be a bachelor all of my life. Boy! I never expected this. Thank you, Father*, he prayed. *Help me be the kind of husband this beautiful lady deserves.*

The pastor, James and Tony were standing at the altar with him. Brother Alexander was beaming.

Tony was not watching Evelyn. He was watching his own beloved. *She's even more beautiful than she was on our wedding day*, he was thinking. *How did I ever come to deserve this kind of happiness?* He glanced at Ally as she stood behind Anna, ready to drop the tiny pink roses. Their dresses were both a dusty rose, with necklines and sleeves alike. Tony's heart was so full he thought it might break.

The chords of the bridal march filled the building. Everyone stood in honor of the bride. Evelyn began the slow walk behind Ally as she dropped the pink roses. She arrived at the front at last, and Jeffrey reached for her hand. The smile that passed between them brought smiles to everyone in the church building—along with a few tears. Anna was among those who were crying tears of happiness.

Ally was all smiles. *Thank you, God, she prayed. Thank you for a good day. Thank you for my Grandma Bo. She looks so happy!*

When Brother Alexander asked the traditional question, "Who giveth this woman to be married to this man?" Anna, Tony and Ally all said in chorus, "WE DO!"

The laughter that this evoked died down as the special music started. Then the auditorium was completely hushed when the vows began. "Do you, Evelyn Dawson Johnston, take this man to be your lawful wedded husband, to have and to hold from this day forward...?"

"Oh, yes I do!" She looked up at the man she loved and they smiled private smiles at each other.

"Do you, Jeffrey Lawrence, take this woman to be your lawful wedded wife, to have and to hold from this day forward...?"

"I surely do!" replied Jeff.

Everybody was smiling at their enthusiasm. His mother was weeping.

When the vows were complete, James removed the rings from the pillow in Ally's basket and handed one to Tony. He gave it to Jeffrey, who placed it on his bride's finger.

"With this ring, I thee wed," he repeated after the pastor, then kissed the hand which now belonged to him.

James handed the other ring to Anna, and Evelyn took it from her daughter. Placing the ring on her beloved's finger, she also repeated, "With this ring, I thee wed."

Brother Alexander then spoke the long anticipated words, "I now pronounce you man and wife. You may kiss your bride."

The kiss was gentle and beautiful, and everyone felt the great love that was shared by the couple.

"Ladies and gentlemen, I present to you Mr. and Mrs. Jeffrey Lawrence!"

The joyful notes of the recessional began. Mr. and Mrs. Lawrence walked down the aisle, followed by Anna on Tony's arm and Ally on James', to form the receiving line at the door. The pastor and Jeffrey's mother stood with them as they accepted many hugs and congratulations.

The guests moved to the fellowship building behind the auditorium. Photos of them were taken, while the bridal party was being photographed in the auditorium. In a short time, the newlyweds joined their guests. They cut a piece out of the beautiful cake, and shared a bite of that first piece as camera bulbs flashed. More photos were taken as they shared a glass of punch, and then they were free to mingle among those who had come to celebrate with them. A buffet of good things to eat became the center of attention for a while, as everyone gathered about it. They all had a good time, laughing and talking together.

Anna had never seen her mother look more beautiful, although there were pictures in an album back home, which showed a similar look on the face of a much younger Evelyn. Anna thought of her father for a moment, knowing that he would be glad that his Bodacious had married such a wonderful man—his own dear friend.

Soon, it was time to depart the celebration. The bride and groom left by the side door, where friends pelted them with rice as they ran to their car. Evelyn threw her bouquet, which was caught by Lynn amid much teasing and laughter. As they drove away to their hotel, they were followed for a short distance by young well-wishers who were honking and waving. At the dinner hour, their families would join them in the hotel dining room. Meanwhile, they would have a couple of hours alone. Tomorrow they would leave for their honeymoon.

Chapter Sixteen

The ringing of the phone stopped Tony in the middle of his breakfast. He went to answer it, and came back with a look on his face that said the something was wrong. Anna's first thought was that something had happened to her mother, but he quickly let her know that it was nothing to do with her family.

"I guess you have to hear this, too, baby," he said to Ally. "I hate to tell you," he agonized.

"It's okay," she said, "I'm almost grown up, you know."

Both adults smiled at that, but it didn't make the telling of his news any easier for Tony. He knelt down in front of Ally and took her hands in his.

"It's your mama, honey. She's escaped again," he told her. "They don't know how she manages it, but sometime during the night she disappeared. They wanted us to know, before it hits the news. I'm so sorry."

A look of terror came over Ally's little face, and she started crying. Tony was frightened by what he saw. He looked up at Anna, wondering how to handle this. They couldn't let this precious child live in constant fear.

"Honey, we have no idea what you went through during the years with your mother," he said at last, "but we do know that you belong to God. You are his child. He loves you so much, and he will keep you safe. We have to trust him for that."

"I hate her!" Ally screamed. "She didn't love me, and she didn't let me be with people. Aren't you mad about that, too? Don't you hate her, too?"

The look of anger was not going away. Tony could understand that, because he was struggling with the same feelings, even though he knew that they were wrong. He knew that neither he nor Anna could let Ally be "eaten up" with hatred. This could change her personality. It could ruin her life. *What am I supposed to do, dear Father?* He prayed. *Please help me.*

He took a deep breath. "Honey, do you remember when you accepted Jesus as your Savior?" he ventured. "Brother Glenn had preached about hell, and you didn't want to go there? Do you remember that you wanted to tell everyone that Jesus had died for them, too, so that they would never have to go to such a terrible place?"

"Yes..." she answered cautiously.

"Do you realize that your mama may never have trusted Jesus to be her Savior?" he asked.

The little head came up. A look of concern was on the troubled face. "I forgot about that. Mama could go to hell, couldn't she?"

"Oh, honey, God doesn't permit us to judge whether other people have believed in Jesus or not. But he does tell us that if we do not choose to accept his wonderful gift of salvation, through his son, that means we are rejecting it.

Ally was staring at Tony. "My mama may not go to Heaven," she said, "and I wasn't even thinking about that. I just hated her. Now God won't love me any more, will he?" She began sobbing.

Anna and Tony looked at each other, relief in their faces. She would be all right now. The tears would heal some of the hurt. One day, she might be able to forgive, even if she could never forget.

"You know that isn't true, baby," Anna comforted her. "God tells us that when we do something wrong, all we have to do is ask him to forgive us. 'If we confess our sins, he is faithful and just to forgive us our sins.' He says that in the Bible. You don't ever have to worry that God will stop loving you. Do you want to ask him to forgive you?"

"Oh, yes! Can I do it now?"

"Let's pray together. I think the two of us may have to ask God to cleanse our hearts, too," she said.

The trio bowed their heads and asked God to forgive them for not having been able to love their enemy. They asked him to help them show his love to others. When they raised their heads there were smiles all around. Their joy was back even though they felt sad and a little afraid, to think of Georgia out there somewhere...

ॐॐॐॐॐ

"There she is! There she is! Grandma Bo, you're home! Look, Mommy, she's home at last." Ally was jumping up and down in her excitement.

"Yes, darling, I see. We're very glad she's home, aren't we? Look, they're waving to us. Just be patient. They'll reach us really soon."

"But, they're just right there. Can't I run to meet them? Oh, I really want to, Mommy."

"Oh, go ahead, you rascal," Anna laughed.

Ally ran across the tarmac as fast as her legs would carry her and was in Grandma Bo's arms in a flash.

"You're home! You're really home, Grandma Bo. I missed you every day."

Anna and Tony reached the couple, and Evelyn turned Ally over to Jeffrey while she hugged her daughter and Tony.

"Mom! Dad! Boy, I missed you both," Anna said, looking at Jeffrey. She turned to give him a hug. "It was really a long two weeks."

Ally turned back to her Grandma Bo and grabbed her around the waist. She wasn't saying anything. Evelyn bent down and kissed the top of her head. "What's wrong, honey?" she asked. Ally just hugged tighter, and didn't answer.

"It's Georgia, Mom." Anna said. "She escaped the prison unit again."

"Oh, no! I'm so sorry. Don't they have any idea where she is?"

"Not yet," her daughter answered. "It's pretty hard on Ally—well, on all of us."

"I know how you feel. I don't feel too happy about that myself."

Tears came into Ally's eyes, and Bo could see that there was something more that she wanted to tell her. "What is it, honey? Tell Grandma Bo what's bothering you."

"We don't know if Mama will go to heaven, and I said I hated her. I should be worried about her, but I'm just so scared..." The tears began again.

"I'm sorry, Mom," Anna whispered. "Your honeymoon..."

Evelyn put her finger to her lips for silence. She stooped down and hugged her little Miss Ally. She understood, all too well, what the child was feeling. Memories of the dreary house; the lack of care; the isolation...all of it imposed on a small child for years...why would she feel anything but fear? Yet, God's word requires love.

"You know, I think it's okay for you to feel confused for a while. You had a bad experience, and it lasted for almost all of your young life. It will probably take some time for you to sort it all out. Grandma Bo knows that you hope your mama will go to heaven. Don't you think that God knows that too? And we don't really know, do we? She may have trusted in Jesus when she was young. She's a very sick lady, in her poor mind. Maybe she wasn't always like that. What do you think?"

"I love you, Grandma Bo."

"I love you, Ally. Now, shall we go home? I may just have a present or two for a certain pretty girl."

"Oh, boy! What is it? Can I have it now?"

"Wait until we get home. That way, you can be excited about it all the way home."

"You're teasing me, aren't you Grandma Bo?"

"Maybe just a little. Let's get our luggage and go home."

Ally had come to love visiting her Grandma Bo in the hotel, but the house that she and Jeffrey bought was full of new adventures.

202

She had gone with Anna to quickly move the few boxes and other things from the hotel to the house after the wedding, and then they had gone back to the house yesterday to make sure all of the last-minute details were ready for the newlyweds' homecoming. She'd explored the rooms again, and found all of her favorite places, and then she went outside in the back for the first time.

The yard was very large, and full of trees and special plants. Autumn flowers were in bloom, and bright leaves were beginning to fall. These now painted the ground with their colors. Each leaf was a special treasure, and Ally skipped along, gathering one of each color.

Wooden chairs and a two-seater wooden swing blended into the earthy background. From one of the larger trees, hanging by strong ropes, Ally found an old fashioned swing. Painted on the wooden seat was the name, "Ally." The little girl slowly sat down on the swing and began crying.

Thank you, God, she prayed. *Thank you that I have a pretty name now. I have a "family." Thank you for my Grandma Bo, 'cause she understands what little girls need. Thank you for my very own swing, with my very own name on it. I know everything's gonna be okay now. They love me. I know they love me, 'cause they made me a swing, just for me. It's almost like I really belong. Everything's gonna be okay,* she wept. *I love you, God. Amen*

Coming to the house now, Ally felt the thrill of "family." Luggage was unloaded, and the delicious lunch, which she and Anna had brought to the house, was enjoyed. Everyone laughed and talked together, just enjoying each other's company. The "grandparents" told of their special honeymoon adventures.

"I had always heard that the Falls were incredible. They truly are absolutely breath taking!" Bo said.

"And there's so much power in them," Jeff added. "The amount of electricity they produce is absolutely astronomical!"

"And they're very romantic in the moonlight!" Evelyn added, smiling.

"It sounds like you had the perfect honeymoon. I'm so glad," Anna said.

"But it's very good to be home. Thank you for all of your hard work. The house and yard both look beautiful. I worry that you have overdone."

"Oh, no, Mother. It was fun, wasn't it, Ally?"

"Yes, I love this house, Grandma Bo and Grandpa J."

"We do too, dear. We will have many happy hours together, here. You may also bring Mews anytime you wish."

"Oh, he'll love that, Grandma Bo. He misses you."

"Well, now, how about those presents I promised?"

"I thought you forgot, Grandma."

"I did get a little carried away with my honeymoon stories, didn't I? Sorry about that."

The gifts came out of the suitcases, and were properly appreciated by their three recipients. Evelyn was somewhat distracted, still thinking about Ally's having called Anna "Mommy" again. Anna had acted as if it were normal. Evelyn knew that Jeffrey had spoken with Anna and Tony about the adoption, but had anyone ever said anything to Ally? *Oh, my*, she thought. *She must think I have broken my promise to her. This has to be remedied.*

The Benskis stayed for another hour, and then the said their "good-byes," and went home.

"Alone at last," Jeffrey teased after they had gone. "I've missed you."

"I've missed you too. But it was really good to see our family again. I guess we're just not ready for the honeymoon to end. Oh, Jeff, our house is so very beautiful, and I love being home with you."

They put the things from their travels away and spent the evening just enjoying being in their new home together.

Chapter Seventeen

The doorbell was insistent and it finally awakened Tony and Anna from their deep sleep. Sunlight was pouring in at the window, and they could hear muted sounds coming from the living room. They had slept late this Saturday morning. The bell rang again, and Ally knocked quietly on their bedroom door.

"Come in, dear," Anna called, and Ally opened the door a few inches.

"Daddy, someone's at the front door. Do you want me to answer it?"

"Okay, honey. I'll be there just as soon as I can get dressed. Go ahead, but leave the chain on."

Ally moved to the door and opened it, leaving the chain fastened. "Who is it?" she asked.

"It's me, Kevin. I need to talk to you. Will you ask Mr. Benski if I can come in? I need to talk to him, too."

"Okay, Kevin. He's coming. Wait a minute."

Tony stumbled into the living room in house shoes, still tucking his shirttail in. "Who is it, baby?" he asked.

"It's Kevin. He wants to talk to you."

"Kevin? The guy who broke into our house? The one who was going to kidnap you? He wants to come in by the front door this time?"

"He's okay, Daddy. Let him in. You're here to protect me."

"You go on into the bedroom with Mommy. Then I'll let him in."

Ally looked at him with sad eyes, but he didn't back down. "Do it, Ally."

She did as she was told, and Tony unchained the door.

"Kevin? This is a bit unusual. Aren't you out on bond, after trying to kidnap Ally?" Tony wasn't feeling too friendly. The last time he had seen this person, he had just broken into his home.

"Sir, I can't sleep. I can't even eat. All I can think about is what Ally said about heaven. You people know something I don't know. I want to know about it, sir. I'm almost thirty years old. I may be going to the penitentiary. People get killed there. I want to know that if I get killed, I'll go to heaven, too. Ally said there was something I could do..."

"Kevin, forgive me. You threatened Ally's safety. I'm having a hard time overcoming that, but your eternity is at stake here. Come on in. If I can't answer all of your questions, I know someone who can."

Anna appeared at the entrance to the living room, looking anxious. Tony spoke quietly to her. "It's okay, honey. I wonder if you could bring my Bible, and then fix us some coffee. This guy wants to know about Jesus."

Anna's face brightened. She nodded her head, and walked down the hall toward the study to get the Bible. After she had given it to Tony, she and Ally went to the kitchen to prepare a late breakfast.

"Mommy, could we pray for Kevin before we start breakfast? I would feel a lot better."

"Of course we can. I should have thought of it, myself. You understand that we cannot pray that God will save him, don't you? God has already done his part. It's up to Kevin now, and he has a free will to make his own choice. Our part is to just tell him what God has done for him, and then ask God to help him understand. Do you want to start, or should I?"

"You start, and I'll finish, okay?"

"That's fine."

The two knelt in front of kitchen chairs. Anna asked God to give Tony the words to say, and to open Kevin's heart to the truth—to help him understand what Jesus had done for him. She asked God to help her stop being angry with Kevin if he sincerely wanted to know about Jesus. When she said "amen," Ally began to pour out her childish heart to him.

"Dear Father, God, I love you, God. I love Jesus. I'm glad you let him come down here, even though you knew people would be really mean to him and kill him. I feel so bad that people hurt him. I feel bad that he had to let them, just because I sinned and he wanted me to live in heaven. Dear God, Kevin doesn't know about Jesus. He wants to go to heaven, too. I don't want him to go to hell, God. Please help him. In Jesus' name, amen."

Anna hugged the child. She felt humbled by the fact that Ally could feel such love for a man who had been a part of her sad years. At the same time, she felt that they probably owed Kevin a debt of gratitude. He was likely the only one who brought any sunshine into Ally's life during that time. She sincerely prayed that he would understand, and accept Christ as his Lord and Savior.

"Let's get this breakfast started," she said, and Ally smiled. They began working, but their prayers kept ascending from anxious hearts as they worked.

They were just about to ask if the men wanted to come for breakfast, when they heard Kevin shout, "I see it! I see it! It's so easy. I was looking for something hard that I had to do. I don't have to do anything at all, do I? Just accept what he did, right?"

"That's all there is to it, Kevin," Tony replied. Just recognize that you are a sinner by nature; that you can do absolutely nothing to save yourself from suffering the penalty of your sin; and that you need a savior. Accept Jesus as that savior, and you are on your way to heaven!"

"I did! I just did that! I can't believe the relief I'm feeling. Thank God for Ally. If she hadn't said what she did that night…"

"She loves you a lot. She really wanted you to go to heaven with her. She'll be very happy when you tell her. Let's do that now."

207

But Ally had heard everything. She met them halfway and threw her arms around Kevin's waist.

"You did it! You trusted Jesus, too. Don't you feel wonderful? Oh, I'm so glad." There were tears in her eyes and a smile on her lips. She was jumping up and down.

"I'm so glad for you, Kevin. I know from personal experience just how wonderful it feels to have your sins washed away. Thank God. The angels are rejoicing right now." Anna was beaming.

"The angels know about me? But, I'm nobody..." Kevin was incredulous.

"That's right," Tony said. "Pastor showed us in the Bible that the angels rejoice when someone comes to know Jesus as savior. That includes you. You are a child of God—the creator of all things. That makes you very special."

"Wow!" Kevin said, shaking his head. "Wow! I feel like jumping up and down too."

"I know. The three of us have only been saved about four months. We could hardly believe it either. Remember, Anna?"

"I'll never forget. Every day I thank God for loving me so much. Kevin, your life has just begun," she told him.

"Can we eat now, Mommy? My stomach is so happy, it's hungry."

"You silly. Everything is ready, Tony, if you're ready to eat now."

He smiled and nodded his head, and the "ladies" began putting things on the table.

"Kevin, you sit there, to the right of Tony. Ally, would you get that sugar bowl, please dear?"

Breakfast that morning would be talked about for a long time, for they spent the time talking about God and the Bible and how wonderful it is to know, without any doubt at all, that your eternity is settled forever—no matter what might happen to you on the earth. They read the last two chapters of Revelation, about the beautiful city that God has prepared for those who love him. They talked of a street made of gold that is so pure that you can see through it. They read about the throne of God; the beautiful green rainbow that surrounds it; the river of life; and the tree of life. The scripture told of the twelve beautiful gigantic gates of single pearls, and the huge walls with twelve foundations of precious stones. They all got so excited talking about it that they forgot the time and spent most of the day together around God's Word.

They finally realized that it was getting late, and there was work to be done. Before he left though, Kevin said that he wanted to be baptized right away. "If I'm sent to the penitentiary," he said, "I really want to join the church first. Mr. Benski, would you call the pastor and ask him for me? I want to be baptized to let people know that I belong to Jesus."

"Sure, Kevin. I'll do that right now," was the response. He walked to the phone in the hall, and dialed the number. Kevin could hear him talking, and waited anxiously for an answer. Moments later Tony was back. He was smiling and nodding his head. "Pastor said 'sure, that's exactly what he ought to do if he has accepted Christ as his Lord. Tell him to come. Definitely.'"

"Thank you so much. I'll certainly be there. I guess I'd better go and let you get on with your day."

"Would you tell me something before you leave?" Tony asked. "It's about Georgia. Have you heard from her?"

"She's back in the criminally insane unit of the prison. She's bad news," Kevin answered.

"She's escaped again. We really need to find her. As long as she is out there, Ally isn't safe. Could you try to find out where she is and let us know?" Tony's face showed his concern.

"I'd do anything for that kid. Sure. I'll try to help you get her back into the facility—for her own safety, too. She isn't competent to be running free. She's going to get herself hurt, if not worse. It's caused by the drugs. She wasn't always like this."

"I know. Anna and I knew her in college. Right now, though, I guess I'm more worried about Ally. I'd feel a lot better if Georgia were safely behind bars again."

"Count on me, sir. After what you've just done for me I owe you. I'll let you know the next time I hear from her."

Tony nodded his head and thanked him as he walked him to the door.

Kevin left, rejoicing, and planning to be baptized the next morning after the Sunday service.

The Benskis invited Kevin for Sunday dinner after church. That morning, he had told the congregation that he could be going to the state penitentiary, and that he was devastated by what he had done. The people had accepted him into the church with a great deal of love and compassion, and then he was baptized. Everyone knew that crimes must not go unpunished. They understood that he could get as much as a life sentence. They were all hoping, however, that his punishment might not be too severe. "We have to leave it in God's hands," pastor had said.

Ally talked incessantly all the way home. She wouldn't let go of Kevin's hand. "If you have to go to jail, I won't get to see you for a long time," she said. "I'd better hold your hand now, just in case."

He smiled back at her, and squeezed her hand.

"You're my special girl, Ally. You told me about Jesus. I can never thank you enough for that."

"But someone told me. That's how people get to know about it. Now you're supposed to tell other people."

"I sure will. I want to tell the whole world!"

The next morning, the entire family was in court with Kevin for his hearing. Ally was holding his hand again, and they walked into the courtroom that way. Jeffrey was there as his lawyer and the family sat down together to wait until his name was called.

The judge walked in, and Jeffrey smiled as everyone rose to his or her feet. He turned to speak to the others. "God has sent us a Christian judge," he whispered. "Just keep on praying. He will do God's will. That's what we all want."

"I don't want Kevin to go to jail. Can't I tell God that?" Ally asked Jeffrey.

"You must let God make the decision, honey. Just pray for his will."

She looked at him wistfully, and then he saw the change in her face as she let God take control. He relaxed and leaned back to wait their turn.

"It's okay, Ally," Kevin whispered as everyone sat down. "I did something really, really wrong. If I have to go to jail to pay for that, God knows best. Don't worry about me, okay?"

"Okay, Kevin, but I don't want you to go."

"Kevin Sheffield."

Kevin took a deep breath, and stood up again. He and Jeffrey moved to the front of the courtroom and stood facing the judge.

The clerk read the charge: "Breaking and entering, with intent to kidnap," and sat down.

The judge cleared his throat, and then gazed down at Kevin. "Mr. Sheffield, this charge is very serious. What do you plead?"

"I did what he said, your Honor. I can't say that I wish I hadn't, though."

"Really? Do you realize that by saying that, you are putting yourself into a very dangerous position, Mr. Sheffield? You are accused of breaking and entering, and of an attempted kidnapping. This is a felony. You could spend the rest of your life in prison, sir!"

"I know that it's serious, Your Honor, but if I hadn't done what I did I might never have learned about Jesus. Ally told me about heaven that night. She was worried because I hadn't accepted Jesus as my Savior. I could hardly eat or sleep for weeks. When I finally bonded out of jail, I went back and asked Mr. Benski to talk to me about it. He showed me from the Bible how I could go to heaven. I accepted Jesus. No matter what happens to me now, I'll always be thankful for that night, because I now know I will spend eternity in heaven. God has forgiven me. Ally and her family have forgiven me, and I'm just about as happy as any man has a right to be. I know that crime has to be punished. You do whatever you have to do, your Honor."

Judge Hawthorn's face registered his surprise, but he quickly recovered himself. "Counselor, I will meet with you in chambers," he said to Jeffrey. "Be seated," he directed Kevin.

Kevin took a deep breath and walked back to his place beside Ally. She grabbed his hand again, and wouldn't let go. "Pray, Kevin. Pray hard!"

"God will do what is best. Don't worry." He squeezed her hand and bowed his head. When he lifted it, there was a smile on his face. He was at peace.

Judge Hawthorn sent word out to the clerk that the hearing would recess for lunch, and resume at two p.m. Tony looked at Kevin and the rest. "It sounds like God is at work in there. This really is a difficult decision for him to make. A crime has been committed, yet God wiped it away when he forgave Kevin and accepted him as his son. As a Christian, the judge knows that, but what must a human court of law do in light of all of this? Not punishing him could send the wrong message to others who have broken the law. But God has forgiven him, as have the family. He knows that prison would serve no purpose in his case. I wouldn't want to be in his shoes right now. We need to pray that God will give him wisdom."

"I just wish I had listened to my mother years ago," Kevin mourned. "She tried to tell me. She took me to Sunday school until I became a teen. Then I rebelled and refused to keep going. I had heard a little about God and heaven, but no one ever really explained it to me like Mr. Benski did. Mom tried, but I wouldn't listen...oh, man! I need to call her. She doesn't know that I found the truth, at last." He ducked his head and looked distressed. "She lives in Black Mountain, North Carolina. I haven't talked to her for years. I'm not even sure she's still alive. I'm the world's greatest creep."

"No, Kevin," Evelyn said gently. "You're a child of God, and he loves you. We do, too, and I know without any doubt at all that your mother will be the happiest mom in the world when she gets that call. There's a pay phone over there. Call her now, while you know that you can. She'll be very glad to receive a collect call from her son."

He walked over to the phone, then turned and looked at Evelyn for a moment. She nodded, and the four of them moved father away from him to give him privacy. When they looked in his direction a few moments later, he was sobbing.

"I love you too, Mom. If I can ever get this mess all cleared up, I'm coming home. I want to live near you, and help you. I love you," he repeated. "Okay, thanks. I need all of the prayers I can get. Bye, Mom...What? Oh, I think so. Just a minute, I'll ask."

Calling over to the others, he said, "My mom would like to ask a favor of one of you. If you don't want to..."

Evelyn smiled, and went over to the phone. "Mrs. Sheffield, I am Evelyn. What can we do for you?" she asked. "Oh, certainly we will be in touch with you and keep you informed if Kevin is unable to call." She paused, and then responded, "I know. We're all very happy for him too. I know this is an answer to prayer for you. Here is Kevin again. What? Oh, you're very welcome."

Tony quietly separated himself from the group and went to the door of the judge's chambers. He knocked, and someone opened the door. He spoke a few words, and was permitted to enter. He disappeared inside, and the door was shut. Anna wondered what he was going to do, but said nothing.

After Kevin had hung up the phone, the four of them left the courthouse to find a restaurant where they could eat lunch. They enjoyed an hour together, carefully avoiding any talk of courts and prisons.

Only the clerk and an officer were in the courtroom when they returned. They walked to the front and sat down to wait. It wasn't long before the judge came in with Tony and Jeffrey following.

All rise, the clerk said, and after the judge had sat down, the two men joined their family.

"Kevin Sheffield, come forward," the clerk called.

Kevin walked confidently toward the bench and stood in front of the judge.

"I'm ready, Your Honor. Whatever God has led you to do; I know it will be for the best."

"This has been a hard decision to make, young man," the judge told him. "It is obvious that your crime must not go unpunished. You already know that. Deciding the punishment has been the difficult part, but I have made a decision. As the family does not wish to press any charges, I do not feel that prison is warranted here. Instead, you will be under house arrest for a period of one year, plus time already served. You will serve the remainder of this sentence in Black Mountain, North Carolina, in the home of your mother. I have already spoken with her, and with the authorities there. This is a very unusual thing to do, but an officer there has been assigned to your case. You will be under the supervision of that officer, and there will be many restrictions. You will, however, be permitted to go to certain places at his discretion. At the end of one year, you will return to this court, so that I may review your case. Is this clear?"

There were tears in Kevin's eyes as he spoke. "Thank you, Your Honor. I promise you that you will never have reason to be sorry for this decision. My Mom will thank you, too. Thank you, thank you," he repeated, shaking his head as though he could hardly take in what was happening.

"Since you are out on bond, you may have one week to tie up any loose ends here in Johnston. You will be transported to North Carolina to serve out the year of house arrest. That is all. You are free to leave, but at the end of one week you must report to officer Duhon, who is standing at the back of the courtroom." The officer mentioned nodded his head, so that Kevin would be sure to know who he was.

The judge continued, "Failure to report to him at that time would result in a warrant for your arrest, and you would then, most certainly, serve prison time."

"I understand. I'll be here. I will definitely be here, your Honor. Thank you."

There were hugs all around as Kevin went back to the family. They went to their cars for the drive to Jeffrey and Evelyn's home. The ladies set out cold cuts and potato salad while Kevin's mother and Brother Alexander were called. The women who manned the church prayer line spent some time calling all of those who had been praying. When he left to return to his apartment, Kevin was rejoicing in his own special miracle.

ॐॐॐॐॐॐ

Georgia was watching covertly as Kevin arrived home. She moved out of the shadows, and over to the door of his apartment building. Slipping quietly up the two flights of stairs, she knocked on his door. When he opened the door, he was surprised to find her standing there. She looked terrible. She had obviously been on the run ever since her escape. She didn't wait for an invitation, but quickly pushed past him and into the apartment.

"Close the door," she commanded.

"No, Georgia," he answered. "I don't want you here. The police are looking for you. I've already spent weeks in jail because of you, and now I'm looking at a year of house arrest because I let you talk

215

me into going after Ally. What do you want with her, anyway? You never even liked her."

"That's my business. She's my kid, and I'm gonna get her back, just like I told Tony I would. You're gonna do it for me. You know you always do as I tell you."

"Not any more, Georgia," he answered. "It's over. I'm not going to do anything for you—not ever again. Get out of my apartment. Now! I'm calling the police..."

He turned his back on her and started to walk to the phone. She picked up a heavy vase from a nearby table and hit him on the head with all of her force. He fell to the floor, and didn't move.

Oh, no! What have I done? she thought desperately. *What was I thinking? My head feels so funny. I can't think straight. I shouldn't have come here. I've got to get out. I-I didn't want to kill Kevin.*

Running from the apartment, she headed for the stairs. She ran crazily down, looking backward to see if she were being followed. She didn't see the little truck some child had carelessly left on the stairs. She tripped over it and fell, tumbling down, screaming, until she hit the bottom. She lay there, quite still, her head turned at a crazy angle.

People poured out of their apartments to see what was going on. They found her there, with the small truck by her side. It was obvious what had happened.

"She must have come from up there," one man said, pointing to Kevin's open door.

"I wonder why he didn't come out to see if she's all right," another person questioned aloud.

"I'll call the police," the first man said. "Maybe you should go up and see what's going on with Kevin. He has to have heard the screams.

"Don't touch her!" he yelled at the onlookers. "If she isn't already dead, moving her could break her neck. Get back everybody!"

216

In just a moment the other man yelled down from Kevin's door. "Call an ambulance!" he said. "He's in bad shape. No wonder she was in such a hurry. She could have killed him." he said.

Two ambulances drove away to different destinations. Georgia hadn't survived her fall. Kevin was being rushed in a different direction, to the hospital. In the ambulance he was beginning to regain consciousness, and was feeling the pain. Then he drifted off into oblivion again, and stayed that way until the ambulance reached the hospital. An orderly found Tony's address in Kevin's pocket and gave it to the receptionist. "Look this guy up in the phone book and call him to tell him his friend is in the E.R." he said.

Tony got to the hospital as quickly as possible, and found Kevin awake. The x-ray had shown no serious damage, and he was about to be released. He looked at Tony and shook his head. "Georgia's dead," he told him. "She tried to get me to go after Ally again. When I refused, and turned to call the police, she did this to me," he said, gingerly touching the knot on his head. "She fell down the stairs trying to get away too quickly. She broke her neck."

Tony sighed, visibly touched. *What a waste,* he thought. *I wonder if she ever did trust Christ as her savior. Well, Ally is free from her now. God has taken things into his own hands.*

"Do you need to go home, Kevin, or would you like to go with me to tell Ally about her mother?" he asked.

"I'd like to go with you. I only have a few days before I leave. It would be a great blessing to see that little face when she learns that she is free to live her life without fear now."

"I don't know what her reaction may be," Tony responded. "Georgia was her mother, in spite of all of the cruelty."

Ally opened the door, and smiled to find Kevin there. She had to gently touch the huge knot on his head, and kiss his cheek before she was sure he was okay. "I'm gonna miss you, Kevin," she said.

"I'll miss you too, baby. We have something to tell you, though. That's why I'm here."

She sensed the tension, and the now familiar look of fear came over her face. "Mama?" she asked.

"It is about your Mama, honey," Tony told her. "But you don't have to be afraid this time. Kevin wants to tell you what happened at his apartment."

Anna was searching her husband's face for some clue to what they were about to hear. She found peace, and a strange sorrow there. She instinctively knew that Georgia would no longer be a threat to Ally. She took a deep breath and waited.

Kevin knelt down to Ally's level. "Sweet girl," he said, "your Mama came to my apartment tonight. She ordered me to get you for her. I refus-"

Ally began screaming. "No! No! I don't want to live with her again. She's mean!"

"Sweetheart, listen to Kevin. Your Mama *will not* get you back. Listen, okay?" Tony's heart was torn by her screams. He just wanted her to know that everything was okay now, but the sobs continued.

"She's *dead*, Ally!" he blurted out.

The screaming stopped. Her little face froze. "Mama's dead?" she asked. "For true?" She looked from one face to the other and saw that it was so. She seemed stunned for a moment, and then collapsed.

"Oh, Tony," Anna said, rushing to the small form. "She's passed out. The news must have been more than she could handle."

"Baby?" she said, shaking her gently. "Oh, dear Father, please help her," she whispered.

She looked helplessly at Tony. "Honey, do something! She's not breathing! She's not breathing!"

Kevin said, "I know what to do." He quickly moved over, turned Ally onto her back, and began artificial respiration. It only took a moment for the child to start breathing again. She opened her eyes and saw the three worried faces around her. She smiled a weak smile, and sat up.

Still a bit dazed, she muttered the word, "Mama?"

The three adults waited, not breathing, not knowing what she would do.

Tony broke the silence at last. "God has taken care of things in his own way, baby," he said. "Your mama wasn't normal in her poor mind. Mommy and I knew her when she was young. She was a lovely young girl. She wouldn't have done the things she did, if she had been normal. It's over, now. You can get on with your life without fear."

The puzzled look vanished from Ally's face, and she said softly, "Okay, Daddy. I love you." There were hugs all around, and gradually the conversation changed to happier things.

When Tony took Kevin home a little later the two sat in his living room and talked for awhile. So many things had happened during this day that Kevin needed to sort it all out. Tony listened to him, and gave counsel when needed. He invited his new friend for supper the next night, and headed for home with a light heart.

৯৽৽৽৽৽

The phone awakened Phyllis from a sound sleep. Her heart froze within her. Late night calls usually meant bad news. Getting out of bed, she made her way to the living room, and picked up the receiver. She paused for a moment before saying anything, and then said a muted "Hello?"

"Is that all of the enthusiasm I get after being gone these many months?" the familiar voice on the other end of the line questioned.

"Tom?" she whispered. "Tom! Oh! Oh! Oh! Where are you? Are you still in Korea? Oh! Is this really you?"

"Hey, pretty lady, let me answer those questions one at a time," he chuckled. "On second thought, all I need to say is that I'm down here at the airport. Come and get me, wife."

Phyllis was crying so hard by this time, she couldn't speak.

"I love you, honey." he said. "Come and get me."

"I...I'll...be there in five...minutes. Don't you go *anywhere!*" She hung up the phone, rushed to dress, and was out of the door in record time. Ten minutes later, she was in his arms.

"I can't believe you're really here," she murmured. "After all of the waiting... Oh, Tom, I thought you would never get home. I was so scared."

"I had a few fearful moments myself, but God was so good to me. My Korean friends kept me hidden, often at the risk of their own safety. I owe them a lot."

"Everyone has been praying for you. They're really going to be happy to hear this. I'm going to call them all tonight," she decided. "They'll want to wake up for this news!"

Tom laughed at her. "I have an idea they can wait until morning, little darlin'. This night is just for you and me."

They left the airport in each other's arms.

Tom held her close as they walked up the steps to their home, and she snuggled against him. "Don't you ever go away again," she said. "Never leave me again—ever!"

He kissed her in the glow of the porch light, then picked her up and carried her into their house.

Chapter Eighteen

Evelyn didn't forget her promise to Ally. She and Jeffrey discussed the adoption possibilities in detail. He felt, as she did, that with Georgia gone, there should be no problem. He had already tried, with no success, to find the father, or some relative. "I think the judge will grant the adoption," he said. "It always takes such a long time to get everything out of the way. Tony and Anna are probably feeling a little discouraged with the wait. I'll talk with them tomorrow about going ahead with application for adoption. Ally needs to know that we are trying, too. She's waited a long time."

When Jeff spoke with Anna and Tony the next day, they were excited with the prospect of making Ally their own, very soon. When she arrived home from school, they asked her if she would like to be their real adopted daughter. She flew into their arms, laughing and weeping. They all wept together, and from that day, Ally called them Mommy and Daddy always.

Jeffrey talked with the judge again the next day. Plans for the adoption were set in motion. Papers were signed, and they waited.

≈≫≈≫≈≫

December was fast approaching, and the excitement was growing. "Baby John" would be making "his" appearance soon. Ally talked to him every day. So did his parents.

Anna was wearing down as the final weeks passed. She had very much wanted to make Christmas special for Ally, but she realized, at last, that she would need to limit her activities. Evelyn would serve the Christmas meal at her house. Tony, Ally, "Baby John," and Anna would have an intimate family time at their own home during the morning, as would Evelyn and Jeffrey. Then, they would all be together for the rest of the day.

One December morning, after Ally had left for school and Tony had gone to work, Anna had a burst of energy. She spent the day cleaning the house, mending clothes that had been in her work basket for a while, and even washing some windows. Taking time out for an afternoon nap, she fell asleep making plans for a special supper. She woke up an hour later to a severe pain in her back. Ten minutes later, she sat up, and the pain hit again. Just about then, Ally came bursting through the front door with her usual excitement.

"Mommy? Where are you? Mommy?" She went through the house looking for her, and found her sitting on the side of the bed. Worried, she ran over and hugged her. "Are you okay? Are you sick? Oh, please don't be sick, Mommy."

"No, no, it's okay, honey. I'm not sick. It seems that 'Baby John' has decided it's time to come into the world to see us. Is Daddy out there?"

"No, ma'am. Do you want me to call him?"

"Not yet. Can you see a clock? I need to know the time."

"It's three-thirty."

"This is his early day, so he has already left work. He should be home any minute. Can you help me out? I need my suitcase. It's on the floor in the closet."

Ally quickly found the suitcase. She brought it over and put it on the bed.

"Now we need to call Grandma so she can be with you while I go to the hospital. Could you go call her for me, and tell her the baby is coming? The number is by the phone."

"You're going to the hospital? Like Grandma did? Oh, no, I don't want you to go."

"Everything will be fine, Ally. I won't be there very long, and when I come home I'll bring the new baby with me. Won't that be wonderful?"

"I don't know…I don't want you to go to the hospital. I'm scared."

"Honey, I really need you to call grandma for me. Please. Right now!"

That got her attention, and she left the room to do as she was told. Anna could hear her talking and she breathed a sigh of relief. Mother would be here soon. Ten minutes later the front door opened and closed, and Tony called her name. She could hear him talking to Ally, and then he rushed into the room. He put his arms around her and started talking excitedly.

"It's finally happening! I can't believe it. Honey, how are you feeling? Are you okay?"

"I'm okay. I think maybe we should hurry, though. Ally called Mother, but we have to call the doctor, too. Would you do that? Then get me to the hospital!"

"We're about to have another grandchild, John," Evelyn said aloud as she drove to get Ally. "Our granddaughter is lost to us, but we will have this little one to love. I hope it will be a boy. Maybe he'll even look a little like you. What do you think? Oh, how you would have spoiled him. And Ally? She would have you wrapped around her little finger. You wouldn't want to leave where you are now, though," she said. "Not even for this.

"I'll need to call Jeffrey. He will be so excited! He'll be a good grandfather for your grandson. No need to worry there. We all think of you often, my dear."

Tony was putting the suitcase in the car as Evelyn drove up. She got out quickly, and went in to check on things. She found Anna near the front door, waiting for her husband to help her to the car. She smiled at her mother and reached for a hug. "This is it," she said. "I can't believe it's real. Oh, Mother, I'm so happy!" She smiled through the pain as another contraction struck.

"Me, too. I'll be glad when it's all over and we can hold that baby in our arms."

"I know. Soon we'll know if we have a boy or a girl. Tony wants a boy so badly. I do hope…"

"We'll love it, whichever God gives you, but I know you would like for him to have a son."

Ally was subdued. Tentatively, she asked, "Can't I go with you, Mommy? I'll be really quiet."

"I need you to stay with Grandma Bo, darling. You can come to see us after the baby is born."

"Okay." Tears were close to the surface, but she didn't say anything else.

Tony came racing back to get his wife. They kissed Ally, said goodbye to Bo, and they were finally on their way to the hospital. Anna relaxed as much as possible. She knew that being tense would make things worse.

"Honey, maybe we should hurry a bit faster. I think it's about time."

Turning on the headlights and stepping on the gas, Tony made the last mile in record time. He pulled up to the emergency entrance, jumped out of the car, and rushed in to find an orderly with a wheelchair. Minutes later, Anna was in the labor room, and a call had been sent out for the doctor.

A couple of hours passed before the nurse finally came out and walked toward him. He stood up, anxious and excited.

"Mr. Benski?" she asked.

"Yes. Are they okay?" He would never forget her words…

"Your wife and son are both fine."

"Hallelujah!" he exclaimed, a bit more vigorously than his surroundings dictated.

She smiled. "You'll be able to see them in just a little while. Congratulations!"

When, at last, he was directed to the nursery, he looked in on his new son. A couple of other fathers were there also, all of them were beaming with pride.

"What a blessing. He looks perfect." Tony was in awe of the wonderful miracle of birth. A nurse found him there and told him he could go in to visit his wife. She led him down the corridor and left him at the door of Anna's room. Gently, he opened it, and was greeted with a tired, but happy smile.

"Did you meet Anthony John Benski?" Anna asked.

He chuckled, and walked over to her.

"I sure did! Thank you, my darling. He's perfect. God is so good, isn't he?"

"Honey, let's thank God for our son together."

"Yes. Let's do that," he agreed. He took her hand and prayed a heartfelt prayer of thanksgiving. After Anna had voiced her thanks, her husband bent down to kiss her. He prayed a silent prayer of gratitude for the wonderful change in her.

"I'd better find a phone and call Mom. She's probably having a hard time keeping a certain little girl from bouncing off the walls."

"You're right. Hurry back, though."

There was a short line for the phone in the waiting room. Tony was getting restless, waiting his turn, and was relieved when the last father had finished bragging and hung up the phone. He dialed Evelyn's number, and she answered on the first ring.

"It's a boy, Grandma! Come on down here."

He could hear her telling Ally, and then heard the squeals, as she reacted to the glad news.

"We'll be there as soon as we legally can." Bo said, and hung up.

Next, he called his own parents in California. They rejoiced with him too, while also regretting that they were so far away from their new grandson. Slowly, he hung up the receiver, and breathed a deep sigh. How he would love to have his parents there with him. "Well," he said aloud, "that can't be right now. Maybe they'll get to come soon. At the moment, I just want to be with my wife." He turned and walked back down the hall, smiling to himself as he thought about his precious son.

Nurse Grey saw Evelyn and Ally as they came in, and went over to greet them. "It's been awhile, Mrs. Lawrence. How have you been?"

"Great! Thank you for coming to the wedding. It was so special to see you there."

"Your wedding was beautiful. I wouldn't have missed it. Are you here for a check-up?"

"No, I'm fine. My daughter just had the baby—a boy. We've come to meet him. Will they let me take Ally in?"

"We aren't supposed to. When you were all here before, she had been part of the accident, and there was the thing about her mother. They were kind of lenient about letting her come and go because of that. Today, I'll need to ask permission. Young children can be carriers of measles, mumps, and such, so there is some danger to the babies, of course. They like to keep them isolated as much as possible. I'll ask, though. Be right back."

Ally stood there with her head down, feeling pretty rejected. First her mommy wouldn't let her go with them to the hospital, and now Nurse Grey wasn't going to let her go in to see Mommy.

"Look, Ally, here comes the nurse. She's smiling, and she has something in her hand. I'll bet it's for you," Grandma Bo comforted, as nurse Grey approached.

"You have to wear a gown and mask, Ally," the nurse said, "but at least they are going to let you go in this one time—only for a few minutes, though. I'm so happy that you have a new brother. Here," she said, handing the gown and mask to Evelyn. "She'll need to wear these when she goes into her mother's room. You can go see the baby first, and then put these on her."

226

"Thank you, so much for all you have done for us. You are such a treasure."

"Your family is so special." Nurse Grey responded. "It's a pleasure to do things to help you."

"Oh, one more thing—would you mind telling Tony that we are here?" Bo asked. "He's going to want to be with Ally when she sees the baby."

"Of, course. Just wait here, and I'll send him to you."

"Thanks, again."

Tony was smiling from ear to ear as he approached them a few moments later.

"If you're ready, let's go see that brother, Ally," he said. "You're going to love this little guy," he assured both of them as they headed down the hall.

"Can we take him home now?" Ally asked. "Can we?"

"Not for several days, honey," Tony responded. "You're going to have to be patient again, I'm afraid. Remember how we had to wait for Grandma Bo? That wasn't so bad, was it? Now we have to wait for Mama and Baby John for a few days. Understand?"

"I want them to come home now."

Tony just laughed and shook his head. They had arrived at the nursery window, and his thoughts were on the blessing of his precious son at the moment.

"Can you believe it, Mom? Just look at him!" he said proudly.

Evelyn was standing there looking at the tiny human that was hers and John's first grandson. She was in a world alone—memories flooding over her.

Tony recognized that this moment was significant, and kept Ally quiet.

"Oh, my," Evelyn said at last. "What if I hadn't come back? There were so many blessings waiting for me here, and this guy…oh, my!" she repeated. "Wouldn't Grandpa John have…well, perhaps he knows."

She changed the subject then, and turned her attention to her son-in-law. It was obvious that he was tired, but totally happy. "What a fantastic day!" she said. "We don't get a lot of days like this, do we, Son?'

"I'm so glad you're here for it, Mom," he replied. "It is so awesome."

"I can't see him good." Ally interrupted. "His bed is too tall."

"Oh, dear. Grandma's sorry, sweetheart. Daddy, what do you think we should do about this?" Evelyn asked, smiling.

Tony looked down at the little girl and said, "Well, let's see. How would you like me to lift you up?"

That brought a smile, and as soon as she had been lifted up and had seen her new "brother" she was back to normal. She began chattering about the things they would do together, and telling him how cute he was.

"I think I'll take Ally to the room to see her mommy now," Tony said a few minutes later. "Mom, are you ready to come," he asked.

"I believe I'll stay with John for a moment more, then go call Grandpa J. Won't he be surprised? Oh, here, let me help you get Ally into that paraphernalia before you go," she offered.

Enveloped in her hospital garb a few moments later, Ally giggled. The gown was from the pediatrics ward, and it fit just fine, but still it made her laugh. "I feel like a nurse," she said, wrinkling her nose under her mask. Tony and Evelyn laughed at her.

A few moments later, both parents laughed together at the strange sight of Ally in the hospital gown. She ran over to Anna and hugged her tight.

"Baby John is here!" she exulted. "I saw him. Can we take him home now?"

"NO! both parents said at the same time. They all three laughed together.

Jeffrey definitely was surprised upon learning how quickly everything had happened. "You must be thinking of John right now," he said to his wife. "I know that I am. I'm so glad we both loved him, so that we can share memories of him and talk about him. His having a namesake kind of gives him back to us in a way, doesn't it? It is okay to talk to you like this, isn't it? I know little John will be ours—yours and mine—but right now I can't help thinking of John, and his claim to his only grandson."

"I was having the same thoughts, and worrying that I was being untrue to your love because of it. I do love you so very much."

"Then it's settled. We both love our memories of John, and we're both very glad he has a namesake to leave in his place. I can't get away from the office for a few moments yet. I'll be along as soon as possible."

"I understand. Oh, honey, have Miss Black order flowers, would you? See if they can put a baby boy and a big sister among them. Ally will love that. Then, red roses for our kids, okay?"

"That sounds perfect. Bye."

"Bye."

There were more calls to make, to friends and family. This took a while, and just as she was hanging up from calling the head of the prayer committee, Jeff appeared. They shared a glad embrace and headed for the nursery. Baby John was wide awake and stretching. Suddenly, he started howling, and nothing short of a bottle would stop the hungry cries. He settled into the nurse's arms and soon was satisfied. His grandparents laughed at this, then headed for Anna's room.

At the doorway, they got in on the tail end of a conversation.

"She is Bodacious, you know," Tony was saying to Ally.

"I know. She told me, the day she said Mews was too small to drink from a bowl." A far away look came into the little eyes.

Standing beside his wife in the doorway, Jeffrey noticed that there was a similar look on her face. What might this mean?

229

The flowers arrived just then, and the moment passed. Ally especially liked the little dark-haired ceramic girl holding a tiny ceramic baby, wrapped in blue.

A short time later, Evelyn and Jeffrey took Ally home to stay with them. They left an exhausted, but happy Mommy. Tony would stay with her until the visiting hours were over, and then join them at their home for a late supper.

Chapter Nineteen

"You look pleased with yourself, dear husband. What have you been up to?" Evelyn asked one evening as Jeffrey came in the front door. She always met her there in the evenings, if she possibly could. He often told her how he looked forward to this as he drove home from work.

"Well, I have just been talking with Judge Walker," he said." I got a surprise. The search for Georgia's possible husband has come up empty, as we know, and both of her parents died in that plane crash when she was in high school. She was an only child and her grandmother died years ago. There is not one relative to be found. I would never have thought that we wouldn't find even a distant relative alive. They have to be out there somewhere, but we didn't find them."

"You mean Georgia was completely alone in the world? No wonder she had problems."

"I know, but we have done an exhaustive search, and have found no one—no husband, no family. Ally has no known relations who would want to take her in. That means an open door for the adoption. We've set the adoption day for January fifteenth."

Evelyn threw her arms around her husband's neck, and wept. "That's just two weeks away! I'm so incredibly happy! Can you imagine how Ally, Anna and Tony are going to react to the news?"

"I have some idea," he responded with a huge smile. "There's another surprise that goes along with that one. Guess who will inherit the house, and its three acres. Go ahead. Guess!"

"Don't tease me, you rascal! Well, it has to be someone I know, or you—oh, of course—Ally."

Jeffrey moved to his special chair, pulling Evelyn onto his lap.

"We'll have to pay the funeral cost, of course, as Georgia had no money, and the house is the only thing that belonged to her. Since the county took care of the burial, that won't be much of an expense, but it will have to be paid by her heir. Would you believe that the house is actually in Georgia's name, and police never thought to look for her through those records? It was deeded to her when her grandmother died. It was an old family property, and had been occupied by renters for twenty-five years. They apparently just left it vacant and moved on to another state. When Georgia came to live in it will never be known now."

Evelyn rose and began pacing the floor. "I wonder if this is wise," she murmured. "There are a lot of unhappy memories in that house. What could she do with it? I know she would never live out there again. She could sell it, I suppose. I just worry that this might bring back the bad memories."

"I hadn't thought of that. It just seemed like Ally should get something for all of those years."

Evelyn stood and reached for her husband's hands. He rose, and took her in his arms. She marveled that she could feel so protected and safe again after all of the empty years. Here she was, though, sheltered in the arms of her loving husband. She smiled at him, and he kissed her on the forehead.

"Dinner is ready," she said, smiling again. And still holding hands, they headed for the kitchen.

"Could we think about this while we eat?" she continued their conversation. "If God has given the house to Ally, then he must have a reason." They sat down to eat at their small kitchen table, each caught up in their own thoughts.

The food was tasty, as usual, for Evelyn was a good cook. When dinner over, Jeffrey leaned back in his chair and sighed. "That was great, honey. It sure beats all of those restaurant meals I settled for during my bachelor days."

232

Neither of them spoke of Georgia as the dishes were cleared away. The subject was on both of their minds, though, and after they had sat down together in the living room, Evelyn turned the conversation back to the judge's decision.

"I do need to go back to that house," she said decisively.

"Georgia's house? Why, honey?"

"Well, everything happened so quickly that I feel as though I left a part of myself there. I need closure. I wonder if Ally feels that way, too. Perhaps the three of us—Miss Ally, Mews and I—need to choose a day and make a trip out there one last time. Maybe we need to say a final good-bye to Misfit and a tired old lady named Bodacious."

Jeffrey laughed at that. Looking at his lovely wife in her nice clothes and make-up—every hair perfectly in place, nails manicured, and the soft scent of her favorite perfume embracing her—well, he could only chuckle. But he recalled the look on her face, and Ally's, that day in the hospital when little Johnny was born. He knew that there was a need of some sort. She was certainly anything but tired and old now, but perhaps it would help her close that part of her life if she went back.

"What I mean," she was saying now, "is that the person I had always been, and am again, doesn't relate to old Bodacious, but she was real. She suffered, and I guess she'll always be a part of me. I learned a lot about life during those twelve years. Maybe I became a better person in some ways. I think I need to tell her good-bye. Yes, I do need that."

"Come here old lady," Jeff said gently. She obeyed, and he held her close.

"God has blessed me so much," he said. "How could it be that I am married to the likes of you? You are the most wonderful woman I have ever known."

"I'm the one who's blessed," she murmured. "God has given me back my life, and more."

233

They sat without talking for a long time. At last, she stirred, and looked into his eyes.

"There really is something to this need to go back to the house, though Honey. Could you get me a key to that lock? If Anna and Tony think it would be a good idea for Ally to go, I'll take her, too. Is that okay with you?"

"Sure. Consider it done, but I have to tell you it's hard to think of you as a tired old lady!"

She laughed then, and snuggled into his embrace.

At Anna's the next day, Evelyn broached the subject of taking Ally with her to the house.

"I need to talk with Tony, Mom, but I don't know of any reason why you couldn't take her. We never saw her the way she was at that house," she continued, "so we can't relate. There's only you. Perhaps she does need to go back and close the door on that part of her life."

"There's one other thing," her mother said. "When Ally found Mews, the only way she could feed him was to steal some milk from a store. I know how that feels. I never actually stole food, but I was sorely tempted at times. Honey, she needs to go back and pay for the milk."

"Oh, my! I didn't know about that. I agree that she must take care of it. I'll talk with Tony tonight and let you know what he says— oh, listen—I hear your grandson waking up. Would you like to give him his bottle? He's always so dear when he's hungry. He can hardly wait. Then he just holds on so tightly to my finger while he eats. It's as if he thinks I'll take his bottle away if he doesn't hold on to me with all of his might."

Evelyn's face gave answer to the question of feeding the baby and they went together to pick him up. Grandma changed him and made him comfortable while Mommy got the bottle ready, then they enjoyed watching him together. Once again, the thought of all that she had missed crossed Evelyn's mind. *My, what a mess we can get our lives into by being stubborn, she thought. Thank God I came to my senses—well, with a rather large nudge from a certain little girl. If I hadn't found my Ally, where might I be right now?*

Mews suddenly went bounding out of the room where he had been overseeing everything, and they heard the front door close. A little bundle of energy entered the baby's room, and the quiet time was over.

"Grandma Bo!" she squealed, "I didn't know you were going to be here." She hugged her with all of her might and kissed her cheek. She nuzzled her little brother, and asked him how his day had been. "I got an 'A' in art," she told him. "What do you think of that? Do you think you'll like art, too? I can teach you when you get a little bigger. I'm gonna teach you lots of things, 'cause I'm your big sister. Yes, I am!"

"Mommy," she said, running to hug her too, "can you come to my school Thursday night? We're having open house. You'll get to see all of my stuff. Would you come too, Grandma? Would you? You too, baby John. Everybody wants to see you, 'cause I told 'em how cute you are."

Both Mommy and Grandma said they would be there, and even little John could go, too. Ally was ecstatic, but she never stayed long on one subject. She was soon telling all of the day's happenings, and then asking what was for supper and, could she go out and swing for a while? Oh, and could she have one of those cookies from yesterday? Two?

When they heard the back door close, both women burst out laughing. "Ally has brought us so much joy," Anna said. "I'm so very glad that God brought her to our family."

"Honey, that reminds me—if you aren't busy tonight, Jeff and I would like to come over. He has been working on the adoption, and needs to talk to all three of you together."

"Oh, of course, Mother. Come any time. Do we have good news yet?"

"It sounds like we may," her mother hedged. "I guess we have to wait until Jeff can tell us."

An hour later, Evelyn headed home after a protracted good-bye with her granddaughter, and quite a few sweet baby kisses. She sang all the way home.

Back at the Benski's some time later, Jeffrey didn't wait long to share the good news. When Ally heard that the adoption was only two weeks away, she started crying. Anna held her, and Tony held both of them. Happy tears were in the eyes of all five of them, and it took some time before they could quiet down enough to hear the rest of Jeff's news.

"There is one more thing," he said. "I'm not sure how you will react to it, Ally, but the judge has said the house is to be given to you. It will be held in trust until you are of age, of course, but it is yours. Your parents will make decisions regarding it, until you are grown."

"I don't want it, Grandpa J."

"I thought you might say that. We'll just leave it in the hands of your parents. You won't have to talk about it or see it. Okay?"

"Okay, Grandpa J. but can I still get adopted?"

"Of course, darling. The house has nothing to do with your adoption. In a couple of weeks you will legally be Ally Benski. You'll want to add a second name, I'm sure, and you could change from Ally to some other name if you like. Any name you choose."

"I won't be the same person any more, will I?" the child said pensively.

"Well, I don't really think much will change, except your name. You may keep the name Ally if you prefer, then nothing would change except your second name. You're already Ally Benski at school, as you know."

"Can I think about it, Grandpa J?"

"As much as you like. Talk it over with your new parents. Take your time. Don't forget that it's only two weeks until you legally belong to us, though. Be happy, sweetheart."

"We need to go, kids," Evelyn said. "I'm so glad we could bring you happy news."

After hugs and kisses, they were gone, and the Benskis sat looking at each other in disbelief. After such a long time, the good news had come all of a sudden.

Ally went to bed that night with a song in her heart.

Chapter Twenty

Christmas was quickly approaching. Ally had never had a real Christmas. Georgia would give her a used book, a pair of used shoes, or maybe a candy cane. Dinner would be hamburgers. If it was a good year, there might be pudding made from a box mix. Preparations for this year's Christmas boggled Ally's little mind.

One day, she went to Grandma Bo's to do some baking. They made "candy cane" cookies, twisting white and red dough together, and then shaping it. On top, they sprinkled crushed peppermint candy. These smelled delicious while they were baking, and Bo removed them from the oven just as they were barely beginning to turn a light brown around the edges. To Ally, they were the most beautiful cookies in the world.

Throughout December, there was a constant round of fun things to do. Shopping was a favorite of the little girl who had never had a real Christmas. She went with Grandma Bo one afternoon to buy her gifts for her family. Tony gave her a certain amount of cash. She would have to budget this to include all of her gifts. This was almost as much fun for Ally as buying the gifts.

Finding a stuffed, toy train in one of the dime stores, Ally laughed. "Johnny would love this forever, Grandma! Don't you thing it's just perfect for him?" The train that was almost as big as the baby.

Evelyn smiled and agreed wholeheartedly.

For her mother, she found a tiny wooden music box in a book store. It played one of Anna's favorite hymns. She also found very nice, carved wooden pencil boxes in the same shop. The boxes included pencils that the shop would engrave with the name of the person who was to receive them. Embossed on the top of the box was an eagle, and the words from the Bible, "they that wait upon the Lord shall renew their strength; they shall mount up with wings as eagles..." Ally chose two of these, one for her Dad and one for Grandpa J. She was very proud of her purchases. She could hardly wait until Christmas Day so that she could watch them being opened.

"I'm not getting your gift today, Grandma Bo. Mommy's going to take me for that, 'cause if you were with me you would know what it is."

"I think I'll wait to buy yours, too," Evelyn teased. "Unless you want to know what it is..."

"No, Grandma, I like surprises! If I saw your buy it, I wouldn't be...Grandma Bo, you're teasing me again," she said when she saw the look on her Grandma Bo's face.

"You figured that out, did you?" Evelyn was laughing, and Ally joined in. They walked up and down sidewalks, ambling in and out of the stores, laughing together. They looked at things they each liked, and just enjoyed each other's company until mid-afternoon.

"Well, it's been fun, but I think we'd better get home, little sweetheart. Grandpa J will be getting there soon, and for some silly reason he likes to find his supper ready," Evelyn laughed.

"Okay, Grandma Bo. I had so much fun. Thank you, thank you!"

"You're very welcome. If you would like, we'll call your mommy and see if you may stay for supper, then we could wrap your gifts. I have a lot of ribbon and paper."

"Really? Oh, boy! Wait till I tell Johnny about this day."

"He likes to hear what you've done during the day, doesn't he? He's so smart."

Out of the blue, Ally asked, "Grandma Bo, do you ever think about how it was for us—before we went to Grandpa J's office that day? Sometimes I get sad. I know I shouldn't but..."

"Yes, darling, I do think of my lost years quite a lot. I caused my own grief, though. You couldn't help what happened to you I understand why you might feel like you lost a large part of your life, but God can even use the bad things to make us better people. Let's try to see how we can use the bad years to serve God in some way. Let's just enjoy the holidays for now, though, okay? You have never had a real holiday, and I have been away for twelve of them."

"Okay. I love you so-o-o much!"

Ally was full of stories that evening after she got home, and she talked nonstop until Anna got her tucked into bed and turned out the light.

"Oh, wait, Ally," she said as she started through the door. "I forgot that you received a package today. Come, let's check it out."

"A package for me? I never got a package in the mail before. What is it? Oh, boy!" She was out of the bed in a flash, Mews dangling behind her as she grabbed him from his box. He couldn't miss something as special as this.

"I left it on the dining room table." Anna was leading the way there, when Johnny began crying. "Oh, honey," she said, "you'll have to go ahead and get it. The baby is hungry. You may open it if you like. Daddy's in the living room."

Ally was really disappointed, and she drew her lips into an angry frown as Anna left the room to feed the baby. Fortunately, for her, Tony was watching them from his chair, and he saw the mad face she made behind Anna's back.

"Miss Ally Benski! What's the reason for that ugly face you just made?"

She was startled to hear him talk to her like that, and changed her face immediately. She tried to pretend it hadn't happened, but he would have none of that.

"Ally, if you pretend not to have done something you actually did, you are lying. Do you want to be guilty before God of lying? He plainly orders his children not to lie."

241

Her eyes got wide, and fear replaced the recent ugly frown. "No, Daddy. I don't want God to be mad at me. He's so good to me. I love him."

"Then go apologize to mommy and come back here to me."

She stared at him, a puzzled look on her face. "But mommy doesn't even know..."

"Does that change the fact that you did it?"

"No, but..."

"It starts with apologizing to Mommy."

Slowly the deflated little girl headed for the nursery.

Boy, this parenting stuff can be difficult to take, Tony thought. *I don't like...oh, now I'm doing it. Forgive me, Father. I don't want to disobey you, either. Disciplining children is the job you have given me to do. I know it's important to love them enough to be rough on them when they need it. It's not pleasant, but it is necessary. I love that little girl so much. I hate being the one to cause her to be sad. It's kind of hard to learn all of this at once. I guess it's difficult for Ally too. Help me do this right, Father.*

"Mommy..."

"What is it, sweetheart? What was in your package?"

"I don't know. I have to say I'm sorry to you before I can open it."

"Sorry? For what, honey?"

"I was mad because Johnny took you away from me. I made a mad face behind your back. I'm sorry, Mommy..." and she started crying.

"Well, I'll tell you what—Johnny is just about through here. Let me get him settled back in bed, and you, and Daddy and I will talk about this. Okay?"

"Can I stay here with you?"

"Of course. Now let's be quiet so the baby will sleep for us."

A short time later, John was fast asleep in his bed and Ally had recovered the package from the dining room table. The three of them were sitting together on the couch, in the living room.

242

"Now, let's get this out of the way so you can enjoy the package. What happened?" Anna was trying to be kind, but stern. The parenting was hard for her, also. All she wanted to do was to make Ally happy. The child had spent most of her life in misery. Her new mommy knew, though, that her future happiness would depend on the way they taught her as a child. For the children's sake, it was necessary to be tough when the situation requires.

"I lied," Ally was saying. "When Daddy saw my mad look I tried to pretend I hadn't done it. Daddy said that's lying."

"What do you think?"

"Do I have to say?"

"Yep."

"Okay, I guess..."

"Now, don't guess. What do you think?"

"I was lying. But you didn't even know, Mommy!"

"Daddy knew. More importantly, God knew. You knew. Even Satan knew. That made Satan happy."

Dark eyes opened wide. "I don't want to make the old Devil happy, Mommy!" She was indignant.

"But," said Tony, "everything we do either pleases God, or Satan. When we lie, that does not please God. He commanded us not to lie. So who do you think it pleases?"

"Oh..." The severity of her simple act of defiance hit her full in the face. Tears welled up and spilled over. "Mommy, I'm really sorry this time. I didn't feel sorry when I told you in the nursery, but I do now. I'm sorry, Daddy. I thought you were being mean to me. I'm sorry, Johnny. Most of all, I'm sorry, God. I don't want to do things you tell me not to do. Amen."

"Is it over?"

"Over?" Tony questioned.

"Brother Alexander said that if we say we have sinned, and are sorry, God always forgives us. Is it over?"

"Yes, if you were sincere. Just saying the word 'sorry' isn't enough, though. It has to come from your heart. I think you are truly sorry. Am I right?"

"I'm sorry. I really am." She was weeping, and Tony put his arms around her.

The hug softened the sadness they were both feeling Anna smiled as she reached out to share the hug and hand the package to Ally.

"It's from Kevin!" Ally squealed. "Hey, Kevin!"

She tore into the wrapping and found a book of paper dolls. The dolls were made of cardboard, and their clothes were printed on paper. There were cardboard "stands" that would attach to the feet, and make the dolls stand up. Everything would need to be cut out. She turned through the book, looking at clothes, pajamas, purses, hats, and coats. There were even a puppy and a kitten printed on the cardboard. A card fell out of the book, and she picked it up and read it aloud. "To my very special friend, Ally. Thanks for changing my life. Love, Kevin."

She found a letter and a photo at the back of the book and handed them to her daddy. He read the letter to them.

Dear Benskis: These months since I left you have been wonderful. I've been permitted to attend church with my Mom, and I have found a girl at church. This house arrest makes it hard to have a normal relationship with her, but she doesn't seem to mind. She tells me that one year isn't so long, and it will soon be over. Every time I get upset about the things I can't do, I remember my crime, and the fact that I could have spent the rest of my life in prison. I ask forgiveness, then, and just feel glad for the wonderful life I do have. Tanya and I are to be married after my year is over. We want to spend our lives serving God. Love to all of you, Kevin

The photo showed him with a pretty, young girl. The woman with them was his mom. She looked older than her years, but she had a loving look, and she was smiling a very happy smile.

"Well, that was a nice surprise. It's good to hear how he is doing. He sure does love you, Ally." Tony was still struggling, wondering why it was always so hard to feel that things are back to normal after a dispute. Then, he realized that he was feeling guilty for making Ally sad. He shook his head, not wanting to feel what he certainly was feeling.

As though she knew of the turmoil that was going on in her husband's heart, Anna suggested, "Why don't we each quote a favorite Scripture verse?"

"Perfect," Tony said gratefully. "God says, 'Thou wilt keep him in perfect peace whose mind is stayed on thee, because he trusteth in Thee.' That's somewhere in Isaiah, I think." He was smiling again. "Peace comes from God. We just have to draw near to him. Quoting Scripture is a great way to do that."

"There's nothing too hard for Thee." Anna was smiling, too. "I don't remember where it is found, but I say it a lot."

"I like 'God so loved the world that He gave His only begotten Son.' That was Jesus," Ally said.

The evening ended on a happy note. All three had learned a lesson this night. Ally would forever be careful about lying, now, and both parents would be careful to guide their children in the truth, even though it might hurt. Quiet settled over the house that night as the Benski family slept in sweet peace.

Chapter Twenty-One

The few remaining days before Christmas went smoothly. Christmas Eve came in on a light blanket of snow—a holiday first for the little southern town of Johnston. Ally spent an hour outside playing in the white stuff, then came in and helped Anna make good things to eat. They were having Phyllis and Tom over in the evening, and Anna wanted to make it special for them.

The day passed quickly, and the family sat down to an early supper in order to allow more time for final Christmas Eve preparations. The excitement was building for Ally, and the adults couldn't help picking up on the emotion. Hymns about the birth of Jesus were playing on the hi-fi, and good smells filled the house as Phyllis and Tom came through the door. They were dressed in matching, bright red sweaters.

"You look like Christmas, Mrs. Phyllis," Ally said. "You're pretty. Mr. Tom is cute, too."

"Thanks, sweet girl. You look adorable tonight. Are you getting excited?" asked Tom.

"Yes sir. I never had Christmas before. I can't wait!"

"Bless your little heart. Well, I know this will be a wonderful one."

"Just look at all of those presents," Phyllis said. "Now I wonder who they could belong to. Do you know of anyone who likes presents, Ally?"

Ally giggled, and went over to sit beside Tony on the couch. Mews immediately jumped onto her lap, and settled in for a nap.

Later, as they sat around the table with hot chocolate and homemade cookies, Phyllis and Tom looked at each other. "Should we tell them now?" she asked him.

"Well, I'm not sure they would really be interested. What do you think, sweet woman?"

"You two," Anna said. "What have you cooked up now?"

The smiles on their faces made it obvious that they had good news and that they were just bursting to tell it to them.

"We're having a baby!" Phyllis was excited, and her hosts joined in the excitement.

"Wow!" Ally said. "I'll be a big sister again."

Tom smiled, and sent a silent prayer above. *Thank you Father*, he began. *I came so close to never coming home at all and now I'm going to be a father. Thank you for your loving mercy.*

An hour later, after a final round of hot chocolate and cookies, Phyllis and Tom thanked their hosts for their gifts, received thanks for the gifts they had given, and headed for the door. They stepped out into the frigid air. Saying good-night, they headed for home, arms around each other; as though they were daring anyone or anything to ever separate them again.

At Jeffrey's sister Alexandra's house, he and Bo had enjoyed a late Christmas Eve dinner. It was a festive evening, with Mother Jeanette, Alexandra, her husband Peter, their five children and seven grand-children. There was gift exchanging, and a lot of fun and laughter following the meal. Then the younger ones disappeared out into the yard to enjoy the snow for a while. Soon the others just had to join in the fun. They left the warmth of the living room in return for snow-ball fights and cold red noses.

Jeff and Evelyn headed home, at last, with thankful hearts. This was turning into a wonderful Christmas! The joy of "belonging" was incredibly special to Jeff this year. He now had a wife and kids and grand-kids of his own. Silently, Evelyn thanked God for her wonderful new life.

Christmas morning began with a little girl peeking into her parent's room. She wasn't making any noise, but they could feel her presence, and they began to stir. Still half asleep, Anna saw Ally standing there. She smiled a happy smile and nudged her husband. "Wake up, Daddy. It's Christmas," she said, "and this Christmas we have kids in the house!"

Tony sat up in bed, fully awake all at once. The joy of having Ally overwhelmed him. He glanced toward the door. There she stood, grinning at him. "Come here, you rascal," he laughed. He held out his arms, and she flew into them.

"Get up, Daddy! It's Christmas!"

"Uh-huh. Could all of this have anything to do with the presents in the living room?"

"What presents?" she asked innocently, grinning again.

"Oh, well, if you haven't noticed them, I guess I can go back to sleep for a couple of hours."

"Daddy!"

The three of them laughed together, hugged, and said "Merry Christmas" to each other.

Sounds from the nursery told them that the baby was awake. Ally said, "I'll get him!" and headed down the hall. She found him in his bassinet, wide awake, making little baby noises. "Come on, Johnny, it's present time! You're gonna like what I got you. Come on baby," and she reached into the bassinet to get him.

Anna had followed Ally down the hall. She stood in the doorway, watching the children together. Tears of joy were in her eyes, and a prayer of thanksgiving was in her heart. For just a moment, she thought of her sweet Megan, and then she put the sadness aside and entered the room.

"Maybe we should change the baby's diaper and make him comfortable first," she said with a happy smile. "What do you think?"

"Oh, I forgot about that. Do you want me to warm his bottle for you?"

"That would be a big help, sweetheart. You have gotten very good at that. Take it to the living room, would you? We'll be right in. This guy can eat while we open presents."

"Oh, boy!" and she was off like a flash. Christmas Day was here at last!

"We know that Jesus wasn't really born on December twenty-fifth," Tony was saying awhile later, "but the entire world is thinking of him at this time. We want to think of him too, and remember the incredible gift he gave to us—his own dear life—so that we might spend eternity with him in heaven. Before we start opening gifts, let's take a moment to thank God for all of our blessings." He reached for Anna's and Ally's hands and each of them held onto tiny baby fingers as they all bowed their heads.

"Oh, dear Father, how can we ever thank you for all that you have done for us? Ally has come to us." He squeezed the hands he was holding, and they squeezed back. "Our baby John is here, and very healthy," he continued. "Mom is safely back and happy. Jeffrey has become part of our family. We have so many blessings, Father, and here we sit in front of these gifts—abundance of everything, beyond measure—but, oh, Father, it is your unspeakable gift to us that is all important. You sent your only begotten son to die for us, and then sent people to tell us about that. Thank you for Jesus, dear Lord. Thank you for your messengers, who told us about him. We love you Father. In Jesus' name, amen."

"I love you, too, Jesus, Lord," Ally piped up.

"And I do too, Father," Anna said quietly. "So much."

"Burp!" said baby John, and everyone smiled. Anna burped him once more and propped him up on the couch so that he could be in on everything.

"Next year he'll really be getting into everything at Christmas. Won't that be fun?" Tony laughed.

"I know. Oh, Tony, we're so blessed. I can't believe how I behaved all of those years, yet God has done all of this for me."

He smiled at her, and gave her a "bear hug."

"He's perfect, remember?"

"I know. Okay. I'll just love him and enjoy all he's done for me."

"Good idea. Let's relieve Ally's misery and let her open these gifts. What do you say?"

"I say 'yes', Daddy!"

"You're sure you want to do this, Ally? I mean we could open them next week sometime, just as well."

"Daddy!"

"Well, okay, if you're sure…"

"Yes!"

He reached for the first gift. "Let's see, this one says, well, how about that. To Ally from Johnny."

"From Johnny!" she squealed, grabbed for it, and ripped off the paper.

"It's a puzzle! Oh, boy! Thank you, Johnny," and she kissed his sweet smelling head. "That means love," she informed him.

"Well, this one seems to be to Mommy. From Ally, it says. Wonder what it could be? Hum-m-m. It feels like…"

"You rascal, give me my gift."

Tony laughed and handed the box to his wife. She opened it quickly, and her eyes lit up when she saw the tiny music box. "Ally, it's lovely, darling. Did you choose it yourself?"

"Yes, Mommy. Turn it over. It has a key." She was bouncing up and down with excitement, anxious for Mommy to hear the music.

"Oh, I see that." She turned the key, and the notes of "The Love of God" came from the intricately carved wooden box. Anna loved the beautiful song which had been part of her Mom's wedding. It had recently come into popularity, because of the famous singer who sang with evangelist Graham's crusades. The hymn was written in 1917, by Frederick Lehman, according to a small paper which was enclosed with the music box. The beautiful music and words were now thrilling the world.

"Oh, honey, I love it! It's just perfect," she said, and gave her "nearly" daughter a hug. Ally's face radiated the joy of having given a treasured gift.

Tony loved his pencil box. He took it immediately and put it in place on his desk. "It's perfect, Ally," he said as he came back into the room. I really needed new pencils, too, and these have my name on them. Love it!" He hugged her, and she smiled at him, happy as could be.

One by one the gifts were opened. Ally was incredulous as her pile grew.

"Anna's gift from Tony was one of the last ones opened. She gasped in delight then broke down in tears when she saw the beautiful mother's ring her husband had bought for her. In the center were the children's birthstones. On each side of those, were tiny hearts, with Anna and Tony's birthstones on the other sides of the hearts.

"Oh, Mommy, don't cry. Don't cry, Mommy."

"These are happy tears, honey," Anna told her. "I have my family at last. That's what this ring says. See. Here is the stone for Daddy's birthday. This one is yours. This one is Johnny's, and here is mine. All of us—all together. The hearts are for love."

Ally was silent. The ever-present fear surfaced. What if the adoption didn't happen? What if she lost these people whom she loved so dearly? Recovering herself, she reached out and gently hugged Anna. After she hugged Tony, she ran to hug Johnny. His train was wedged in beside him. It was almost as large as he was.

After they had opened all of the presents in the pile, Tony feigned surprise.

"Oh, Mommy, wasn't there something else for Ally. It seems like there might have been. Help me out here, would you?"

"Oh, yes… I remember. Didn't we put something in the wash room last night, dear? Could that be it?"

"Oh, sure—silly me. How could I forget? I'll go see if it's still there."

Of course they had Ally's attention by this time, and her eyes were wide with excitement as Tony's voice came back from the wash room... "Can't find it. I must have been mistaken—oh, wait, I think this may be it. I'll bring it out so you can see..."

As he walked through the kitchen door into the dining room Ally gasped. He was pushing a shiny new pink bicycle. There was a large name tag, with "To Ally" printed in big letters, hanging from the basket. She was stunned. "I have a bike," she said at last. A grin started at the corners of her mouth, and then just got bigger and bigger. She jumped up, ran over, got onto the bike, and sat there laughing. "I have a bike of my very own, just like the kids in my books. Thank you Daddy! Thank you Mommy! It's the most wonderful present any girl could ever get. I love you." She jumped off of the bike and ran to give them each a hug.

What a wonderful morning—that Christmas day at the Benski house! Once they had opened all of the gifts, they spent a little time looking them over and enjoying them. Tony and Anna had a wonderful family time, watching Ally with her toys, and snuggling little John. Anna finished preparing her part of the dinner to take to Grandma and Grandpa's house, and soon it was time to leave.

"I got a bike!" Ally was the first one through the door, and just had to share the news with her grandparents. She ran through the whole list of her gifts, of Johnny's and her parents'. Evelyn and Jeffrey were well informed about every single one of them.

"What did you get, Grandma?" She asked

Grandma told her of their gifts, knowing very well what would come next.

Sure enough, Ally was inching closer to the pile of gifts to which Tony was adding by bringing theirs in from the car. Ally kept cutting her eyes over at them, trying to get a peek—to see if she could spot her name on any of them.

"Ally, come help Daddy arrange these," Tony said. He and Evelyn exchanged knowing glances, and tried to hide their laughter from the excited little girl. It was no use. They were soon laughing aloud, and Ally knew she had been found out. She grinned and made a dash for the gifts.

"Don't touch!" Evelyn warned. "You might guess what's inside and ruin your surprise."

"I'll put my hands behind my back," Ally responded, and Evelyn laughed again at the comical snooping that was going on as she inspected the gifts. Each time she found something with her name on it, she would look knowingly at Grandma Bo, with wide eyes. When she found one particularly pretty package, she got really excited.

"When will we open presents Grandma?"

"Oh, I thought we would wait until after we've had dinner, and things are cleaned up. Okay?"

"Oh… okay, Grandma Bo…"

"Just kidding! We'll do it as soon as we all get settled down here."

"Oh, boy!" She ran over for hugs, and then went to tell Johnny.

"That child will be talking before he's five months old if Ally has anything to do with it," Jeffrey said, laughing

"She talks to him constantly," Anna said. "She tells him everything, and has been doing that since before he was born. She completely ignores the fact that he never answers back. I do believe it might mean that he'll talk early."

Tony was just bringing in the last of the food they had brought. He set the final two dishes down on the counter beside the others. "There, that empties the car," he said. "We have enough food here to feed a small army."

"Now, Grandpa J? Please, now?" Ally was getting impatient.

So many gifts—so much love. All of the lonely people, who had come together, now spent their first Christmas Day as a complete family. How they enjoyed each other! What fun to watch Ally, for she thoroughly loved every single moment of the day. They played games together after lunch and brought out the food again for the evening meal. At last, it was time to separate.

"There are a couple of presents that we were saving until last," Tony said, quietly. He went to get them from their hiding place and brought them into the den. Pretty green bows complemented the bright red foil wrapping paper.

"These are for you, Mom, and for you, Ally—from Jeffrey, Anna and me. They're given with lots of love. Here you are," he finished, and handed them to the surprised pair.

"This is unexpected," Evelyn said. "Shall we all sit down? I think maybe I need to..."

Everybody found a spot, and they sat down together.

"Shall we open them at the same time, Ally?" Evelyn's hands were trembling, slightly. It was almost as though she already knew what was inside of the beautifully wrapped gift box.

"Okay, Grandma Bo," was the response, and they began removing the ribbons. Then, before un-wrapping the paper, they looked at each other.

"Ready?"

"Yes. Are you?" The child had picked up on Grandma Bo's emotion and a serious look was on her face.

"Let's do it."

They each unfastened one end of the paper, and looked at each other. The rest of the paper came off in one big swoop and revealed simple white boxes. They looked at each other again, and began opening the boxes. They lifted the tissue paper to reveal...

"Oh, my," breathed Bodacious.

"Oh," whispered Miss Ally.

Inside of the boxes, they found lead crystal plaques made to sit on a piano, dresser, or mantel. Burned by acid onto the crystals were identical pictures. A small girl was on her knees on the floor. Beside her, a tiny kitten was looking up at her from a bowl of milk.

The girl was looking up at an older woman who strongly resembled Evelyn. The child looked much like Ally. Both were bedraggled, and their faces were solemn. Beneath the pictures, simple captions which read, *Bodacious and Miss Ally*, left no doubt concerning the identities of the pair.

Both sat, staring at their plaques, for a long moment. Then they went into each others' arms and wept. They wept for lost years and lost joys—and they wept for the overwhelming gladness that was theirs, at last.

Regaining her composure, Evelyn said, "I'm speechless, you three. I don't know how you managed this, but it will always be one of my dearest treasures."

Ally couldn't say anything. She simply moved over to Anna and Tony and wept in their arms. They wept with her, washing away some of the hurt. They knew that no one can ever really know the pain endured by an abused child. Ally had been given a second chance at life, but the scars would always be there. The plaque was a bridge between the bad years and the wonderful new years to come—for that moment when the two had met in the run-down kitchen had been the very start of their new lives.

All of the fun gifts were forgotten—suspended in time for a moment. Nothing else mattered, except those lovely pieces of crystal. At last, Evelyn got up and went over to Anna and Tony for hugs. Then she walked over to her piano and set her plaque in its place. She knew that it would remain there, a dear, dear treasure, for as long as she lived. Turning to her husband, she went into his waiting arms.

It was unspoken, but the looks on their faces left no doubt that Evelyn and Ally would definitely have to go back to that house for a final good-bye.

As though on cue, Mews came running, and jumped onto Ally's lap. This brought smiles, then laughter, as he turned around and around looking for the best spot to settle. He was soon purring contentedly, and more than anything else could have done, he brought comfort and healing to his young mistress.

Just then, Johnny decided it was time to eat, and he put an end to the tears by howling in hunger. He was really loud, and soon everyone was laughing.

The glad day ended on a gentle note. The Benskis drove home that evening midst softly falling snow. The baby was sleeping peacefully, but Ally was still excited. When they got out of the car she plopped down on the front lawn, and made a "snow angel" in the inch or two of Christmas snow. Tony had one arm around his wife's waist as they headed for the house. The other arm carried John. He leaned over, kissed Anna, and sighed happily.

"A most merry Christmas to you, Mrs. Benski," he said. "I love you."

She smiled up at him, and repeated the precious words.

Phyllis and Tom had heard their car turn into the driveway. They poked their heads out of the front door to call out, "Merry Christmas!" The Benskis all responded in kind, and then entered their house, closing the door against the cold wind.

"What a happy day," said Anna.

"Indeed it was, my darling. Indeed it was."

They put John to bed while Ally looked through all of her "loot," which Tony had just brought in from the car. He went back for dishes and his and Anna's gifts, then shut the door for the night.

Looking in on Ally a little while later, they found her and Mews curled up on top of the covers, sound asleep. Mommy and Daddy smiled happy smiles. They covered their sleeping "daughter," and left the room, thanking God for a perfect day

As they settled into their bed that night, they got out the pictures of their little Megan, and spent a few moments remembering their lost child. They prayed for her—prayed that if she were still alive, she was happy. Then, turning to the last page of the album for a final look, they saw it.

257

In one of the photos, their tiny daughter Megan was clutching a stuffed kangaroo in her arms. Anna had written the word, "Kangy" beneath the picture. It had been Megan's favorite toy, and "Kangy" was her very favorite word. Her kangaroo had disappeared with her that dreadful day. Memory dawned for both of them at the same time—a memory of Ally, opening her birthday gifts. "A Kangy! A Kangy!" she had cried when she opened Jeffrey's gift. They recalled the unshed tears in her eyes as she spoke those words, and suddenly they knew.

They knew beyond any doubt…

Chapter Twenty-Two

Tony appeared at the home of his parents-in-law early the next morning. Evelyn and Jeff had just finished a leisurely breakfast, and Evelyn had gone in to have her morning shower. Jeff got up to respond to the door bell. When he opened the door, and saw the look on his son-in-law's face he knew not to question him until he had had his say. Something heart rending was tearing at him.

"Come on in, son," he said. "Whatever it is, I'll do my best to help."

"Thanks, Dad," Tony answered. He was struggling to stay controlled.

"There's coffee ready in the kitchen, if you'd like…"

The young man shook his head, and began pacing the floor.

"Have a seat and tell me about it, son."

The pacing continued, and then he stopped in front of Jeff. His face was contorted with anger, and he was trembling.

"She stole our daughter, Dad!" He was almost screaming. It was all he could do to control himself. "She cost us seven years of the worst kind of agony. I have never been so angry!"

"Calm down now. Can it really be that bad? Have you had news of Megan?"

"It's *Ally*! Ally is *Megan*, Dad! All of these months we've had her back and didn't even realize it. *Ally is Megan!*" he repeated. "Georgia must have stolen her to get back at me for dumping her for Anna. I had dated her for a couple of months, and when I realized that she was thinking that I would marry her, I stopped asking her out. She was nice enough, but I had no thoughts of marrying her. She was so mad when I started dating Anna, that she said she would get even with me for leading her on. I didn't, Dad. I just asked her out a few times. Who would think that someone would steal their little child as payback for that?"

Tony was weeping uncontrollably, and Jeffrey just stood with his arm around his son-in-law's shoulder and wept with him.

"Let's pray," he said at last. It was difficult to speak around the lump in his throat, but he asked God for peace, and for guidance; then, realizing the incredible impact of this thing, he began to praise God for the wonderful discovery. Megan was back! She was home with her own parents! Evelyn had seen the granddaughter she thought she would never know, and she already loved her. He was weeping in earnest now, and Tony, letting go of his anger in the realization of the incredible truth, was sobbing—for joy. He also began thanking God, and the elation that filled the room was almost physical.

"Megan is back," Tony whispered. "God has given my baby back to me. I have to go. I have to talk to Anna. I have to tell Ally…"

"You'd better wait about telling Ally, son. Let's make real sure, so that there is no chance of her getting hurt again. Isn't there a footprint from when she was born?"

"Sure. It's in her baby book. I saw it last night. Will that prove anything?"

"Yes. We'll have an expert compare Ally's footprint with the one in the baby book; then there will be no confusion. Okay?"

"You're right. I won't say anything to her, but Anna and I talked about it all night. I'll have to tell her everything."

"Of course. Let's leave it at that. We'll go ahead and take Ally down to get the footprint done. We can tell her that it has something to do with the adoption. She already knows about that. Can you be ready in an hour?"

Tony nodded. "That's good for me. Thanks for helping me see this in perspective," he said. "I'm afraid I was a little out of control. I'll just thank God now, and try to put the anger behind me.

Georgia's dead. She can't hurt us anymore." He turned, as he headed for the door. "We'll be back here in one hour."

"Okay, son. We'll get this done as quickly as possible. Your family has been through enough. Be sure to bring the album. I'll call in some favors and get everything set up while you're gone."

"Thanks, again," Tony said as he went through the open door, leaving Jeffrey standing there, shaking his head in wonder of the miracle which had just happened. He turned around when he heard Evelyn enter the living room. She had bathed, and was dressed for the day.

"I thought I heard yelling while I was in the shower," she said. "Did you have an angry client? Is everything okay?"

"Much more than okay, sweet Grandma!" he said. As he told her the news, she started crying. She was trying to assimilate the glad truth, but she was overwhelmed by the suddenness of it.

"Megan," she said. "Ally is our Megan. She suffered all of those years without her parents because of a fit of jealousy. No wonder Georgia kept her hidden." She felt angry, and then had to reprimand herself. Megan was alive and well. No thanks to Georgia, but she was safely back home with her parents. God had been so good, and she would never have to give her Ally up. She was her real granddaughter. What a thrill!

"It's a little bittersweet, isn't it, darling?" Jeffrey asked. "Of course we can't be legally sure until we get the test back, but there really isn't much doubt. It looks like God used you to bring it all together. No one is more thankful for that than I am! Are you still taking Al...uh, Megan to the house this morning?"

"Is it okay? Should I wait until another day?"

"I think it might be better to get it out of the way before she finds out about this other, then she can just be Megan from now on. What do you think?"

"You're right. It's going to be hard not to tell her, though. Oh, Jeff, what will we do if it isn't true? I..."

He took her in his arms and held her a moment. "Let's leave it up to God, okay?"

"Okay. I want to be excited, but there's still that small possibility that we're wrong isn't there?"

"We can't be positive until after the test. That's why we can't let her know what's going on. It would be hard enough on all of us, but think what it would do to her. Let's just be patient. We should know by the end of the day."

A horn honked, and Jeff kissed his wife good-bye. He left her standing in the door watching, with a prayer in her heart, as they drove away.

A couple of hours later, a very subdued little girl climbed into Evelyn's car, and they headed for the small store from which Ally had taken the milk.

Evelyn parked the car in front of the store and got out. Ally was still seated and showed no sign of moving. Evelyn walked around to her side of the car and asked, "Did you change your mind, sweetheart? This has to be your decision. Grandma Bo is not going to make you do it."

"I want to, but I'm scared. What if they put me in jail?"

Bo had to suppress a smile. "Not likely, as they don't usually put little children in jail for taking a can of milk."

"Two cans."

'Yes, well, if you don't plan to go in, I'll just get back in the car." She started to go around the car, but Ally called her back.

"I'm going. Please wait for me."

Evelyn held out her hand. Ally opened the car door, grabbed the hand, and they walked to the front of the store. She had a "death grip" on her Grandma Bo as they went through the door. Bo was struggling to keep from laughing, but she also felt sorry for Ally. This was a major trauma for her.

"Good morning. May I help you?" The clerk seemed pleasant enough. But the small hand tightened even more on the larger one.

"Hello. How are you today?" Evelyn responded.

"I'd be a lot better if it weren't for the thieving kids around here. They come in, look around, and walk out with merchandise hidden in their clothes somewhere. I'm going broke. My husband passed away four months ago, and it's been hard. I live in a small room upstairs, so I don't have a lot of bills, but there isn't much business here, either. I'm sorry. I'm just rambling on. How can I help you?" The pressure on Evelyn's hand had increased even more dramatically as the store owner spoke of the thefts. She looked down into a face of stark terror. Quickly, she returned the pressure, and spoke softly to the child.

"It's all right, Ally. Remember why we're here, okay?"

Ally nodded, but her lips were compressed, and Bo knew she would have to help her out with this one.

"Well, what we have to say may help you feel a little better," she told the woman. "I'm Evelyn Lawrence, and this is Ally. You may have heard about her. Her mother deserted her almost a year ago. They had been living in a house very near here, and Ally was never permitted to see anyone, or go anywhere away from the house."

"Oh, yes, someone told me about that. I couldn't believe that nice lady could have done such a thing. She was one of my best customers. Did she really leave the little girl alone for weeks?"

"I'm afraid she did, and that's what we want to talk to you about. Ally became somewhat desperate after her mother had been gone for a few weeks. She took two cans of milk from your store. Now she wants to pay for them."

Ally still said nothing, but she reached into her pocket and removed the money. She laid the coins on the counter and looked into the woman's face. Tears were streaming down her cheeks. "I'm sorry I took the milk," she managed to say.

"Oh, child," the woman responded. Tears came into her eyes too, and she opened her arms to embrace the little girl. "If you had only told me you needed help, I could have taken care of you. There now, don't cry. It's all right. There, there," she soothed.

Ally stood still for a moment, and then asked, "Grandma Bo, can we go now? I feel so bad that I took that milk."

"I think that the nice lady is trying to tell you she forgives you, dear."

"Oh, of course I forgive you," she assured the child. "I feel terrible that you were so close, and needed help so badly, and I didn't even know. My, you must have been frightened. You just forget about the silly milk. It wasn't anything."

Ally looked into the kind face of the lady. "Thank you for not sending me to jail," she whispered.

This caused both women to have to struggle really hard to keep from laughing. They lost the struggle, and soon all three were laughing together.

"Is it over?" Ally asked at last. She was ready to be finished with all of this.

"It's over, dear. Are you ready to go, then?"

"Yes, I'm sorry Miss—what's your name? I don't know what to call you."

"Dorothy Gleason," was the response. "Just call me Miz Dot," she added. "Everybody does."

"Thank you Miz Dot. We're gonna leave now, so I don't feel so sad."

Dot leaned down and kissed the smooth forehead. "You mustn't feel sad. Everything is okay here. You made it all right. I'm real proud of you. Good-bye, dear."

"Thanks, Dot. This was hard for her. You made it a lot easier."

"Do come to see me again. I feel like I have two new friends."

"We might just do that. Good-bye."

Outside once more, Ally relaxed a little. Evelyn reached down and gave her a hug.

"I'm getting hungry. Are you?" she asked. "Shall we go have our picnic before we go by the old house?"

"Yes. I don't feel very hungry, though. I'm sad."

"Remember—if we ask God to forgive us, and we do our best to make things right with the people we have sinned against—then we have to forgive ourselves and be happy again. If we don't do that, Satan can make us miserable, worrying over something that's already been forgiven."

"That old Satan! Does God want me to do anything else?"

"No, dear. You have done exactly what he tells you in his Word to do. He forgave you. Miz Dot forgave you. That's it. You're the only one who hasn't forgiven you. Do you want to do that now?"

"How do I do it, Grandma Bo?"

"Just accept the fact that it's over. We can go back to normal—be happy, even. Okay?"

"Yes, 'cause it feels good to be happy. Can I do it now?"

"Right now." Evelyn took her hand and began skipping to the car. A happy smile lit up the gloomy face, and by the time she jumped into the front seat, she was giggling again. It was over, at last.

ও৶ও৶ও৶

"Well, that was a nice picnic, wasn't it?" Bo was saying as she returned the last of the remains to the basket. "Are you ready to go say 'good-bye' to our old lives? I sure am."

"Yes, ma'am. How about you, Mews?" She reached down and petted him. He hadn't been a little kitten for some time, but they both seemed to just keep thinking of him that way. Perhaps it was time for him to leave the "kitten" behind with Old Bodacious and Miss Ally. He was a cat now. He responded to his name and began purring happily as his mistress stroked him.

"Before we go, I want to be sure that you understand something. The court has given the house to you. It belongs to you. Do you need me to explain that?"

"No, ma'am, but I don't want it. It makes me feel sad."

"I thought you might say that, but I have a brand new idea. What would you think of letting Miz Dot live in the house?"

Her face lit up with a happy smile. "Could I do that? That would make me real happy."

"Me, too. Let's go on to the house, and say our goodbyes. We'll ask your parents about Miz Dot when we get home. Grandpa J can handle it for you, if they agree, and she wants to live there."

They walked up to the newly repaired and painted fence, and looked at the house. They saw that the lawn had been nicely trimmed at summer's end, and the grass was now wearing its brown winter coat. Some of the old feelings left Evelyn. It was only a house, after all—and a rather nice one, at that. With repairs, it would make a wonderful home for Miz Dot. With her living in it, it would be a happy house. Maybe they could even come to visit her, and make some nice memories here.

"Well, shall we go in?" Evelyn opened the gate, which was sporting its fresh new look, and walked through it, into the yard. She turned to look at Ally, who hadn't moved an inch.

"Would you close it, please, Grandma Bo?"

Feeling puzzled, she closed the gate and watched as the little girl released the catch and stepped onto the lowest board. She swung her way through the opening and jumped down. Her face was a study of controlled emotions.

"That isn't fun any more," she said. "Now I know what real fun is."

Evelyn took the key from her purse and extended her hand to Ally. Wordlessly, the two approached the door together. Each struggled with her own emotions as they entered.

How stark everything was. How very old and worn the furniture looked. Evelyn remembered the relief she had felt upon passing through this door for the first time. Real furniture! A real bed! A place to rest and to escape the approaching storm! How closed her heart had been—until a little girl and a tiny kitten had pushed their way inside it. She looked down at the little girl now and lifted a prayer of thanks to God for the wonderful change in her. The small face was at peace as she looked around the room.

Ally walked down the hall and into her old room. She sat down on the bed. Mews jumped onto her lap, and she stroked his fur, absently.

Back in her old room, Bo sat down on the bed. *How could I have helped thanking you for this place, Father?* She prayed. *Not only was it a much needed refuge in time of trouble—but it also brought me back to my family. Thank you so much for all you have done for me since that day. Thank you, Father. Thank you, my dear, dear Lord.*

She looked through tears to see Miss Ally standing in the doorway, Mews clutched in both arms.

"You're not Old Bodacious any more. You're my Grandma, and I love you," she said.

"And you certainly aren't little Miss Ally. Let's say good-bye to these memories and go home. What do you think?"

"I say good-bye. But is it funny that I don't feel sad any more, Grandma? It's like this is over, and I'm safe and happy now. I don't have to worry, do I?"

"It isn't strange, sweetheart. God is letting us heal from the bad years. That's what this goodbye is for. The things that happened to you here, and the things that happened to me during those twelve years were bad, but that's all over now. We have a choice. We could go on feeling sad about things we can't change—or we could just thank God for all of his blessings, put those bad times behind us, and live the rest of our lives for him. Obviously, that's what we are choosing to do—so how could we feel sad about that?"

Together, they walked to the front door and turned around for one last goodbye. It wasn't a sad goodbye. It was triumphant! They had chosen to let God heal their hearts, so that he could use the rest of their lives in his service.

Evelyn closed the door behind them and turned the key in the lock. Holding hands, they walked down new stepping stones to the gate. Passing through it, they closed it ever so gently and turned for one last look at the past.

"Say goodbye, Mews," Ally said quietly. She looked up at her Grandma Bo and together they smiled happy smiles.

They climbed into the car and headed for home.

All the way back, Evelyn was praying. It would be difficult for them if this report came back negative. She was thankful that Ally didn't know what was happening. At least *she* wouldn't be disappointed.

As she pulled into the driveway at her daughter's house, she tried to calm her anxious spirit. *God will have his way. I have just seen what he can do. He always knows what is best. If this turns out to be a negative, we'll just make it a positive by adopting her...*

She knew in her spirit that this was true, but her heart longed for the blessed news that her granddaughter, Megan, was alive and well.

Ally opened the car door and hopped out, chattering and laughing. The trip to the old house had indeed released her from hurtful memories of the past. She now knew, beyond doubt, that her present was secure. In a few days the adoption would be final, and she would truly be a member of this family that she loved. "Come on, Gramdma Bo!" she called as she ran to greet Anna and Tony, who were standing in the open door.

Evelyn breathed a deep sigh, praying for good news. Hurrying to catch up with Ally and Mews, she entered the door just behind them.

"Hi, Mommy and Daddy. We said goodbye to our old house." She hugged her Mom around the waist, with Mews in between them as he so often was.

"Oh, baby, I'm so glad." Anna smiled down at her.

Tony stood nearby, holding a sheaf of papers. On the top was the paper with the foot print from that morning. He stooped down to Ally height so that he could look into her face. Anna joined him.

"Honey, we have news for you," he said.

When she saw the paper with the footprint, fear gripped Ally's heart. Grandpa J had said, "We need to do this because of the adoption."

Everybody's acting so funny, she thought. *What if something is wrong? What if they can't get permission to adopt me? Will I have to leave my family I love so much, after all?* Tears formed in the dark eyes. She took a deep breath, and waited for the bad news.

"Sweetheart," Tony said, "you remember this footprint we had made this morning, right?" He held the paper for her to see.

Wide-eyed, lips compressed, she nodded cautiously.

"And do you remember Megan's baby book?" You looked at it when you came to our house that first day."

There was another somber nod.

Tony took the book from beneath the papers, and opened it to the page with Megan's tiny footprint on it.

"Honey, this footprint," he said, pointing to the one in the baby book, "and this footprint," he pointed to the one they had done that morning, "are the same. Precious—*you* are our Megan! Our beloved baby girl, all grown up into a big nine-year old. Look! Here is your name on the birth certificate."

The tears left the dark eyes and spilled down her cheeks. She looked from one beloved face to the other as she tried to comprehend the incredible news.

Both parents were weeping and laughing and hugging her all at the same time. She began shaking her head, wide-eyed. What did all of this mean? What was she supposed to do?

Just then, she heard Grandma Bo sobbing. "Jeffrey, is she really ours? I haven't lost my only granddaughter, after all? Ally really is Megan?"

"Yes, my darling. Wonderful miracle, Ally is Megan!"

"Grandma Bo?" It was barely a whisper.

Instantly, Bo realized that all of this was too much for her granddaughter to understand so quickly. She rushed to her side, and began talking softly. "Honey, do you remember that day at the old house, when I told you that we would get you a real name—all three names? Look, here," she said as she reached out to Tony, and he handed her the birth certificate. "This is the answer to that promise. It says: 'Megan Lei Benski, born June 14, 1941. Mother: Anna Jeanne Johnston Benski. Father: Anthony Lee Benski.' This is your name—Megan Lei Benski. Your—own—real—name."

"For true, Grandma Bo?" She put her hand over her mouth, as the wonderful truth began to sink in.

"Yes, darling. For true."

"Oh, Grandma! You said you would find a family for me—and you found my very own family! Now I *belong*! I have a real name, just like everybody else! You kept your promise, Grandma Bo. I love you!"

She moved into the open arms of her very own grandmother, and they held each other in a joyful embrace as all that remained of Old Bodacious and little Miss Ally slipped gently away into a distant memory…

270

CPSIA information can be obtained at www.ICGtesting.com
Printed in the USA
LVOW080341130712

289906LV00003B/5/P